A CRYING SHAME

Renate Dorrestein

Translated from the Dutch by Hester Velmans

BLACK SWAN

A CRYING SHAME
A BLACK SWAN BOOK: 0 552 99990 3

First published 1996 by Uitgeverij Contact as *Verborgen gebreken*.
English translation first published in Great Britain by Black Swan,
a division of Transworld Publishers

PRINTING HISTORY
Black Swan edition published 2003

1 3 5 7 9 10 8 6 4 2

Copyright © Renate Dorrestein 1996
English translation © Hester Velmans 2003

With thanks to the Foundation for the Production and Translation of
Dutch Literature for their financial support of this translation.

The right of Renate Dorrestein to be identified as the author
of this work has been asserted in accordance with sections 77 and
78 of the Copyright Designs and Patents Act 1988.

Set in 11/13pt Melior by
Kestrel Data, Exeter, Devon.

Black Swan Books are published by Transworld Publishers,
61–63 Uxbridge Road, London W5 5SA,
Addresses for companies within The Random House Group Limited can be found at:
www.randomhouse.co.uk/offices.htm

The Random House Group Limited supports The Forest Stewardship
Council (FSC®), the leading international forest certification organisation.
Our books carrying the FSC label are printed on FSC® certified paper.
FSC is the only forest certification scheme endorsed by the leading
environmental organisations, including Greenpeace. Our
paper procurement policy can be found at
www.randomhouse.co.uk/environment

MIX
Paper from
responsible sources
FSC® C018072

Printed and bound in Great Britain by Clays Ltd, St Ives PLC

appear at the
Heart of Stone and
novels published in English, a
Black Swan.

Hester Velmans' translation of *A Heart of Stone*
won the Vondel Prize for Translation in 2001.

Also by Renate Dorrestein

**A HEART OF STONE
WITHOUT MERCY**

and published by Black Swan

This is an insignificant book because it deals with the feelings of women in a drawing-room.

Virginia Woolf

A CRYING SHAME

One

In the beginning God created the heaven and the earth. And God said: Let there be light. And there was light. And God called the light day, and the darkness he called night.

Genesis 1

1

Chris could always tell from his voice. From the way he said, 'Hey there, kiddo,' when he came home. It felt like an elephant landing on her. Her knees buckled and the air was squeezed out of her lungs. Oh, God, not again! Yet even so, every time was the first time. It sometimes felt as if her life had the hiccups – another thing it was best not to think about, because thinking about it only made it worse. Her teacher had said people sometimes died of the hiccups. Her teacher looked like Barbie. Only her hair was shorter. She had stopped by one afternoon just before the holidays for a little chat because she was concerned about Christine. That's what she'd said, anyhow. And then she'd left for the Canary Islands.

Everybody loved going on holiday.

Chris started biting her fingernails. Now that his voice had given him away, it scared her, the way he hooked his thumbs through the belt loops of his jeans. The way he walked to the kitchen, the way he came back with a can of beer and popped it open. 'Aaah,' he said after the first swig. Foam on his upper lip. His Adam's apple bobbing up and down. They were going to Scotland, all five of them.

'Christine!' her mother said. 'Stop chewing your nails.'

She hastily bit off one last corner of her thumbnail, and then let her hand fall. The sweat ran down her back in rivulets. It was still unbearably hot, though it was already past six. The new lawn chair's checked cushion was stuck to the backs of her naked knees. The neighbours on the left had the same chairs, except that they had flowered cushions, and a barbecue with sausages sizzling on it. The charred smell came wafting up from other gardens as well, and from all around came the sound of clinking dishes, glasses, forks and knives. As far as the eye could see, half-dressed people were eating and drinking behind the newly planted hedges. By the looks of it, some of them had takeout chips from the new shopping centre. SUMMER AND WINTER A LITTLE SNACK FROM THE SPRINTER. Once the streets were paved, the new housing estate would be completed. There wouldn't be any sand to play in any more, no sewage pipes to hide in. Soon there would be street lights, speed bumps, paving stones. Jaap had said it was only a matter of weeks.

'Hard to imagine,' her mother had answered. Her mother found everything hard to imagine. She only believed in what she could see with her own two eyes.

Involuntarily, Chris kicked the table leg. She was wearing her new trainers, pink and white striped ones, a pink shoelace in one and a white one in the other. Girls' trainers. She had asked for basketball shoes. Shoes for running away, shoes for kicking.

'No kicking, Christine,' said her mother, who had insisted on being called Sonja ever since taking up with Jaap. Sonja was forty, Jaap nowhere near that old. 'Careful of your new shoes. And of the table.' She sent

14

her daughter a warning look. Don't spoil it now. We've all got to do our best. Then she pushed her chair back a little, stretched out a long, tanned leg and rested her foot on her lover's knee. She knew she had great legs. And an attractive, youthful face, especially when she remembered to keep it set in a slightly surprised expression. She preferred not to dwell on what went on in the middle, between those legs and that face. She had written off her torso as hopeless, after three babies.

Jaap folded his fingers over her toes and then let go again. 'Shall we have another one?' he asked lazily.

'Good idea,' came the unsolicited opinion of her eldest son Waldo. He didn't look up from the sports magazine he had been reading since getting home from his paper round.

Sonja got up. She went into the kitchen to fetch beer, Coke, mineral water and fresh ice. At least it would be that much cooler in Scotland. She bent down, pulled the strap of her high-heeled sandal a notch tighter and teetered carefully outside with the loaded tray. 'Waldo,' she said, 'did you check the camping stuff?'

Her son pulled a sulky face. 'Not yet,' he said. He was at that hopeless age when body parts seem to grow at independent rates: his nose was too large and too angular for his face, his arms were too long in comparison with his narrow shoulders. One day you were still giving them their bath, powdering their bottoms and feeding them Heinz, and the next they were sprouting blackheads and pubic hair.

'I'll take a look at that tent later,' said Jaap.

'No, that's his job. Come on, Waldo, you were going to look after your tent. Jaap is doing ours.' Her own words made her uneasy. Our tent. Yours. She shouldn't be talking that way, it only made everything more complicated. Didn't 'our tent' fall into the same category as 'our bed': a seething source of dark, distressing thoughts for an adolescent? When Waldo was younger she never had to worry about that sort of thing. She thought, I've always given him too much – I should – I shall – in future I will.

'Waldo and I will check on that stuff later,' Jaap offered soothingly. He was lying back in his chair, his legs spread wide, the short sleeves of his T-shirt rolled up to his shoulders so that his muscles showed. A pair of sunglasses sat on top of his almost frizzy black hair. She didn't know anybody who was as laid-back as he was, yet also gave you the impression he could spring into action at any moment if he were so inclined.

'Fine,' said Sonja.

In the ensuing silence a neighbour on the other side of the hedge could be heard saying to his wife, 'Did I ever *say* you were a bitch on wheels?'

From a little further on came the noise of a child whining, a dog barking, a TV set broadcasting laughter; someone was hammering something together in a slow, rhythmic tempo: another pergola of course, lots of people had already put up a pergola next to their tool shed, and had bought a baby's breath plant, or a clematis. We'll have a grapevine, Sonja decided, clasping both hands round her cold glass of mineral water, a lovely white Van der Laan, which would grow in any soil. She'd always wanted a house with a garden. She didn't know why she was feeling so blue.

'And what's eating *you*, anyway?' she asked her daughter sharply.

Christine shrugged and hung her head. Despite the heat, she was wearing her favourite sweater, the one with the appliqué of a galloping horse. Sonja thought to herself, if she mentions just one more time that she'd rather go to that pony-riding camp – if she has the nerve – well, she can just melt to a puddle in that hot sweater of hers, see if I care. 'Well?'

'Nothing,' said Christine in an unhappy voice.

'Shall I go get us some chips?' asked Jaap.

'Yes, please,' said Sonja gratefully. 'And I'll bet Christine will want a fried croquette as well.'

Her daughter shook her head without looking up. Sonja had the almost irresistible urge to scream, right, I've had it with you. I've HAD it with you!

'What *would* you like then, love?' asked Jaap. 'Or do you want to take a ride over there with me, so you can choose?'

'No,' said Christine.

'No, thank you, Jaap,' Sonja corrected her. Don't give one-word answers. Look people in the eye when you're talking to them. And comb your hair. And stand up straight. And wear something nice. Be nice.

Waldo said, 'Make it a fried sausage with extra mayonnaise, for me, Jaap. As a matter of fact, I'll go with you.' He put down his can of beer, stood up, and stretched. His black T-shirt was hiked up above his belly button, rendering the dripping red letters illegible, but Sonja knew what they spelt out across her son's narrow chest: *If in doubt, knock them out.*

'That's nice,' she said. She massaged her aching forehead, smiling at him wearily. She was thinking, unreasonably, I've been at work all day too, you know.

Sonja sold henna products to beauty salons.

Jaap sold freezers to hotels and restaurants.

They had met in a car park.

'Can I have a couple of guilders for the slot machine?' asked Waldo.

'You can take it out of my purse. Five, Waldo. No more.'

Christine sat up suddenly. 'Mum, I haven't had my allowance yet.'

Sonja said sarcastically, 'By God, she's talking. Did you guys hear that? A whole sentence. She spoke a whole sentence.'

'Come on, let's go,' said Jaap.

'When am I getting my allowance?' said Christine stubbornly.

Sonja swatted at an imaginary fly and shut her eyes. Her daughter had been born on a freezing day in January, so painlessly and rapidly that for days afterwards she had found herself waiting for the labour pains, for the ordeal still to come. She'd felt cheated; the little creature she had been carrying all those months scarcely needed any intervention from her at all to come into the world. Christine had managed it all by herself, she had snuck up on Sonja like a thief in the night, stealthily and without warning. Sonja didn't like the unforeseen; life had taught her that what occurs unexpectedly is seldom a good thing.

'Mum! Sonja! When am I getting my allowance?'

Sonja opened her eyes a fraction. 'You're not getting a cent for another four weeks,' she said curtly. 'As you perfectly well know.' At the memory of it, her headache moved like a thunderstorm from her right-hand temple to the left, zapping her whole skull with static. Christine's teacher, perched uncomfortably on the edge of the new leather couch, had briefed her in a low voice. Then they had both looked at the girl; Sonja in dismay, right there in the middle of her new living room, with the new teapot in her hand, the teacher

18

shaking her head, lips pursed. 'I'm really a little worried about you, Chris,' she'd said.

Christine, red as a beetroot and biting her nails, had just sat there with shaking shoulders. It had taken a few seconds for Sonja to realize that her daughter wasn't crying, but giggling nervously. That had been the worst. She hadn't had the courage to tell Jaap that evening that the child had gone for a classmate's face with a rusty nail, just like that, for no reason; she'd been waiting for the girl by the bicycle rack with that nail in her hand. A girl who wore glasses and braces, too, an easy target, the sort of girl who flunks PE.

Sonja had also failed to tell Jaap that later she had found Christine's Barbie dangling from a noose, the lovely hair cut off, the naked, perfect body bescribbled in red felt-tip. It had been such a sinister tableau that the hair on the nape of her neck had stood on end. Panting, in a cold sweat, she had freed the doll with trembling fingers, and wiped it clean. She'd given it a dress to wear, and a sweater on top, and over that a coat, as if she might protect the doll from her daughter's strange malice that way; she had put it to bed in Barbie's Dream Home and pulled the covers right up to the little button nose.

She had always wanted a daughter who would play with Barbie dolls, a daughter whose face would light up at the sight of those tiny red plastic shoes the size of your fingernail.

She sat up. She said gruffly, 'Why don't you go and see where Tommy's got to, that way we can all sit down to eat in a little while.'

Silently her daughter got up from the checked cushions opposite. Her thin blonde hair straggled in her eyes. Shuffling her feet, shoulders hunched, she set

19

herself in motion. As if she's dragging an elephant along, Sonja thought irritably – I *must* do something about her posture.

On the bed of sand that was shortly to be their street, cobblestones lay stacked on pallets in readiness for the street pavers, but the rusty metal strips over which the lorries had been driving back and forth for months had not yet been cleared away. Their ends sprang up, they were just crying out for fingers or toes to get caught under them. Chris jumped on one of the strips, let her weight come down on it three or four times. Then she aimed a few karate kicks into the hot, sizzling air. *I am an angel with a double-edged sword, I am the Angel of Justice.*

Knowing was always the worst. To see that look in his eyes, and then to have to sit and wait for the entire evening to crawl by. She pulled the collar of her sweater up over her chin and began chewing on it. It tasted salty. As salty as tears. But she never cried. She had simply put up bars in front of her eyes.

'Tommy!' she called. 'Where are you? I know you're here somewhere! Come out or you're in big trouble!'

Her little brother promptly came trotting out from behind the site trailer. He didn't look where he was going, he stepped in dog poo, he had his arms stretched out to her, he cried, 'Chrissie! Chrissie!' Tears as big as marbles rolled down his chubby cheeks.

Chris pulled down her sleeve, used it to wipe and mop, said sternly, 'And now blow your nose.'

Tommy blew his nose into her sleeve.

'Come on,' she said, 'now think of something nice.'

He grabbed her thigh with both pudgy little hands and nestled his head against her hip.

'Just imagine that it's your birthday and you got a Space Man.'

'But his le— his le— his leg,' the child faltered.

'Broke off right away,' Chris helped him. 'Well, just think of something else then.' He was perfectly capable of talking. He was four, after all. It was just that he didn't want to. Or maybe he was scared he'd spill the beans.

'We're having chips,' she said. 'So you don't have to have any salad.'

He sat down in the sand. She bent down, grabbed one of his legs and pulled. 'Do you want to get dragged home on your bum?'

He nodded gravely.

Chris turned round, clamped a leg under each arm, leaned forward and plodded through the sand, dragging her brother along behind her. She still remembered how she used to push him around in his buggy when he was a baby. She used to pause every once in a while, in front of a cracked paving stone for instance, or where something green had worked itself up through the cement, and she'd point at it. And she had pointed out the birds in the sky, the raindrops, the stones, the gutters, the shops, the cars. She had shown Tommy the world and taught him the names of all things. He belonged to her.

It was too hot to eat. Naturally. Evidently. Everyone knew it. But that was no reason not to make some attempt at it. Sonja pleaded and begged. You can't go on holiday tomorrow on an empty stomach, Christine! Wrong thing to say, of course, all wrong. Why didn't they just let her stay at home in that case? Triumphant eyes in the pale little face. Let her stay at home? Like

21

hell she would. That isn't an option, Christine. Reasonable voice, no bickering at the table, no fighting. Let's keep it pleasant. And eat something, please, after all the trouble Jaap went to for you . . . Wrong, all wrong.

Sorry, Sonja signalled to Jaap. She was thinking, you princess-and-the-pea – you and your moods, your crabby sulking and moping – get out of my sight – for God's sake – even ten minutes would be a blessing – I'd just like to sit here for ten minutes, that's all, without having to work at keeping the atmosphere pleasant – give me a break, will you? 'Selma asked if you'd drop by before we left.' The lie almost made her blush.

Christine jumped up. Gone was her glumness. Her whole body expressed one desire: *Selma*.

'Don't stay out too long, all right?' Sonja automatically called after her. Tommy started banging both fists on the table. His cheeks were turning a deep crimson.

'Me,' he yelled, 'me, me, me too!'

Sonja grabbed him by the arm. Without thinking, she deftly applied the torque known as the Chinese burn. Her little boy shut up at once, startled. His eyes filled with tears as he rubbed his arm.

'Crybaby,' said Waldo. 'Blubberer. Weepy worm.' He brought his face up close to the toddler's and started pulling horrible faces.

'Come on,' said Sonja. 'Please.' Under the table she shook her fingers, appalled at herself.

'Cigarette?' asked Jaap neutrally.

She took one from his pack, bent over towards his lighter, inhaled. 'Shouldn't we – I mean, there's still the washing-up to be done and we have to pack yet and I do want to leave the house tidy, or we'll be coming back to a pigsty in two weeks.' She couldn't believe how stodgy that sounded, how square.

'What are you getting all uptight about now?' he asked. 'We have the whole evening ahead of us. Shall I put this little piggy to bed, incidentally?'

'No,' cried Tommy, 'no!'

'Yes,' said Jaap, 'oh yes indeedy.' He picked up the child and threw him over his shoulder, laughing. 'Goodnight, Mum. Sleep tight, Waldo.'

Tommy howled.

'It's time for the grown-ups now, poppet,' said Sonja. 'See you in the morning.' She hated it when Jaap called her 'Mum'. For some reason it made her think of a cow with an enormous udder. She drew so hard on her cigarette that all she tasted was burning paper.

Opposite her, Waldo was writhing in his chair. 'Hey, Mum,' he began. He made a pretence of slapping himself around the ears. 'Hey, Sonja.'

'Oh, stop it,' she said. 'Who gives a damn, anyway?'

They both had to laugh, and Sonja finally relaxed. Her aching head gave an almost audible sigh of relief. Her restless hands fell idly into her lap. She kicked off her shoes with her toes. Of all her children, Waldo was the only one in whom she recognized herself. The other two reminded her of their fathers, and often it was hard not to hold it against them. It was quite a job, to have to love the consequences of your own stupid mistakes.

Her son patted his knee invitingly. She moved her chair closer and laid her feet in his lap. 'Oh!' she sighed when he began pulling at her toes one by one, gently and expertly. With his other hand he scratched the soles of her feet, her ankles, her calves. 'Keep going,' she murmured.

'Only if you'll listen to what I have to say,' he said.

'OK. I'm listening.' She rubbed her heel against the

23

palm of his hand. When she'd been a hairdresser, old women, lonely women, ugly women, would sometimes press their scalps against her fingers while their hair was washed, hankering for touch: dependent on the kindness of strangers. 'A little lower, to the left,' she mumbled.

'Your nail varnish is chipped.'

'Oh no, is it really? I only just did them.'

He leaned over her toes. 'You just slopped a new coat over the old one, slut.'

'I was in a hurry.' Her feet tingled and begged, keep going, keep going. But he had let go. He was tugging at the earring in his left ear. He'd recently shaved off all his hair on one side. Sonja was almost used to it by now. 'What's up? Shoot.'

'I was planning to do some cruising around on my own, in Scotland,' he said. 'Climb a few mountains and that.'

'Over my dead body, kid. You're not going off on your own until you're seventeen.'

His voice cracked. 'But I might be dead by then.'

'By God, you're right,' she said, 'By God, if you haven't hit the nail right on the head, Waldo.'

He shook a cigarette out of Jaap's pack, lit it and blew the smoke into her face. 'I'm serious, Sonja.'

'Me too.'

'Just a couple of days.'

Sonja saw in her mind's eye rocks, mist and desolate beaches. She thought, we'll be bored out of our skulls and the little ones will be impossible to manage. She suddenly panicked at the thought that her son might really walk out on her. Stalling for time, she said, 'Here, give me one too.'

He offered her Jaap's cigarettes, gave her a light. She

stared at his skinny wrists. She ought to forbid him to smoke. Or drink beer. But didn't all boys his age do it? Uneasily Sonja shifted her weight in the new deck chair. She had only the vaguest notion of what boys his age were like. Maybe he already had a secret girlfriend with whom he did unspeakable things. The heat was really getting to her now. Sometimes she'd catch herself hoping he was gay, as if that would make everything less complicated.

'Coffee, anyone?' asked Jaap. He was standing in the patio doorway.

'Yes,' said Sonja, 'or, no, I mean, we really have to get a move on.'

'Does she always act this way before going on holiday?' Jaap asked Waldo.

Her son said, 'Wait till you see her in the morning.'

They both gazed at her with compassion.

Piqued, Sonja crushed out her cigarette and got to her feet. You could bet on it that tonight, late, at least one of the inflatable mattresses would be discovered to have a leak and need patching, that the zippers of various musty sleeping bags would be stuck, that the tent stakes wouldn't be in the tent bag and the groundsheet would be mouldy. Passports nowhere to be found, one half of every pair of socks mislaid, shirts and trousers missing buttons, indispensable stuffed animals too bulky to fit in any bag or rucksack – where was the blue rucksack anyway, and the coolbox?

'What are you making such a fuss for?' asked her lover. 'We'll fix a few sandwiches in the morning, and then we'll just shut the door after us.'

'You should learn to travel a little lighter, Mum,' said her son.

Sonja felt her temples pounding again. She remarked,

25

as brightly as she could, 'Weren't you going to check on that tent?'

From the bedroom window, Tommy screeched desperately, 'Mummy! Mummy! I'm so hot.'

Without looking up Waldo roared, 'Leave your mother alone!'

Their next-door neighbour promptly came into view, leaning indignantly over the hedge: 'Hey, Sonja, get those kids to pipe down, will you, we can't hear ourselves speak over here!' His head was too small for the rest of his body; he always made her think of a dinosaur. Perhaps it would be better if she dropped off the house key at No. 11 instead.

'Sorry, Fred,' she said, 'but it's live and let live.' She flashed him a conciliatory smile. 'Are you going away anywhere?'

She made interested noises as he began elaborating on his caravan. Was it silly to iron clothes before packing them? But a pressed shirt always seemed so much cleaner.

'Yes, Limburg *is* gorgeous,' she said. 'Well, see you in a couple of weeks then, Fred, and have a good time.'

It wasn't until he'd disappeared behind the hedge once more that she noticed Waldo and Jaap still hadn't budged.

Her son yawned and scratched himself beneath his T-shirt. Lazily he said to Jaap, 'How about getting yourself one of those cool tattoos? Hey, Mum, doesn't he have the perfect arms for it?'

'Mummy!' her youngest whined from the first floor.

'Not very sexy,' said Sonja.

'Not very sexy?' asked Jaap. He looked at his arms.

She jumped. She had voiced her thought out loud, apparently: her life simply wasn't very sexy. She wanted a black Fiat Panda without dents or scratches, and legs that were permanently shaved; she must, she should, from now on she would.

'What's wrong with my arms?' asked Jaap. 'Or you mean you think tattoos aren't very sexy?'

She was sure to forget Christine's ear drops if she didn't put them out right now. She sat down again. She said, 'I think I wouldn't mind a glass of white wine.'

'Her name is Sonja Maria,' said Waldo. 'Hey, man, how about having that on your arm? SM, a heart, an arrow . . .'

Sonja thought, he's punishing me. She thought, why is he punishing me?

The cement stones of the new terrace scorched the soles of her feet. Rummaging around for her sandals under the table with her toes, she brushed Waldo's leg and instantly felt his hand grip her ankle; she sank back and placed her foot in his lap.

Overhead Tommy was lisping, 'Mum? Mummy?' It wouldn't be long before he fell asleep from exhaustion, right at the windowsill.

'So no-one wants any coffee?' asked Jaap.

'She wants wine, amigo,' said Waldo. With his free hand he snapped his fingers.

'Is there any wine left?' Jaap asked her.

He had parked his Volvo next to her old Toyota in the car park and they had got out of their cars at the same time. She with her sample case under her arm, he carrying his portfolio of shiny brochures. Waiting for the lift, they'd both stood stamping their feet against the cold. As they stepped into the lift, Sonja had dropped her gloves. She hadn't meant anything by it. She knew herself well enough to know she had definitely not meant to fall in love again. Love led to

27

babies, in her case anyway, and enough was enough. When she looked at her children, she was sometimes struck by the feeling that life kept eluding her, it had knocked her around, it had turned out completely differently from the way she had expected it to and she had become someone she had never meant to be: a single mother with children fathered by three different men.

Or to put it another way, she had wanted to make up for her first mistake with the second, and for the second with the third.

Either version was equally depressing.

A normal family, that was all she'd ever wished for. It seemed such a small thing to ask. There were whole streets full of normal families, street after street, each one more normal than the next. In her mind, those homes invariably smelled of freshly baked bread, as if it was always breakfast time, that happy time of the day when one's good intentions haven't yet turned into a complete joke, when they are still intact, neither spoiled nor dog-eared. Saucers and teacups on the table, next to cheerful cereal bowls filled with healthy muesli. In that kind of family, no child wore a latchkey on a string around its neck, no child had a leaky ear requiring yet another visit to the doctor, or was dressed in outgrown clothes in dire need of replacing. All the appliances worked. The tax forms were filled out on time. And when a child lost a tooth, the tooth fairy paid a visit that very night.

Sonja hadn't realized how tired she was until she met Jaap, half a year ago. In spite of all her sensible resolve, she had fallen gratefully into his arms as if he were an easy chair.

She pulled her foot off Waldo's knees. She said, 'Why

don't you get us some of that wine? I've yet to see you lift a finger today.'

'Is that so?' asked her son calmly. He lifted his pale, grimy hands and examined them intently before loudly cracking his knuckles, one by one. Then he stood up, sent her a withering look, and with long strides stomped out into the garden. Slamming the gate behind him, he briefly turned back and lifted the middle finger of his left hand.

2

Ringing her bell loudly, Chris pedalled up the drive, veered left at the fork and raced to the last of the six white bungalows. Her bicycle was called Mister Ed and it was really good at rearing up on its hind wheel, especially when people were watching. And there were plenty of spectators around here: the residents sat in little groups under the trees in front of every building, their hands folded over their stomachs. Their heads stopped nodding when Mister Ed came galloping up and began showing off his one-wheeled tricks.

'Hey, Chris, will you leave just a little of the lawn intact for us?'

'Willem!' she shouted. In the midst of completing a double wheelie, she jumped off her bike. Mister Ed landed on his side in the grass.

'I was afraid you'd gone off on holiday without saying goodbye to us.'

'No way, José,' she yelled. She hopped around him, fists clenched, aiming at his stomach. He was the fattest of the group leaders, but he was quick on his feet, and if you got hit by him you weren't a happy camper. She didn't really want to spar with him, actually, it was much too hot, but having started she could hardly quit now. That was the way these things always went with her. Out of politeness she dealt him a couple more blows, then dived under his arm and started running. She raced into the bungalow where her aunt lived. She knocked on her bedroom door, out of breath, and heard shuffling footsteps inside.

'Chrissie!' said Selma, poking her head round the door. Her wide, flat face beamed with pleasure at the sight of her niece. When she laughed, her nostrils opened wide; when she cried as well. She wasn't like other people in any way.

'Hey,' said Chris.

Selma was still wearing the red shirt of her uniform. Of late, the bus had been dropping her off at McDonald's every morning. She could slice tomatoes as well as anyone, she cleaned tables, she scooped chips into paper cones, she did everything in fact, except take money at the till. You only had to tell her something once and she'd remember it for always. The manager said that as far as he was concerned, the experiment was a great success. The newspaper had a picture of him and Selma standing side by side. It had made Sonja furious. 'My sister isn't a circus attraction,' she'd said, and after that they'd all been offered a Big Mac for free.

Whenever Chris felt that nothing in the world could ever cheer her up again, she usually went to Selma's McDonald's for a milkshake.

They sat down together on the bed in the small, stuffy room, in front of the blaring colour TV. On the screen a music video was just ending and a new one starting. In an empty, smoky space, six half-naked girls writhed to the throbbing music as if they were getting zapped by electric currents. Chris watched intently.

Next to her Selma was tapping her stubby fingers on her thigh to the beat; her mouth hung open a little and from time to time she'd slurp some saliva back inside.

The video hadn't even finished yet when Chris sighed a sigh of contentment. The worm that so often wriggled around in her intestines, gnawing at her insides, was nowhere to be felt. The elephant, too, was gone. And there was nobody nagging her head off. No questions asked. Questions were the worst. Because how were you supposed to answer if you weren't allowed to tell?

The next music video was starting. She'd already seen it, and she tore her eyes from the TV screen to glance at the photo on the bedside table. Sonja had taken it, at last year's Christmas show. Selma had been an angel, in a high-necked nightgown of starched white cotton, with on her back two gigantic wings that Willem had cut out of foam. In the photo she was cradling a candle in both hands. Beneath the cardboard halo, her face glowed with a deep, exceptional solemnity.

Chris thought it was the best photograph she'd ever seen. It was a photo that was real, it was the truth. A lot of people thought angels were sissies. They didn't realize being an angel was hard work.

The television belched out the last chords of a hard-rock number. Then the credits started rolling. Her aunt sat up indignantly, her whole body went rigid and she cried out, 'No Michael Jackson!'

'Maybe tomorrow,' Chris said consolingly.

At that, Selma immediately relaxed again, and yawned. She nestled her head on Chris's shoulder. Together they sank back and, happy as clams, watched the first round of a quiz show. The questions weren't hard, and Chris gave all the correct answers in her head. The nonstop applause was so loud you couldn't tell if the telephone was ringing somewhere else in the house. But maybe Sonja had forgotten the time because she and Jaap were having a nice little tête-à-tête. She pictured her mother's face, laughing and talking. She started biting her nails. What if Willem wasn't around to answer the phone and call her? He might well still be outside.

Selma was asleep. She smelled of rubber.

Carefully Chris got up. She propped a pillow under Selma's nodding head. She turned off the television. Softly she said, 'OK then, bye.'

Outside, it wasn't dark yet. The road surface was sweaty and smelled of dogs. The streets were deceptively quiet: something was definitely going on. The world might very well end before she got home.

She rode as slowly as possible, but you couldn't hold back time. The evening was definitely almost over now, almost over. At the corner of her street she braked. She came to a standstill. Then she leapt back in the saddle, clicking her tongue to spur on Mister Ed. He bucked a little, and then shot forward, elated at being given free rein. Chris sensed almost immediately that he wanted to head for her school. The prospect gave her goosebumps. *I am an Angel with a double-edged sword, I am the Angel of Justice*.

She parked Mister Ed in the bicycle shed, where she had pounced on that dork Irene. She hadn't thought it through properly, that time. This time she'd think of something better. Her hands thrust deep in her pockets, she ambled into the deserted playground.

33

She kicked a Coke can against the wall. The clanging sound reverberated across the entire playground. When she got to the climbing frame she took a flying leap, pulled herself up and swung back and forth, arms outstretched, and then flopped down into the sand. She was as strong as the Hulk.

She could see into her classroom from here. In there, only a few days ago, just before the holidays, they had learned a new song. 'I had such an ama-ma-ma-mazing dream, it was a cra-cra-cra-crazy scene.' How cheerfully they had belted it out! And her teacher merrily tapping the beat. It was a song from *Children for Children*, a show on video and CD. The kind that had happy kids energetically dancing while singing their heads off. You know, so that it made you think, boy, are *they* ever lucky.

The stones around the climbing frame had been carelessly laid. You could easily get your fingers underneath. In slow motion Chris saw a couple of fat lice crawl away, she saw her own hands come up ever so slowly, grasping the grey brick. The next moment there was an ear-splitting crash and she had to duck because it was raining glass.

She waited, tense as a strung bow, for several minutes. Her breath came in short, rapid puffs. But nobody came. Nobody came for her. Nobody came to take her away.

The paper bags from the snack bar had been left lying on the kitchen counter. IN SUMMER AND WINTER A LITTLE SNACK FROM THE SPRINTER. If Selma ever found out where they got their chips, she wouldn't understand. Her nostrils would grow wide and indignant.

'Christine?' called Sonja, from somewhere in the house. 'Is that you at last?'

Quickly Chris opened the fridge and poured herself a glass of milk. Her mother stormed into the kitchen with a pile of clothes slung over her arm. She snapped, 'Do you have *any* idea what time it is?'

'Quarter past eleven,' said Chris.

'That's no time to be wandering around the streets by yourself, as you perfectly well know. Anything could happen!'

Jaap called from upstairs. 'Sonja! The tent stakes aren't in the bag!'

'Don't think I've finished with you yet,' barked her mother and darted out of the kitchen again.

Chris took her milk out into the dark back garden. The chairs had been put away in the shed. She sat down on the rubbish bin by the kitchen door. In the lit window of the bedroom she saw her mother and Jaap walking back and forth. They were busy packing. But when the back gate banged shut, Sonja immediately stuck her head out of the open window. 'Waldo?' she cried eagerly.

'Yeah!' shouted Waldo, walking up the path.

'Oh, good! We've lost the tent stakes.'

'Doesn't Chris know where they are?' Waldo called. He pointed at her, sitting on the rubbish bin.

Now Jaap, too, leaned his head out of the window and looked down. 'Come on, Chris, out with it. We've got to get up early tomorrow.'

When there had first been talk of moving, Sonja had told them it was very special for someone to be prepared to live under the same roof as someone else's children. She'd said that they should all be glad Jaap wanted to, of his own free will. 'I think,' she'd said, 'that we're pretty lucky.'

Chris had immediately produced a drawing of a horse for him. Her pencils had pranced with hope and expectation.

'No,' she shouted back. 'How should I know where the tent stakes are!'

'But why does Waldo say you do, then?' asked her mother out of the window, in a voice of splintering steel.

Chris threw her brother a nervous look. Sometimes she had this feeling there were two Waldos, a dangerous one and a nice one, one for the night-time and one for the daytime. 'It's just his age,' her mother always said in a tone that implied that she didn't want to hear one bad word about him, 'he's having a bad time with his hormones.'

Chris often thought back with longing to the time when Waldo didn't yet have hormones. She thought of the smoke bombs he had taught her to make when she was four or five and wore red dungarees with braces – empty jam jars into which he'd blow smoke from the cigarette they'd nicked from Sonja before quickly slipping the lid back on. He'd run around the battle-field with his smoke bomb while she nursed the wounded behind the lines. When the gunsmoke lifted, she would jump on her scooter, she'd scooter up to him as fast as she could and stick a plaster on his arm.

She pulled the collar of her sweater up over her chin again. It was beginning to get a little cooler in the garden.

'Christine! Are you going to answer me or not?'

'I don't know where the tent stakes are, Mum, really I don't, Sonja!' she shouted.

'You're lying, Christine! I can hear it in your voice.

36

It's always the same thing with you! Nothing but lies and fabrications!' Her mother slammed the bedroom window shut and a little while later she stormed outside on angrily clicking heels. 'If you think you can sabotage our holiday, young lady, you are sadly mistaken.'

'Oh, come on, Mum,' said Waldo serenely. He scratched his bare arms. They kept sprouting more hair. He was wearing a black leather strap round his left wrist. 'I was only asking if Chris had seen those stakes. She just always seems to know where everything is.'

'You see!' cried Chris.

'Up to bed, you,' said her mother. 'Right this minute.' The words came hurtling out of her mouth like bricks and Chris instinctively cringed, pulling her head down between her shoulders. She jumped to her feet, ran upstairs and slammed the door to her new room behind her.

She threw herself on the bed, she pounded her knees with her fists in her fury, she tore at her hair. Nothing but lies and fabrications! What lies, what fabrications? She let herself topple backwards.

Her alarm clock ticked. The sound was soft but relentless.

She listened to it, suddenly incapable of moving.

Right now, everyone was still barging around downstairs. But in a little while it would grow quiet. And if tomorrow she told what the night had had in store for her, her mother simply wouldn't believe her. Even worse: if she *did* believe it, she'd never look happy again.

She turned over, threw her arms round the pillow and rolled up into a ball. It was too hot to get under the covers. What difference did it make, anyway? Under the covers wasn't any safer. She tried to see what time it was again, but it felt as if she was looking at her alarm clock through the thick bottom of a glass jar. Sonja had never known about their smoke bombs. Waldo always said their mother didn't have to know everything.

She pinched her arms, her legs. She was already *this* close to not feeling a thing. In a little while the door to her room would quietly open.

3

From the moment they arrived in Scotland, it rained cats and dogs. It was unbelievable, the way it rained. In the campsite the grass was spongy and muddy, water gurgled in trenches everywhere. All their things got wet while they were setting up the tents. Jaap was the only one who was still in a good mood, but even that was over by the second day when Chris threw his sunglasses out of the car window. Her punishment was that she wasn't allowed to leave the camp ground. What a shitty thing to do to her. She had to just sit here counting her toes in the pouring rain while the others were off having fun.

Every time she wiped her dripping hair out of her face, raindrops with angry little faces popped up, clearly and distinctly, on her sleeve. She sniffed loudly and stuck a piece of gum in her mouth. Then she decided to go and sit on the campsite's fence again, rocking back and forth.

The bad weather allowed little to be seen of the surroundings. The grey on one side was the Highlands, the grey on the other the sea. You could stuff it all, as far as she was concerned; only the town interested her, Oban. It lay nestled in the curve of the bay, it smelled of diesel oil and fried fish, and it was packed with penny arcades and ice-cream stalls. There were pubs and souvenir shops along the quay, backing up to a warren of interesting alleyways. Chris desperately wanted to be there. There wouldn't be another chance to play pinball in Oban tomorrow, tomorrow they were moving on, to some shitty island that had nothing on it but nature. Her mother and the boys had already been to the harbour master's office to buy the ferry tickets.

She fumbled in her pocket and found a few coins. Listlessly she slid down off the fence and trailed to the camp shop where she bought a bag of crisps. As she walked outside, munching, she saw the row of pay phones. A Hell's Angel was standing in one of the booths. He wore a leather waistcoat and there were chains dangling from his clothes. He was talking into the receiver. Shitty weather here, he was saying, in English. He raised a huge bare arm and scratched himself under his headband. His rippling muscles made the blue wing tattooed on his upper arm look as though it was flapping. Chris stood there mesmerized.

'Hello,' she shouted hopefully when he came out.

'Hey, kiddo,' he said, grinning. His teeth were square and set far apart.

'Can I have a ride on the back?' she asked in Dutch, pointing at his motorcycle.

He swung a colossal leg over the saddle, revved the motor and with a huge boot kicked the stand out of the way. He held up his hand. 'Cheerio,' he said. And off he went in a fountain of slush.

'Hey, wait!' she screamed, wiping the mud off her face. He turned out of the gate right before her eyes and disappeared from sight.

She should have offered him some crisps. He looked

as though he could put away quite a bit. If only she'd had enough money to buy him a cheeseburger. The kind that Selma made, with extra ketchup on it, so that you had to hold the bun in both hands to prevent the pickle and tomato slices from slipping out.

But she knew very well that Selma's cheeseburgers wouldn't have helped her: after all, it only took one glance. He had given her the once-over and had pushed off pronto because he could tell: this isn't a nice little kid, she's bad, that one; serves her right that she's got an elephant sitting on her, and that's nothing compared with what it feels like to be left alone in the night with this girl for a single minute, oh boy, this kid deserves at least ten elephants.

Never mind, she told herself, never mind. She returned to the tent. Her sleeping bag felt clammy, but since there was nothing else to do she crawled inside.

When she opened her eyes again, it felt warm and pleasant all around. A soft yellow light shone on her. For an instant she thought she was dead and in heaven, and her heart pounded with joy.

She sat up. The air mattress rippled beneath her. The sun shone in through the tent flap. Over there were the plastic bags that Sonja had slipped over Tommy's feet because he didn't have any dry socks left. The torch lay over there. And the bag of crisps, back there. With the sleeping bag clinging to her hips like a sausage skin, she wriggled towards it. Suddenly a shadow fell over the tent. Her outstretched arm stayed hovering in the air.

The zipper opened a crack. 'Hey, Chris.' He folded himself double in order to get in.

Startled, she pulled the sleeping bag up to her chin.

41

'Time for a little talk, just you and me.'

When he put his hand on her knee, she scooted backwards as far as she could. Her throat tightened. 'Where's Mum?'

'I came on ahead.'

'Leave me alone,' she stammered.

He ran both hands through his hair. She hated having to hurt him, because he was friendly and good and it was A-OK with her that he loved her mother, but if he thought he could just come and give her the third degree, he had another think coming. 'This is *my* tent,' she hissed. 'So sod off!'

He glared at her, no longer patient but angry now. 'Why are you being so nasty?'

She pried her chewing gum off the underside of the mattress and stuck it in her mouth. It had hardly any taste left. She chewed as hard as she could. If he got mad, it made things easier. Then she could simply yell back at him.

He yanked at the foot end of her sleeping bag. 'Jesus, girl, are you going to act this way the whole trip? And throw a pair of sunglasses out of the car every day?'

'Well, I'm sorry,' she said shrilly. 'But I've been punished, haven't I? What more do you want?' She wanted to sit on his lap and have him say silly things in her ear like 'misschrissypuckissy', or do magic tricks with coins and then say, 'OK, that's for the Mister Ed fund.' He knew she was saving up for a pony. But a bicycle can be a magnificent steed too, he had assured her, and together they had gone out to buy fluorescent paint, and the tip of his tongue had come poking out of the corner of his mouth as he painted MISTER ED on the crossbar with a fine brush.

When you couldn't sit still, he never said, 'A chair

has four legs.' And he never said, 'My arm isn't a shop sign, you know,' when you didn't rush to take something he was holding out to you.

'Those sunglasses were a gift from Sonja.'

She wriggled her toes inside the sleeping bag. Maybe she could bring on a fit of the giggles. That always made people nervous.

'Isn't Sonja allowed to give me any presents, then?'

'Why should *I* care!'

His chin went all square. 'You're a first-class brat, Chris.'

'And you're a complete jerk!' she screamed. She knew at once that she really meant it. She was furious with him, furious. Sonja had said everything would be different as soon as they went to live in the new house with Jaap, she'd promised, but everything had stayed the same as before, his presence hadn't made a bit of difference, and all she could do now was make him mad, just as mad as she was; tomorrow she'd wreck something else of his, and the day after, and every day, until he saw that she was an angel, an angel with a double-edged sword, the Angel of Justice. She aimed a kick at his shins through the sleeping bag.

But he didn't flinch. He took a cigarette out of his breast pocket and stuck it between his lips.

She snarled in a menacing tone, 'It's No Smoking in here.'

'Oh yeah?' He raised his lighter and lit his cigarette. 'It's a drag, isn't it, when someone does something you don't want them to do. Well, that makes two of us, Chris. Or, rather, three of us. Because the way you're behaving isn't making Sonja happy either. She's really upset that you're acting so impossible.'

She grabbed a lock of hair on her neck and yanked on it, hard.

'That's the worst thing, really, as far as I'm concerned. That you never think of your mother. She's always had to manage on her own with you children, and now that she finally has—'

'Come off it, she had Waldo, didn't she?'

'Oh,' said Jaap. 'Please forgive me. Your brother, the boy wonder! The man of the house!' He seemed on the point of saying something else, but suddenly he shook himself like a wet dog. He chucked his cigarette out of the tent opening. The canvas billowed on all sides as he got to his feet. 'The best of luck with Waldo then,' he said bitterly.

Chris raised her hand without looking up. 'Cheerio,' she said, as cool as a Hell's Angel.

4

'Twelve o'clock at the ferry,' said her mother. 'Not one minute later. Do you hear me, Christine?'

'Yes, Mum.'

'And the same goes for you,' she said to Waldo.

'You can forget *that*,' he said.

Sonja sat down on the rolled-up tent. Her eyes were red. 'We're not going to go over that again, Waldo. You're coming with us, and that's that.'

'I'll come and look you up in a couple of days.' He stuffed a pair of socks into his rucksack.

Sonja was silent. 'Where's Jaap?' she finally asked plaintively.

'At the car,' said Chris.

'Christ, child, haven't you left yet? You wanted to go into town, didn't you? Get going then! We'll never be packed up in time with all of you getting under my feet here.'

Chris grabbed Tommy by the hood and reluctantly started off. There was no fun in going into Oban any more. They shouldn't shoo you away when important things were being discussed.

They hadn't even reached the camp gate when it began to drizzle again. They ran the whole way.

In Oban they looked in the shop windows at slick pottery Loch Ness monsters, at boxes of coloured shells and candles with glued-on dried flowers. From a rack in a doorway they nicked a card with a bagpipe player on it, for Selma. They walked into three casinos, but they were thrown out every time before they'd even had a chance to put a coin in a slot machine. In an alley they kicked over some rubbish bins. They discovered a dead fish in the gutter. Tommy wanted to take it with him, but it didn't fit in his coat pocket. Then they went down to the wharf to watch the boats. It was still raining. Tommy had to pee.

There were busy comings and goings where the boats were docked, but further on there was hardly anybody. Chris dragged her little brother along by the sleeve. They had to step over weathered lengths of rope and torn nets and watch out for the iron rings sunk into the cement.

Next to a deserted shack she unzipped Tommy's trousers and pulled them down. 'Don't piss on your shoes,' she warned.

She saw the sea foaming behind his naked legs; it was high tide, and this section of the wharf had no sea wall. There was all kinds of stuff floating in the water, yellow foam, plastic bags, slimy seaweed, milk cartons. Intrigued, she walked over to the edge. Rings of slate blue, poison green and yellow bobbed around on the surface, fanning out in mysterious patterns.

'Are you going to take a dip?' a voice asked, right behind her.

It gave her such a shock that she almost lost her footing.

He was carrying his rucksack and wore his U2 T-shirt under his open jacket.

'Pull up your pants,' she snapped at Tommy.

Waldo's hand shot forward and grabbed her by the shoulder. 'We still have to say goodbye, little one.'

'Are you really going then?' stammered Chris.

'I told you, didn't I, that I can get a ride to Skye with that fat bloke from the campsite.'

'Yes, but Mum—'

'Isn't it my holiday too? Am I expected to babysit for two whole weeks while the two of them go at it like rabbits?' He pulled her a little closer. His pale, smoky eyes were, as always, brimming with secrets he'd never tell you, secrets you wouldn't even want to know in the first place. Defiantly he said, 'I'm going to climb a couple of mountains on Skye.' Then he stuck his hand in his back pocket and pulled out a ten-pound note. 'Here, buy an ice cream for the little squirt, and something nice for yourself.'

Gulping, she took the money.

'And take care of yourself while I'm gone.'

She shuffled her feet. Ten pounds was a lot of money. They only gave you as much as that if they really loved you.

'Well, am I getting a kiss, Chrisso, or what?'

Her arms swung up of their own accord, her heels came up off the ground and then she was hanging from his neck.

He tugged at her hair gently. 'And don't get your mother all upset, OK?'

'I won't,' said Chris. She wouldn't tell. Of course she wasn't going to tell. How could she ever tell? What *would* she tell anyway? She let go.

Her brother kicked at a stone, which flew over the edge of the slimy wharf and landed in the water with a splash. He raised his arms in a triumphant gesture.

Like the sergeant in *Hill Street Blues*, he yelled, '*Go do it to them before they do it to you!*'

'Oh, yeah!' Chris yelled back. She wanted to jump up and slap him a high-five, it was pretty awesome, except that she wasn't feeling elated enough. The worm was biting her insides and the elephant was sitting on her shoulder, and she stood paralysed on the slippery stones, helpless and confused, staring into Waldo's eyes, the only eyes that ever really saw her, the only eyes that took the trouble to really look at her. His hard, angular body. His clammy skin, his probing fingers. His breath in her ear, his hoarse voice. And the incomprehensible pity she always felt for him afterwards: if she didn't exist, he wouldn't have to do this, at night, in the dark. Every time, the realization: her fault. If only he could be saved from her.

Standing at the edge of the wharf, he called to Tommy, 'Your turn! *Go do it to them . . .*'

Again her arms came up and again her feet left the ground. *I am an angel with a double-edged sword, I am the Angel of Justice*. She struck him smack in the middle of his chest.

He fell over backwards. He made no noise at all. The look of surprise on his face. The only sound the crack with which the back of his head hit the wharf. His hands clutching at the air. The speed with which he slid along the edge and tumbled over it, into the water.

Chris stared at the spot where he'd been standing. Promptly her mother's face loomed up before her, as clear as if she were suddenly standing there: her mother's special Waldo face, eager, gay, provocative, happy, teasing.

Shaking, she grabbed her little brother by the arm and began to run.

5

'Where have they got to, for God's sake?' said Jaap. He drummed his fingers on the steering wheel and through the fogged-up windscreen kept an eye on the ferry boat, which was waiting at the dock. The funnel was already belching out thick clouds of smoke. 'The boat is about to depart any second! Everyone's already on board, and we're still twiddling our thumbs out here. You've got to make better arrangements with those two, Sonny. This just won't do.'

As if to underscore his words, the ship's foghorn gave an urgent blast.

Sonja opened the door for the umpteenth time and got out in the rain. She made a gesture of despair at the man in the orange oilskins who had long since loaded the other cars into the ferry's hold. By way of reply he stuck three fingers up. Three minutes? She looked around. She shouldn't have fought so long with Waldo. She should just have let him go. Now Waldo had disappeared without even a proper good-bye, and who knows how long he'd stay away, mad, to try her.

'Well, I'll be . . .' shouted Jaap, jumping out of the car. 'There they are, and you didn't even spot them!

Over there! Call them! They're heading in the wrong direction!'

Among the tourists shuffling at the water's edge Sonja was able to make out her two youngest. Looking neither left nor right they were trotting along, heads down. Like a couple of whipped dogs, by God! Any other kid would be over the moon at being on holiday, hers acted as if it was a disaster.

Sonja thought, can't you just think about me, for once! Fists clenched, she started giving chase.

Two

And God said: Let there be a firmament in the midst of the waters, and let it divide the waters from the waters. And God called the firmament heaven.

Genesis 1

1

The smell of fish, iron, diesel. A cloud of seagulls, screeching, pitching and plunging on the air currents. The sea is the colour of silver under low white fogbanks. The desolate hills of the mainland are still just about visible in the distance; mile upon mile of misty coast, the slopes strewn with boulders, the coves exposed to the elements. Firths bore their way deep inland and turn the arid soil brackish. How hard life must have been here once. Until the tourists came.

Surrounded by tourists, Agnes Stam stands at the railing of the *Caledonian MacBrayne* ferry. She can remember a time when this crossing was made largely by nature lovers and other devoted eccentrics. You'd acknowledge them with a conspiratorial nod when you ran into them later on: a handful of knickerbockered ornithologists on the cliffs, the odd elderly couple with canvas rucksacks strapped on their backs, purposefully stomping in single file up to the top of Ben More. Those days are gone.

These days, you need to make reservations in Oban for the boat to Mull. On board, there's a turmoil of rustling scarlet and canary yellow rain gear with orange stars, purple stripes, blue trim. Everyone is girded with belts, ropes and bum bags, draped with Ordnance Survey maps inserted in transparent sleeves, binoculars, cameras and compasses. Enormous backpacks of fluorescent material, from which dangle pitons, sets of cooking pots and pickaxes. Velcro closures. Miles of Velcro. Agnes wonders what can possibly be tucked away in there that is so indispensable for climbing Ben More's quite accessible slopes, or for observing the seals in the coves.

She half closes her eyes and peers out over the water. In just a short while Duart Castle will come rising up out of the mist, primitive and menacing, perched high up on the rocks. The clicking of cameras will be followed by a chaotic stampede to the other side, because almost simultaneously Craignure's lighthouse will display itself for a snapshot on the starboard side, with the blue silhouette of the island right behind it. Then the loudspeakers will start crackling. Will drivers of motorized vehicles kindly proceed below deck and await further instructions from the crew. Pushing, jostling on the narrow metal stairs.

In anticipation of that moment, Agnes stands at the railing. Agnes Stam, for whom Mull holds few secrets any more. She knows the glens and the lochs inside out, and she never tires of them, either. She knows every twist and turn in the narrow road which will soon take her to the northern coast, to the house one of her brothers bought for a song some fifty years ago. White walls, blue window frames, a slate roof. A view of Skye when the weather is clear. Right outside the back door, a beach that's safe for the children, for Agnes's nieces and nephews, for her great-nieces and nephews, for the youngest batch of little ones, her brothers' great-grandchildren.

Isabel, Jasmijn, Tobias, Claire, clingy little Dennis, Effie, Flora, Coralie, Vincent, Alice who was allergic to food colouring (or was that Alex?) Roy, nicknamed King Kong, Joris, Anne Marijn, Noortje, Barbara, Elisabeth, Joost, Gemma, the inseparable twins Dirk and Johanneke (one of them has since become an ENT specialist in Toronto, the other a Doctor Without Borders), Mi Ying, deaf little Chris, Ariane, the giggling sisters Ida and Ada, Sennemi, Micky, Erica: they have all stood here next to Agnes at the railing as the ferry chugged through the water. Look! Over there! That's Lismore, and there's Morvern, do you see it?

Innumerable snapshots in innumerable photo albums prove that generations of young Stams have been to the island with Aunt Agnes. They have picked berries there, and hunted for seashells. They were awarded tuppence for every oyster they found, they ate flan out of the old, cracked fish mould, and repeated the bird names after Agnes. Razorbill. Puffin. Cormorant. Guillemot. Tern. Curlew. Plover. Oyster-catcher. Gan . . . what? Now think! Gannet.

The ship swings round to the left. Agnes brushes the whipping grey hair out of her face, clutches at her collar. Her one good eye is watering. Children run past her across the deck, shouting into the wind. A toddler barrels into her and grabs hold of her tweed coat for a moment. She bends over, is about to murmur some-thing kind, but immediately a scarlet arm comes out of nowhere, reclaiming the child. Don't talk to strangers, love.

Agnes finds somewhere else to stand. She takes out a sweet. The gulls dive after the fluttering wrapper.

A sudden uproar: Duart Castle left and Craignure lighthouse right. Exclamations in various languages, including, inevitably, Dutch. Then the stampede to the vehicle deck.

Her Volkswagen is at the front of the line: she'll be driving off the boat first. If she can find her keys, that is. Then, as she's fishing around for them in her coat pockets and bag, she sees they are still in the ignition. The door is unlocked. She doesn't know whether to be upset or relieved.

'Aunt Agnes is getting so absent-minded, have you noticed?'

Well, just try stealing a car on a ferry, on the open sea! The subconscious instinctively takes that sort of thing into account, and therefore casts to the wind all precautions one might otherwise scrupulously heed. Seated behind the wheel, Agnes unbuttons her coat and puts her scarf on the seat next to hers, draping it over the urn containing Robert's ashes.

Just in time too: the ramp starts rattling into motion inches from her car's bonnet. Daylight floods into the hold, that mother-of-pearl shimmer which envelops Mull even on cloudy days. It gently embraces Agnes and her ancient VW as she drives onto the pier of Craignure and then heads up the coast road north.

She loves the stark landscape, the rocks glittering with mica, the scraggly trees groping the air with their gnarled branches, the bluebells along the road, the heather in bloom. Water everywhere, gurgling down the slopes. The mosquitoes must be working overtime.

She drives slowly, glancing in her rearview mirror from time to time to see if she is holding up the traffic behind her. At one point she thinks she sees two children's faces in the rectangular frame, just like old times, but it's just a flash, the next moment they've disappeared, and she says out loud, sardonically, 'Could Aunt Agnes be getting a little senile?'

The gnawing suspicion that there's been a family meeting, behind her back. Sausages sizzling on the barbecue. A little more wine, anyone? Gemma's inevitable potato salad, Joyce's bare legs. Floris finally engaged to be married, and so are we all straight on Aunt Agnes then? 'We've already made other plans for the summer.' Other plans, that sounds good. Riding camp for Margriet and Natalja, we're taking the whole family to Tuscany, and other excuses too: Ruben just had scarlet fever, Basje a new set of braces, Willemijn's broken wrist means she can't go swimming, Jeroen has to re-sit his exams. Agnes, darling, it's just that we don't have any room in the car, or else you could have come with us to Taulignan; really, Aunt Agnes, I couldn't possibly saddle you with Ton any more now that he's turned into such an impossible teen.

But it could just as well have been the children themselves. Grinding their skinny hips to the music of the Artist Formerly Known As Prince. Picking oysters for 10p? Pudding moulds in the shape of a fish? Aunt Agnes? Come on, give us a break.

In the main town of Tobermory she drives past the brightly painted houses along the waterfront, the ships, the pubs, the old Ledaig Whisky Distillery, where on a guided tour an expert will explain to you the ins and outs of malting, mashing, fermentation, distillation, maturation. It's an intriguing whisky that is distilled here, with a hint of seaweed as well as of peat; fresh and smoky at once. Agnes's well-thumbed copy of the whisky bible, the *Malt Whisky Companion*, gives it a rating of only 67, oddly enough.

The sun breaks through as she turns onto the road to Dervaig. The distances are fairly short, but the one-lane roads with their many sharp bends and blind crests call for a cautious speed. Past Loch Cuan, the water tinted lavender in the soft sunlight, she takes the turn-off to Croig. The road is little more than a track here, dead-ending at the ramshackle wooden pier. They used to catch crabs here. But what's past is past.

Agnes stops the car in front of the last farm along the dirt lane. On the stone wall, pots of homemade jam and fresh eggs are offered for sale, next to a rusty tin for the money. This display has always struck her as uncommon evidence of trust in human nature.

She gets out and walks into the front garden, past a row of fuchias in bloom and wild honeysuckle. Moments after she knocks on the door, it is the daughter-in-law who opens it, the younger Mrs Flynt, lean and tanned, a dirty plastic apron over her clothes. Ah, welcome. Did you have a good journey? I've got some scones set out for you. Scones with strawberry jam and whipped cream.

'*Agnes!*' the younger Mrs Flynt exclaims as if she's seen a ghostly apparition. 'We werena expecting you at all.'

'No,' says Agnes, 'I'm sorry . . . but I . . .' Her command of English flies out of the window at the realization she completely forgot to tell them she was coming.

Mrs Flynt recovers. She grabs Agnes's hand. 'Ah, but my sincerest condolences, of course. I was meaning to write to you one of these days. Such a special man, such vitality, for his age. I just canna believe it.'

'Cancer,' says Agnes.

'Aye, that can be very quick.'

Agnes is silent.

'Aye, we'll surely miss him. And you, of course. But come awa' in, you'll be having a cup of tea? Mother-in-law will be happy to be seeing you again.'

Agnes is dying for a cup of tea. But she shrinks from dredging up the memories: Robert this, Robert that. She isn't ready yet for the reminiscences of others. The time will come when she'll welcome all the anecdotes, that's the way it was with her other brothers, but not yet, not right now. 'Actually, I just came for the key,' she says.

'Oh dearie me,' answers the younger Mrs Flynt, who is sixty, only ten years younger than Agnes herself. 'If I'da only known you were coming. I woulda cleaned the house and got in some food for you.'

'I'd normally have come about this time anyway,' Agnes can't help remarking. 'I always come in August.'

'Aye, of course, that's right, only so soon after . . . We werena counting on it that anyone from the family, considerin' . . . But I'll get Muriel to nip along in a wee while with some vegetables and milk. So that you're set for today at least.'

Muriel is the youngest Mrs Flynt. Younger Mrs Flynt and youngest Mrs Flynt live together on a hostile footing. The farm is a theatre of perpetual trench warfare; old Mrs Flynt refuses to take sides, while the male Flynts confine themselves to making pacifying sounds every once in a while.

'Wonderful,' says Agnes.

Mrs Flynt disappears inside and returns a little later with the key. She is clutching it as if she has something else on her mind. Downcast eyes. A blush on the weathered cheeks. She says, 'Might ye have a mind to sell the house? I mean, it was Robert's house, was it no'? Was he no' the owner? Nae offence meant, of course, but my husband and I have been interested in Port na Bà for years – ye kent that, did ye no'? And we could save ourselves, all of us, a wee bit o' money by coming to an understanding ourselves. Will ye be thinking it over, Agnes?'

Agnes wants to tell her that there is no question of selling. The words are on the tip of her tongue, curt, blunt. But Mrs Flynt seems to realize that she's chosen the wrong moment. Hurriedly, and a bit too jauntily, she says, 'But first you're going to have a wonderful holiday. Here's your key. I hope that everything's in order over there. Which of the bairns did you bring this year?' She peers past the fuchias and the honeysuckle at Agnes's car on the drive. 'Have they been here before? I dinnae ken them, do I?'

Astonished, Agnes follows her gaze and turns round.

There are two children sitting in the back seat of her VW, a little boy and a girl.

When the car stopped and Agnes got out, there was no need for them to stay hidden on the floor, out of sight of the rearview mirror. They're both sitting up and looking around inquisitively. Are we there yet?

2

There used to be a cattle trail crossing the entire width of Mull, from north to south, starting at the beach of Port na Bà, which means 'Port of Cows'. The livestock were brought over from Coll and Tiree, and even from the more distant islands. But today there's not a trace of it left. Port na Bà can now be reached only by driving across the pasture, a sea of flowering weeds, a route demanding considerable driving skill, because what from afar looks like a smooth expanse of grass is in reality a series of ledges, shaped like giant draughts pieces: tertiary basalt, solidified from seething lava many millions of years ago and patiently polished by the elements. Scattered around in the grass are crumbling walls of what were once barns, houses, even an inn, possibly.

Old, old, everything on Mull is old, as old as the story that's existed since time immemorial, before man walked the earth.

Agnes is silent the whole way, concentrating on salvaging her exhaust pipe. Behind her the children are conferring in whispers about hunger, thirst, the need to pee. Dutch children.

The last curve, and now the house can no longer

keep itself hidden in the folds of the landscape. White walls, blue window frames, a slate roof. Oh, it's such a friendly house, lying there so serenely in its abandoned state – like someone who has learned, simply by living long enough, not to be afraid of being alone any more. It looks out over the quiet bay of Port na Bà, over miles of bright white sand and rocks covered in bright green algae. On the beach you can find chunks of basalt, gneiss, granite, sandstone, sometimes even marble or schist.

Agnes turns off the engine. A flint of schist, flaky and crystalline: she can almost feel the stone in the palm of her hand.

She flings open the car door and breathes in deeply the honey-sweet scent of the flowering bushes, the smell of salt and seaweed and wind. One by one she lowers her feet onto the springy carpet of grass. Birds screaming overhead. Grey heron. Eider. Goosander. Tern. Snipe. Fulmar. Robert sitting by the blazing fire with a bird guide open on his lap. 'A *kittiwake*, Agnes. I'll give you three guesses.'

Which reminds her, is there enough firewood? The Flynts are the best caretakers anyone would wish for, but when no-one's expected, no-one's expected. Pragmatic islanders. 'I'll give them a ring,' Agnes mutters to herself.

'Who are you going to ring?' demands a child's voice. The little girl clambers out of the car. She is blonde and pale; her sharp little features are tense. Nine years old, possibly ten?

Agnes turns round and crosses her arms. 'Well now,' she says, 'that's right, we have some passengers.'

The little boy climbs out of the car too. He has straight, black hair, chubby cheeks and somewhat slanted eyes. Not a day over four. It's not easy to tell if they're brother and sister. 'I'm Agnes,' says Agnes, rather caustically for her.

The children first exchange glances, then look at her. The girl is chewing gum. The little boy allows himself a longing survey of the beach.

'And *you* are stowaways,' says Agnes. 'So. What's the meaning of this?'

'Your car was open,' the girl says quickly. 'We could just climb in, just like that, on the boat. We didn't force the lock, honest we didn't.'

'Heaven forbid.' She turns to the little boy. 'And you? What have you got to say for yourself?'

Distressed, he looks at his feet.

'He has to go,' says the girl.

'Well, come on then. Let's take care of that first.' She inserts the key into the lock, pulls the handle towards her. She turns it once, twice. She can smell the boots before she catches sight of them: a whole row of wellies, in all possible sizes, underneath the hanging wet weather gear. The faded linoleum in the hall, the yellowed calendar from 1984 on the wall. To think one can be that fond of linoleum, or an old calendar.

She points the children towards the loo and walks into the living room. The low beamed ceiling, as always, gives her the pleasant sensation of being a giantess suddenly, as if stepping into this room has put her under a magic spell. Yet it is a very ordinary room, with walls of pale yellow distemper and comfortable furniture: two snug sofas upholstered in beige corduroy and a couple of wicker chairs that creak when you sit on them; and in the corner one indisputably lovely chest, which Robert used to claim had more drawers in it than all the secrets of a lifetime. Her eyes take in Frank's canvases on the wall, the photos and framed children's drawings, the binoculars hanging faithfully from their nail by the window, the seashells on the windowsill. She opens the window to let in the fresh sea breeze and flings her coat over a chair. 'Thank you, Robert,' she says out loud.

The children are hardly bashful or shy, quite the contrary: they're bored, yawning broadly, after their long trip. The girl flops down on the couch. The boy wanders about with his thumb in his mouth. 'I want clisps,' he lisps. 'Crisps.'

'Later,' says Agnes, the same thing she has said to droopy, starving children for the past fifty summer holidays, wondering meantime what, if anything, she'll find to eat in the kitchen. Baked beans, no doubt, and packets of instant soup.

'Later?' asks the girl. 'What about right now?'

'First we unpack the car. That is the way we do things around here.'

'That's not our job,' says the child defiantly.

'Then you shouldn't have come,' answers Agnes. She turns her back on her uninvited guests, leaves the room, and now it's her turn to head for the loo off the kitchen, to figure it all out. She fastens the catch on the door and frowns: as a rule, what are you supposed to do if you find yourself saddled with two children you've never laid eyes on before? But *is* there such a thing as a rule in this case? OK, let's say you happen to find a couple of kids. A reasonable starting point. It can happen to anyone, clearly. Well, presumably you notify the police at once.

Her gaze rests on the bar of soap shaped like a bear

lying next to the sink; she bought it last year, for her great-great-niece Willemijn – or was it the year before? Willemijn had just turned seven but was already quite adept at vanishing without a trace; she'd hide out in the ruins of the old barn for hours at a time. Some children feel the need, every so often. Agnes considers. She remembers how little Mi Ying would stubbornly wander off if something wasn't to her liking – all the way to Calgary Bay, if need be. Dennis, in his stiff-necked phase, had gone off and built himself a fully furnished hut somewhere secret. Dennis was never coming back, never, do you hear me, Aunt Agnes! But in the middle of the night, the owls and bats had sent him scurrying back to Port na Bà.

She never intervened, never went after the children to make them come back home. Running away has always seemed to her a matter to be taken seriously, an undertaking not to be undermined by adults. And hasn't experience shown her that every child wants only one thing in the end: to get home again safe and sound? This is the kind of situation that will resolve itself eventually. And besides, Agnes thinks, tucking in her clothes and washing her hands, it would have looked downright ridiculous to young Mrs Flynt if she'd gone and admitted back there, 'Those two, in my car? I've never laid eyes on them before.'

When she goes outside she sees that the children have started unloading the luggage. Items lie scattered all over the ground: her video camera, her bags. The little boy is seated on the grass on top of her scarf, examining the urn. As soon as she spots Agnes the girl begins tugging at a suitcase with a great show of industry. But her furiously gum-chomping jaws betray what she's really thinking: here we go again, having to cater to the whims of yet another grown-up, from the frying pan into the fire.

Agnes says considerately, 'That suitcase may be a little heavy for you. Why don't you carry in that overnight bag instead?'

'I can manage.' She drags her load into the house, comes marching out again immediately with determined step, large dark eyes flashing in the mousy little face: now for the other stuff. Standing on the path, Agnes looks on. She wonders if she ought to be amused or alarmed at so much helpful exertion.

Huffing and puffing, the girl starts hauling the next suitcase. Agnes takes it from her and says, to distract her, 'Well, how do you like it here, then?'

The child looks around politely, knits her brow. What does she see?

'When my brother bought this house, it was a total ruin. We had to restore the whole thing. We did it ourselves. Every wall. Do you see, over there—'

The girl interrupts her nervously, 'Is your brother here as well?'

'In a sense,' says Agnes. She turns round and hurries over to the little boy. He's still sitting in the grass and, clumsily holding the urn in both hands, is giving it a thorough shaking. There is nothing about him to remind you, as in the case of other children, of the fragility of existence. He has the compactness of a seal, the ruggedness of a young Eskimo. Inuit, you're supposed to call them nowadays. This child is the type for a name like Ivatuq Hviid, or Kingüü Qaavigaaq. Hey, slow down, Agnes tells herself; remember, when you're admiring a litter of newborn puppies, as soon as you catch yourself thinking 'Flossie' or 'Spot', the next thing you know you're Flossie or Spot's owner. The act of naming is tantamount to adopting. She smiles at the boy with the lanky hair, who, impervious, goes on shaking the urn.

She sits down beside him on the ground. Behind her murmur the waves, a soothing, numbing sound. She ought to turn round and enjoy the view. But the thought of moving is suddenly too much for her. It's only now that she's sitting down that she realizes she's bone tired. On the road all day long, and she still hasn't even had a cup of tea. 'Aunt Agnes is getting rather decrepit.' Perhaps it's true, too.

At that moment the sound of an engine is heard, and she looks up to see Muriel Flynt riding towards them over the pasture, zigzagging nimbly along on her mini-tractor. The island has an abundance of unusual transportation devices, and Muriel's pride and joy consists of a three-wheeler mounted on caterpillar treads, with a plastic crate screwed to the back for transporting tools, fishing traps, buckets brimming with berries, a sick lamb. The vehicle is Muriel's own design, she assembled it herself.

Muriel, negotiating the last few metres, is wearing a down-filled waistcoat over her plaid shirt. Her jeans are tucked into muddy boots. A baseball cap is pulled down over the short, carroty curls. Let there be no mistake about it: Muriel is as good a sheep shearer as any man, she can drive a fencepost into the ground and can drink her husband and father-in-law under the table. But her greatest claim to fame are her muffins, crusty on the outside, moist on the inside, powdered with cinnamon, dripping with honey.

She turns off the tractor's engine.

The little boy Ivatuq Hviid next to Agnes scrambles to his feet and runs off. The urn tumbles to the ground.

Agnes quickly picks it up and tucks it deep into her coat pocket. Then, stiffly, she gets to her feet.

'Hello, Agnes,' says Muriel. She remains seated in her saddle. 'How are you doing?'

Agnes suspects that the question is supposed to count as an expression of condolence. The youngest Mrs Flynt is a woman of few words. That's Muriel for you: welding, drilling, hammering on an anvil are more her style.

'Very well, thank you. As are you, by the looks of it.'

Muriel is studying the dirt under her fingernails. Agnes comes to her rescue. 'I was just going to make myself a cup of tea.'

'I've to cut the rhubarb yet, the rain's no' far off.'

Dark clouds are racing in from the south, where Ben More's two-headed hump looms, heavy and volcanic. 'We're getting a taste of all four seasons of the year today, aren't we?' Agnes begins. 'This morning it was—'

'Aye,' says Muriel philosophically, 'that was this morning.' Only tourists talk about the weather. Endlessly. With infinite enthusiasm. As if they don't have any weather at home, where they come from. 'I've some supplies with me. Shall I take them in for you?'

'The children can do it.' Agnes looks around. The boy has vanished. The girl, too, is keeping out of sight.

Without wasting another word, Muriel dismounts. She picks up a crate of groceries, tucks it under her arm, snatches up a few plastic bags that are lying in the grass on her way in and strides into the house. Nobody needs to show Muriel Flynt the way.

In the kitchen she unpacks two pots of jam, a dozen eggs, tomatoes, a large head of lettuce, potatoes fresh out of the ground. 'I'll be by in the morning and chop you some wood,' she says over her shoulder.

'Oh please,' responds Agnes. 'Thank you, that's wonderful.'

The youngest Mrs Flynt slaps down four generously-sized golden-brown muffins on the counter. She looks at Agnes expectantly.

'Oh Muriel,' says Agnes, 'what a treat.'

Muriel links her enormous fingers. She glances appraisingly around the kitchen, quick and efficient. Her homely, freckled face lights up: it takes on a dreamy expression. Then she says, 'You could put in a bigger window.' She runs a hand over the sill, immediately bringing to Agnes's mind memories of endless days of sanding and planing with her brothers.

There's Justus: thoughtful, an irritatingly slow worker, but reliable, and so even-tempered. Frank: sketching on the back of an envelope, making plans – if we were to knock down the chimney, no, I mean it, just hear me out, and then we did something about the f-façade – is anyone listening to me? Robert: no-one's having a drink until we're finished with that last wall, that last skirting board, not until then. You'll all thank me later. And Benjamin: come on Agnes, everyone has to spend at least twenty years scraping paint off the woodwork, you're getting off easy here. And the way he would then stretch out on the couch, hands behind his neck. His teasing stare: Agnes, Agnes. I used to be the youngest. And then you came along. For you I've had to relinquish my privileged position in the family!

Memories.

'I think that window is perfect the way it is,' Agnes tells Muriel before she's realized she isn't being asked for her opinion. From their trenches, the two warring

71

Mrs Flynts have come up with the selfsame solution to the problem of how to get rid of the other.

Muriel sighs and picks up the empty crate. She nods at the muffins. 'A couple more for you tomorrow? It's nae bother, Agnes.'

3

Her nieces and nephews and their offspring like to
speculate about her amongst themselves; sometimes
they give it away by asking her oblique questions. They
suspect an unhappy love affair, in the distant past. A
fallen soldier. Or a man with 'other commitments'.
Anyway, there must have been some tragedy or other,
otherwise Aunt Agnes would have been married.

Agnes won't say yes, Agnes won't say no. Agnes has
her own opinion on tragedies. As far as she is concerned, there is nothing dramatic to speak of buried in
her past. Unless you count a happy childhood, a
childhood spent with four adoring older brothers, the
kind of men you'll never come across again in your
lifetime, men who laugh heartily at your jokes, who
always forgive you no matter what, are proud of you,
think you're clever, take you seriously. Quite a tall
order, for a husband.

She finally drinks her tea. After the second cup
she grows drowsy; the third remains untouched in
front of her. She dozes off on the couch, overcome
with nostalgia. Justus, Frank, Robert, Benjamin. She
couldn't so much as scrape a knee or her brothers
would immediately start plotting reprisals: did you

fall, or were you pushed? And the games, the rituals! The filtered light of summer at the water's edge. A muddied white frock, sailor suits with the collars askew. Salamanders. Frogs' eggs. Do you have the guts? Should I? Oh, I dare you! Her icy nose rubbed warm in winter by two giant mittens, hands supporting her under the armpits, inky-black ice, and now left, right, left, right. What if we fall in? Then I'll pull you out.

'Just jump, Aggie,' if she didn't dare climb down from the tree house. Arms outstretched.

There were always arms to catch her.

She wakes with a start as it begins to pour outside. Still a bit groggy, she closes the window. It's turned dark, though it's only half past five. The hour at which it's perfectly acceptable to have a glass of Scotch. In the cupboard in the living room she finds a bottle of Tobermory single malt that's nearly full.

But all it takes is the first sip for everything to come crashing in on her. The panic that's been hovering nearby for the past few weeks, like a danger you can tell is heading for you out of the corner of your eye, now suddenly grabs her by the throat. No more brothers. She gets to her feet. Pulls on her coat in the hall, a sou'wester, a pair of wellingtons.

The rain pelts in her face when she opens the door. She walks round the back of the house towards the beach. Feeling as though the props of her life have been knocked out from under her, she makes her way down to the water's edge. The wind tears at her clothes. She should have put on an oilskin, her shoulders are already completely soaked.

It's not as if she has ever claimed to be superwoman. So it shouldn't come as a surprise, suddenly, that this has knocked her for six. The last time – no, this time

74

it's worse. Robert's death, for one thing, places her own existence in a frightening new light. She is no longer the youngest one. She is now the only one. The last one. The next to go.

From force of habit, she sets off again. Through the wet sand she goes, following the curve of the bay. Robert used to say there was nothing finer than a rain shower in Port na Bà. He maintained that it would wash away your worst sins and your deepest sorrows. Oh, do take that silly sou'wester off your head, Aggie.

But the rain appears to be letting up. In the west the sky is already growing lighter. It's quite possible that in half an hour it will have cleared up completely, and there will be a spectacular sunset.

Under the scudding clouds, in sunlight, tempest or hail, the landscape is always changing, lovely one moment, desolate the next. What used to be blue becomes green, what was grey turns violet or black or a foamy white, and what appeared solid seems to melt into the mist – but in the end nothing really changes: Mull remains Mull, impregnable, magnificent, breathtaking. It always remains the same, no matter what. To master that same ability yourself, you'd have to be made of stone. Humans weep, complain, pray, beg, hope, take fright. Perhaps the lesson to be drawn here is that it's best not to take one's emotions too seriously. After all, they're only feelings, Agnes thinks, and feelings are constantly changing; they're only qualms, hopes, fears.

Sensible Agnes.

The tears come on suddenly, like water being wrung out of a stone. Robert's thin hands resting on the sheet. She was able to pick him up in her arms, the world was all topsy-turvy, she lifted him effortlessly and set him

75

on the bedpan. How much could he have weighed, in the end? The end: her brother in the hospital bed, with the covers kicked off. A catheter in his penis, which he'd been trying to pull out in his sleep. The utter certainty that he'd never have wanted her to see him like this. Castor and Pollux, that's what they were. Marco Polo and Amerigo Vespucci. Sir Galahad and Sir Gawain. She had pried his hand off the irksome tube and covered him up again. Never before had she touched a man so intimately.

She tries to find something with which to blow her nose. Her coat is hanging lopsided from the weight of the urn in her left-hand pocket. She takes it out. Everything has a price, a drawback. That goes for being the adored youngest one as well. It means you get to bury them one by one.

She takes the lid off the urn. One should never postpone something that's painful. It's just a moment in time, over before you know it. She's not going to make a whole production of it. He wouldn't have wanted that. She clears her throat. 'Port na Bà,' she says out loud, 'take Robert unto you.'

The ashes scatter in all directions, and at the same time the sun breaks through. Through the mist the other islands become visible in the distance, Coll, Tiree, Rhum and even Skye. It's the kind of moment that would certainly have made him glance up from his bird guide. Agnes! Did you see that?

Her hands buried deep in her pockets, she walks back to the house. An undeniable sense of relief, of satisfaction even, washes over her. She has carried out her mission. In a little while she'll call Robert Jr. He was the one who suggested, 'As long as you're going to Mull, Aunt Agnes, why don't you take Father's ashes?'

Suddenly her mood changes, and she is flooded with resentment. The dead, sure, she's allowed to take care of *them*. But the children have to go to camp. We'd rather send them to camp than entrust them to Aunt Agnes ever again! An insult, if you think about it! And a break with tradition to boot. In August Port na Bà is supposed to be teeming with robust, sunburnt little bodies. There ought to be children running back and forth clutching their treasures, a sea urchin, a piece of driftwood, seashells. Salt-stiffened hair tousled in the wind. Excited voices: 'An otter!' 'No, it's a seal!'

Whoever spots a sea otter is allowed to decide what's for dinner. It's much more likely you'll spy a seal, but even there you have to watch very carefully and have plenty of patience. One moment you'll catch a glimpse of one in the waves, the next moment it's disappeared. On the rocks they are completely invisible. It's only when you know the shape of every single rock like the back of your hand that you can even begin to tell where the seals are.

Agnes's heart skips a beat. Over there! The glint of a round, wet, black, bullet-like head. Then her eyes widen in disbelief. It is the head of the little Ivatuq Hviid, soaking wet, his hair straighter than ever. Next to him, huddled among the rocks, sits the girl, her lips blue with cold.

4

Every part of the island has its own stories. Stories of shipwrecks of long ago, of forest fires, foot and mouth disease. Stories of long, severe winters in the even more distant past, when people went mad from hunger and little children mysteriously vanished without a trace. Tales of the MacLeans of Duart Castle, who evicted their emaciated crofters and set fire to their miserable hovels so that they could not move back in. Or of the clan chieftain who beheaded his own son in the tower of his castle – and how, ever since that day, on stormy nights, a headless rider can often be spotted galloping along the shores of Loch Buie.

Tonight Agnes chooses something a little less blood-curdling for a bedtime story. Sitting on the edge of the bed, she tells them in a low voice about the galleon of the Spanish Armada that was sunk off the coast of Tobermory, and is waiting for someone to come and lighten her of her load of golden ducats. She paints a picture of a magical undersea world teeming with nosy little fishes swimming in and out of the shattered portholes.

'Are those Spanish blokes' skeletons still down

there?' asks the girl, who's listening in the doorway, pretending to be bored to death.

'Quiet,' Agnes whispers. 'He's sleeping.' She tucks Ivatuq in a little more securely and checks the hot water bottle at his feet. Then she stands up, takes the girl by the arm and shuts the bedroom door behind her. 'He still pees in bed sometimes,' says the child reproachfully. 'You should have made him put on a nappy.'

'You *could* have mentioned that earlier. And take that gum out of your mouth, or from now on I'll have to call you Chiclets.'

'It isn't Chiclets,' says the girl. She blows a pink bubble. 'It's Bazooka Joe.'

Agnes steers her down the stairs. In the sitting room she throws the last log on the fire and pulls two wicker chairs up to the fireplace. She sits down. Coming straight to the point, she asks, 'How long were you two intending to stay here, anyway?'

The child chooses to squat down by the fire instead. She shrugs her shoulders sullenly. She is wearing a pink cardigan that Alice once left behind in the house, an old pair of pyjama bottoms belonging to Jeroen and a pair of forgotten socks left in the back of a drawer somewhere. The child's own clothes are hanging in the scullery to dry. How impractical, thinks Agnes, to stow away in a stranger's car without even bringing a wind-breaker. 'And also, do please tell me,' she says kindly, 'why did the two of you run away?'

Bazooka glares at her. 'You told on us, didn't you.' she blurts out instead of answering the question, 'when that lady was here this afternoon.'

'Of course not. I never tell on anyone. Listen, Muriel, I seem quite by accident to have picked up two

79

children on the ferry, complete strangers to me, actually'. Agnes remarks neutrally. 'But I suspect that at this very moment there are a couple of very anxious parents out there somewhere.'

'So?'

Agnes laces her fingers together. What's the best way to handle this?

'I'm not telling, anyway. And my brother won't tell either.'

'Oh, is that your little brother?'

'Half-brother. Can't you see that for yourself?'

'Half-brother,' Agnes repeats. Two different fathers. Or mothers. The modern family seems to her to be an arduously complex arrangement for a child. There are cases like that in her own family as well. Impossible to explain, the relationships are so complicated. 'In any case, we'll have to call your . . . your parents to tell them you're spending the night here.'

'We can't,' says Bazooka quickly.

'And why not?'

'They're camping.'

'Where?'

'Dunno.'

'How can you not know? Surely you know which campsite . . .'

The girl says indignantly. 'Yes, of course, but we never stay at the campsite we were *supposed* to be at. We always drive around. And round and round. And then we pitch the tent somewhere, and then we take it down again anyway, and then we put it up somewhere else again, and then we take it down again and then we drive around some more and then—'

'Very tiresome,' Agnes interrupts her. 'But that's still no reason to run away, it would seem to me.'

Bazooka is silent. Nervously she scratches her neck, tugs at her hair and then laughs suddenly, a loud, forced laugh. She isn't a very attractive child: too sharp, too angular, too scrawny. But her flaxen hair is clean, the clothes hanging in the scullery are bright and quite new. Everything, down to her underwear, points to meticulous care and attention.

Agnes tries another tack. 'You're old enough and smart enough to understand that you can't stay here. Why should I let two children I don't know stay under my roof when they won't even tell me what's going on?'

'Your house is big enough. There are lots and lots of beds. Why is your eye so funny?'

'It isn't real, it's made of glass. But now you listen to me. You can be sure that your parents called the police as soon as they discovered you were missing. And if I were to do the same – hello, I've just found two young Dutch kids – then that'll be that.'

The girl bows her head and pokes at the fire. Sparks fly all around. Then she looks up. Softly she says, 'But if you do that, then we'll tell them you kidnapped us, so there.'

Agnes is taken aback for a second. 'And why should I kidnap a couple of kids, for heaven's sake?'

Bazooka narrows her eyes. She jumps up, points at the video camera on the bookshelf. 'For sex videos, of course.' She's elated. 'You lured us away for sex videos.'

'Don't talk rot,' Agnes cries.

'The first thing we had to do when we got here was take our clothes off, wasn't it?'

'Did you want to walk around in those sopping wet things?'

The girl grins triumphantly.

'A respectable old lady like me,' Agnes begins. Then she all but bursts out laughing. The idea that anyone would believe such a story! Next she supposes she'll have to phone her nephew Joost, who is a lawyer. And then her thoughts immediately take quite a different turn, as so often happens these days. She wonders how Joost's adopted daughter is doing now, her darling Sennemi? Sennemi from the Ivory Coast, who used to smell of sandalwood and cinnamon when she was a baby. Not an easy child, but fascinating. Full of questions. Full of mischief. Well, certainly, the greater the imagination, the greater the problems. Goody-goody two-shoes and mummy's boys will give you less trouble, but then, those are so boring. No question of being bored with Sennemi. Heavens, the way she played the game Mrs-Jansen-goes-to-market; she was brilliant! As a four-year-old she was already joining in, as if she'd been born a true Stam; she could slip into any role. A crack improviser, observer, mistress of every situation, our Sennemi.

Generations of Agnes's nieces and nephews and their offspring have played Mrs-Jansen-goes-to-market, a game without any set rules, object or particular point, a game that simply made an appearance one day and has stuck around ever since. No-one has any idea how long it's been in the family, who invented it or how it should be played, exactly. Sometimes it disappears for a couple of years, but sooner or later the memory of it will surface again, and then some young Stam somewhere will whisper, 'Let's play Mrs-Jansen-goes-to-market.'

The only thing you need to play the game is a shopping basket, and a lot of imagination. The more players, the better. Everyone has the right to be Mrs

Jansen, that's the whole object of the game, but nobody ever actually manages to become Mrs Jansen, and that's what makes it go on for ever, days, weeks, months, endless spells during which, by cunning strategy, one may contrive to become a postman, marchioness, guardian angel, lion tamer or airline pilot, but never Mrs Jansen, never, ever Mrs Jansen.

There have been instalments that were so brilliantly played that people still talk about them at birthday parties. Because even though the Stams, as a family, are certainly not short on imagination, as far back as anyone remembers no-one has yet succeeded in creating a credible Mrs Jansen, even if it was only a matter of missing it by just two points (or twelve – there is some disagreement as to the scoring system).

Bazooka bangs the poker on the floor to get Agnes's attention. 'Are you listening?'

Agnes gazes at her. Sex tapes, no less: the child is cut out for Mrs Jansen, clearly. You could probably explain the whole game to her in two words, and the two of you would have days of fun with it. 'Yes, no, of course I don't want to go to jail.'

'In one of those stripy pyjamas.' Bazooka puts in. Her cheeks are burning with two bright red spots.

Agnes goes one further. 'And a ball and chain round my ankle.'

'And handcuffs.'

'Most unpleasant. So I'd better not call the police, then. I'll just have to get you to leave.'

Bazooka blanches. 'But it's raining outside.'

'Oh well. Your clothes are already wet anyway.'

'And it's dark out!'

'True, but I should think that anyone who's got the

guts to run away from their parents can probably stand up to a couple of knocks.'

Head bowed, the little girl deliberates. She tugs at her hair, fiddles nervously at the hem of Alice's cardigan with nail-bitten fingers. 'But how can we . . . in the middle of the night . . . maybe there's scary . . .' She bites her lip, as if calling herself to order. This is one who doesn't like to give anything away.

Agnes is ashamed of herself: when they're so cocky and impudent, you sometimes completely forget how young they really are. 'I was only teasing, you know. Don't worry.'

'Me? I never worry.'

'No, I don't suppose you do.'

'But for you can't be much fun being here all alone, either.'

Agnes stands up, moves a book on the coffee table, sits down again. Who'd ever have thought, she thinks, that some day I'd find myself in Port na Bà all alone? OK, I'm going to do a lot of reading, naturally, and of course there's always the Flynts. I can certainly drop in over there from time to time for a little chat or a . . . and suddenly her thoughts go into a tailspin: the younger Mrs Flynt saw Bazooka and Ivatuq sitting in the car this afternoon. She's seen her arrive with a couple of kids, as is her wont, and Muriel, too, must at least have noticed the wee lad. If the two little ones are gone tomorrow, it will make them wonder, to say the least. And then it will make them worry about her, when they hear the explanation. 'But Agnes, why didn't you say so from the start?'

In her mind's eye she sees the Flynts conferring at their kitchen table. Should they, as responsible care-takers, call the family in the Netherlands to inform them of Agnes's peculiar behaviour? 'We even asked her whose bairns they were when she first arrived, but she pretended not to hear. It wasn't until those two had gone that we found out what was really going on.'

The Stams gathered in similar conclave. Baffled, embarrassed: Aunt Agnes has flipped her lid. Just as we feared. Robert's death was the final blow. Poor Agnes. It's a blessing in disguise, really, that we didn't let her take Laura, or Bas, or little Ruben; we've seen it coming, thank goodness, for quite a while now. In spite of their dismay, their faces are smug, because what is more satisfying than having your opinion confirmed?

Abruptly, Agnes gets up again. She catches sight of her reflection in the glass and automatically pats her hair. *It wasn't until those two had gone that we found out what was really going on.* The children's lemonade glasses from this afternoon are still on the table. She stacks them up and carries them into the kitchen, where she rinses them under the tap, carefully and deliberately. She wipes the counter clean, switches off the light. There's nothing for it, it's time for bed.

Hundreds of miles from here, in Wassenaar, Robert's widow, Elise, must be performing the last routines of the day too, as slowly as she can, in order to postpone the time when she has to pull back the covers of the empty bed. Poor Elise, thinks Agnes. All alone. Elise with her irritating habit of always finding fault with everything. Elise, who in all her life has never been caught in a single impulsive or subversive act.

Oh, there are so many rules, written or unwritten, rules made by men and rules made by the authorities, rules of morality and rules of decency, rules of hope and rules of fear, rules of winning and of losing, and those of Mrs Jansen. Who on earth will tell you which of these rules to obey, when they're all calling out to you at the same time, follow me, follow *me*?

Agnes returns to the sitting room. Beside the dying fire, the girl wearing Alice's cardigan looks at her anxiously, stubborn and hopeful at once. She may be just a little on the old side for potato cut-outs, but she's surely not too old for seashell boxes.

Three

And God said: Let the earth put forth grass, herb yielding seed, and fruit tree bearing fruit after its kind, wherein is the seed thereof, upon the earth. And it was so.

Genesis 1

1

In the morning Muriel's muffins have disappeared, and
so have the clothes in the scullery. It is quiet in the
cottage.

Agnes looks in all the rooms.

She even looks under the beds.

And still she can't believe that the two of them have
actually sneaked out.

In a tizzy, by way of breakfast she wolfs down a
couple of tomatoes, standing at the sink. Perhaps she
shouldn't have mentioned the police last night. The
police, for God's sake! As if she were dealing with a
pair of criminals on the run, instead of two naughty
little scamps. In her mind's eye she sees Bazooka and
Ivatuq scrambling over the cliffs; the rocks are slippery
and the sea crashes below, but the children barely
mind where they're putting their feet; panicked, they
keep glancing back over their shoulders. Hounded.
Wearing only sandals, in their flimsy cotton clothes,
ignorant of the treacherousness of the terrain, of the
vagaries of the weather. If something were to happen to
them, would it be her fault? Would she be responsible?

Her unease increases. It was years ago, oh, years and
years. Two bedraggled, abandoned dogs on the beach,

almost certainly not answering to the names of Kawa and Saki. She'd immediately gone out and bought a couple of tins of dog food, and then she'd phoned Robert. Robert was the kind of man who understood such things, who'd even approve. His encouraging voice on the phone: you'd better give them some vitamins, Aggie, and dab some iodine on the mangy patches.

But one afternoon four weeks later, when the dogs had begun to look sleek and healthy again, when they no longer ran away when you tried to come near, when they were all frisky again, always merrily wagging their tails when they weren't soundly snoring, Ben Flynt, Muriel's husband, son of the younger Mrs Flynt, had been able to pick them up just like that and had stuffed them into a burlap sack – perhaps they'd even licked his hands as he was doing so – and then he had hurled the sack, weighted with stones, into the sea, because, said Ben, sooner or later they'd be going after the sheep, and you couldn't just sit back waiting for *that* to happen.

You'd think it ought to be easy, simply being a good person, until you see the awful mess your good deeds can cause. But does that exempt you from your duty to try and do what's right?

Impulsively, Agnes grabs her coat and an umbrella, and steps outside. It's a wet, grey day: no view, no islands in the distance, no cloud formations vying for attention. A day for thinking about other days. As she walks across the grass, straining her eyes, she tries to remember what it was like to be Ivatuq's age, or as old as his jumpy sister. What do you think about at that age, what frightens you, what makes you roar with laughter?

There's a picture of herself as a toddler in one of the many family albums, a yellowing, crenellated-edged snapshot. A caption in faded letters: AGNES DISCOVERS THE WORLD. In the photograph she's sitting on the grass dressed in a white pinafore, three or four years old, a contemplative look on her face. In her hand she holds a dandelion puffball. Out of view someone is saying, '*Go* on then, blow!' She remembers to this day the shock when she did indeed puff at it, and discovered she had decimated an entire universe. How strange, that from the very first breath you take, they encourage you to put your own stamp on things, to leave your mark, to make your presence felt.

In the photo you can't see how far the little para-chutes were scattered. She had seen them drift off in every direction, as if on a wide cinema screen. Out of the corner of one eye she'd seen them floating over the privet hedge; out of the other she'd observed the rest wafting into the neighbours' garden on a breath of wind. Without turning her head she could stretch her field of vision like a piece of chewing gum, not really knowing how she did it. You'd think, wouldn't you, that she'd have forgotten that sense of unparalleled width and breadth eventually. But, merci-fully, it is pain that is banished from our memory, not delight.

In hospital the following summer, her injured eye was carefully bandaged after the surgery. The nurses assured her gaily that she was now a real pirate. But Agnes didn't want to be a pirate, pirates were bad men. She cried and said she was Marco Polo, and her brother was Amerigo Vespucci. They glugged their rum straight from the bottle, they ate dry biscuits and shouted, 'Land ahoy!' Their ship was a table turned upside down, and sometimes they'd go fishing and reel in a shark.

In her bed on the children's ward she counted the days until she'd be allowed to go fishing with Robert again. Agnes carrying the little tin of earthworms and the treacle sandwiches, Robert with his homemade rod and net, setting off together across the fields. The muddy smell of the stream, the shade under the hawthorns, the buzzing silence, the gravity of the whole enterprise. In her hospital bed she dreamt she caught an enormous carp, its gills as large as silver guilders, a carp weighing as much as five kilos.

Robert's elated laugh, his proud, 'Agnes's caught a whopper *this* big!'

Nobody told her that after the accident, their mother had taken the rod with the errant fish hook and had broken it into a hundred pieces.

Under her umbrella, in the drizzling rain, Agnes lets out a wistful sigh. She tries to picture her mother in the act of snapping a fishing rod over her knee, in the act of doing anything at all, in fact. She can't. At the time of her birth her parents were already quite old, they were like a fairytale that brings a smile to your face but that you don't really believe in any more. They were usually to be found sitting in their armchairs, and they reeked of peppermint. They argued about whose reading glasses were whose. It wouldn't have occurred to them to be anything but this married couple, *they* didn't feel the need to get divorced and start new families.

All of my brothers, Agnes thinks with nostalgia, were my whole, not my half, brothers: Justus, Frank, Robert and Benjamin. I don't know what it's like to be

Bazooka, or Ivatuq, I simply can't put myself in their shoes.

She walks to where the dirt road starts. It veers to the left at the Flynts' farmhouse and then right again before disappearing from sight. The futility of her search hits her: Mull has thousands of paths, lanes, byways. Dozens of glens, so vast, so lonely, that it's possibly only the grim monotony of mile upon mile of desolate emptiness that makes them so imposing. There's an infinite number of remote creeks and isolated cliffs; plenty of places where you can vanish without a trace. Scattered over the hillsides are umpteen dilapidated barns and sheds, and every beach boasts a few rickety boats that will never put out to sea again: hiding places everywhere you look.

Abruptly Agnes turns and marches over to Port na Bà's mailbox, hanging from a tree limb at the end of the path, to give her futile expedition some purpose after all. But of course there is no post for her yet, just a brochure advertising holiday homes. She slips it into her pocket and walks back. The pasture is marshy, it's hard-going, and the wind yanks at her umbrella.

Normally she loves this stroll. What does it mean, if you can't enjoy the ordinary everyday things any more? Does it mean you're depressed? Angrily she brings her foot down in a mud puddle, on purpose. You're expected to be happy all the time, nowadays. As if life doesn't present you with one insurmountable difficulty after another. You're expected to accept your losses, you're supposed to bow to the inevitable, you have to face up to your shortcomings, you have to forgive yourself and others. Lord, as if it were nothing.

Back at the house, she leaves the wet umbrella on the mat and shrugs off her coat. She thinks, I'll never forgive myself – in their sandals, too, and in their thin cotton clothes.

In the kitchen she makes herself a cup of Nescafé. She doesn't have the peace of mind to sit down, she drinks it standing at the window. Don't think that you'll ever have any say about this window, Muriel! We installed it together, the two of us, it was a boiling hot day, a day when he wore just a pair of shorts, he was all sweaty, steam rising from his chest, and when he smiled at me I could see the corner of the bottom tooth that had once been chipped by a hockey stick; I mean, I didn't see the missing chip, that bit was gone, and gone is gone. It was so hot that day, the window putty wouldn't set.

She rinses her cup.

She walks into the living room. She turns on the radio. And turns it off again.

Maybe she ought to write a few postcards right now, to get it over with. Dear Elise. But she isn't in a mood to make herself feel even worse. Dear Alice? That's better. Dear little Alice, can you guess what I just found? Your pink cardigan! Won't you come and put it on again, soon? Big kiss from your Aunt Agnes.

Suddenly she feels an itch behind her glass eye, a sensation usually associated with tears. Is there anyone left on this earth who still thinks of her, who wishes *she* would come? In the past, when she was a teacher, there was always some little one whose eyes would light up: Miss Stam, Miss Stam! She taught countless children to read and write, she combed the nits out of their hair, she talked to their parents about their report cards and about their special talents. There were times when she even found herself having to intervene in a child's life at home – some jittery little thing, nails

96

bitten to the quick, an unhappy, confused child, battered or suffering from extreme neglect. At no point did she ever hesitate to step in when she suspected child abuse.

But all that is far behind her now. She no longer has any homework to correct, bruises to report or maps of the world to draw on the blackboard; her days are no longer filled with the sort of activities and deeds that prove you're alive and have a role to play.

She thinks to herself: oh, *come* on.

She pours herself a second cup of Nescafé and carries it over to the sofa, where she sits down.

She could phone the elder Mrs Flynt for a chat. Or would that be intruding? She picks up the telephone and lifts the receiver to her ear. After a moment's hesitation she dials her own phone number in the Netherlands.

There is no answer, and she dials the number again. Where can Joyce be, the great-niece with the long legs and the black nail varnish, who has offered to look after Agnes's flat for the month? Has she gone out, just at the very moment when it occurred to her great-aunt it might be a good idea to remind her what to do in case of white spot in the fish tank? ('No, you have to add the medicine to the water first, understood?')

But hadn't Joyce muttered something about a boyfriend who was going to keep her company? Maybe they're still in bed. In *my* bed, thinks Agnes, and she is flooded with memories, in *my* bed. She doesn't want to think about how furious she was, that time – so unfairly, too – and hangs up.

She carries her cup into the kitchen.

In the hall she takes the holiday rentals brochure out of her coat pocket. She wouldn't mind knowing how much per week the average tourist has to pay for a house on Mull. On her way to the living room she starts leafing through it. There's the cottage at the intersection at Croig, there the mill that has stood empty so long in Dervaig, and here, admirably photographed, at its most picturesque, is the house at Port na Bà: white walls, blue window frames, slate roof. SLEEPS TWELVE, it says. Well, not quite, thinks Agnes, perching on the corner of the coffee table, with a little determination and good will this place will actually accommodate fourteen. The rent quoted under the photo is so ludicrously low that she feels insulted. And then it finally occurs to her to wonder, what are *we* doing in this brochure? We're not for rent. She must put an end to this misunderstanding at once.

Agitated, still clutching the leaflet, she grabs the phone. Island Rentals in Tobermory. She dials the number, impatiently tapping her foot on the floor while waiting for the connection.

Somewhere, at this very moment, a stranger's hands may very well be handling this same glossy leaflet, a stranger's fingers may be pointing: 'Might this be something for us?' The fact that it's a mistake that will be put right in a minute offers little comfort, and now she's stamping her foot in frustration. It's simply unbearable, for some reason, the thought that someone would even *think* Robert's house might be for rent. 'Come on!' she mutters into the mouthpiece, and then it finally hits her: the line is dead. Her telephone isn't working.

Now this. And why now, for heaven's sake? Because there's always *some*thing that needs to be repaired in a house that stands empty for most of the year, that's why. Things don't malfunction when they receive regular use; it's when they're never touched that they break down, a phenomenon which has often made her wonder, and which sometimes leads her to worry apprehensively that the same thing might be true of people as well – of her, for example. But now is not the time to feel sorry for herself. First she has to drive over to the Island Rentals office. Then, as long as she has to be in Tobermory anyway, she can take care of the telephone at the same time.

In the hall her folded umbrella is still dripping on the mat. Should she leave the door unlocked, just in case . . . ? But those little rascals could very well be on the other side of the island by now.

Her car is parked to the left of the house, as usual, its nose facing the grey sea. She sits down behind the wheel and wipes the fogged-up windscreen clean. And at that very moment, at some distance along the wet beach, she sees Bazooka's skinny form hauling buckets of sand. Her little brother follows close behind. He too is dragging two buckets, which Agnes recognizes as having come from her shed.

It seems so normal, so unremarkable, the two children playing in the cove, so exactly the way it ought to be, that her initial surprise and relief ebb away immediately. She gets out of the car and walks towards them, her hands thrust into her pockets. So, it appears the two scamps were simply where they were supposed to be all morning long: here, on the beach, with her.

It is unclear what, exactly, Bazooka's and Ivatuq's game consists of. It seems to be prompted largely by a grim determination to move as great a quantity of sand about in as short a time as possible. The beach has been completely overhauled. The girl shouts instructions at her little brother, who looks up at her with grave awe. If God thought His beach was fine the way it was, then there's a surprise in store for Him once Bazooka is through with it. Trotting after her the way the dog Kawa used to trot after Saki, Ivatuq does his very best to assist her in bringing her concept to fruition.

Oh dear, was ever devotion so poorly repaid? There is much scolding. Finger accusingly pointing at sand dumped in the wrong place. But the little boy stands his ground. Despite the furious tongue-lashing, he doesn't flinch. He fills his buckets again, dumps them in the spot where his sister is assertively stamping her foot; he hurries, he scurries. More sand! More!

Why so feverish, why so grim?

Not made any the wiser by the joyless hollering, Agnes walks towards the children. At every step, their enterprise comes to seem to her more primitive, wilder, as if they were trying to move all the sand on earth to cover something over, as if to bury some great and monstrous secret, and she stops short, quite shaken suddenly.

That's when the little boy spots her and lets go of his buckets. There's snot coming out of his nose, and his trousers are falling down. He glowers at Agnes from under his black pageboy hair. And then bursts into tears, flinging himself against Bazooka and pulling at her T-shirt.

The girl glances at Agnes, then puts an arm round her brother's neck and with gruff tenderness hugs him to her chest. 'Crybaby,' she croons indulgently, 'scaredy-cat, you needn't be scared of Agnes, it's only Agnes, remember, the one we live with now?'

It's-only-Agnes knows she ought to snap at them, 'Hang on, hang on, what do you mean, *live* with?'

'He's cold,' says Bazooka, rubbing the boy's bare arms. Her eyes dart from side to side as if she smells danger.

Agnes hesitates. Then she says, 'In that case let's quickly go in and get something hot to drink.'

In the kitchen the children sit side by side on the old painted yellow chairs that have long been a thorn in Elise's side. Agnes puts steaming mugs of tea down on the table. 'You certainly were up early this morning,' she says.

'We didn't make any noise, right?' Bazooka defends herself quickly. Dark circles under her eyes. That one didn't get much sleep last night, by the looks of her.

'You may get out the sugar, it's in the bottom cupboard, there,' says Agnes. She casts a surreptitious glance at the little brother's tear-stained face. A toddler who doesn't wail for his mummy when he cries. That's odd. Pensively she takes a sip of her tea.

'Yuck!' Bazooka yelps, squatting by the kitchen cupboard.

'What is it?'

'Mice!'

'Oh no! Really?'

With a reproachful scowl on her face the child produces a packet of pancake mix with its bottom chewed open, flour flying in all directions. In her other hand she brandishes a bag that's leaking sugar.

'Not *that* again,' says Agnes, getting to her feet wearily. She opens a drawer and takes out a rubbish bag. 'Let's throw everything out that was in that cupboard. Just dump it all in here.'

Now Ivatuq too pipes up. 'Not the crisps,' he whines.

'We'll buy some more. We're not going to keep anything that's been near the vermin.'

'It'll kill you,' Bazooka tells her brother as she pulls packets and bags out of the cupboard and stuffs them into the rubbish bag. 'They have a kind of bacteria in their saliva, a sort of AIDS or something, and . . .' She jumps back with a yell. 'There it goes!'

The mouse makes a dash for it, past Agnes's shoe. It runs for its life to the safety of the skirting board, emitting pitiful squeaks, remarkably loud for such a small creature. It's a grey field mouse, it belongs in the meadow, among the plumed grasses, sitting up on its hind legs and looking around with alert little eyes, like the one on the mug Agnes gave Sennemi for her birthday. Doesn't the mouse know that? What kind of intelligence *does* a mouse have? Does it have any conception of the world? Of day and night, sun and moon? Of buzzards, owls, hawks, crows, eagles?

Bazooka's spindly leg shoots forward. With the toe of her shoe she flicks the mouse off the floor and kicks it viciously into the air. It does a complete somersault high overhead and for just a moment, spread-eagled, it seems to be floating in space; then it comes barrelling down.

Agnes sees the little black eyes bulging with terror. Her mouth goes dry as a cork. From far away, in some other time, she hears someone shouting, 'Watch out!'

Robert, it was Robert who yelled it, at her other brothers. Robert, who had emptied his whole piggy-bank to buy a doll with real hair for her when she was discharged from the hospital. Her injured eye had healed, the world was wide and deep and splendid once again. In the garden, at her homecoming, amidst

102

cries of joy, Justus had tossed her up in the air and caught her in his arms again.

'Watch out!'

Frank had flung his bike down on the gravel to run to greet her. Benjamin had tripped over the front wheel in his haste to join in the fun. 'There's cake, Aggie,' he'd shouted, crashing into Justus as he fell.

'Watch out!' Robert yelled as Justus too took a nose-dive. And Agnes squealed with delight when she felt Robert grabbing her out of the air, and as they tumbled to the ground together she was still laughing. Robert, clutching her tight, fell on top of her with all his weight, and with a crack that felt as though her whole skull was splintering to pieces, the tip of Frank's handlebar was driven deep into her eye socket.

The mouse lands on the stone floor with a dull thud. 'Dead,' says Bazooka with satisfaction. She picks up the little corpse by the tail and waves it around.

Out of pure habit Agnes ponders, it could all have turned out *so* much worse. Something else could have happened, after all, something for which her brothers would never have forgiven themselves. 'Oh, dear,' she says, 'we *could* just have let it go outside, you know.'

With a crushed look on her face, the girl lets go of the mouse; it falls to the floor. 'I only wanted to help! I never do *anything* right.'

'Of course you do,' Agnes hastens to correct herself. Praise. You can never praise a child enough. 'Because at least now we won't get sick from that nasty mouse disease. What a smart girl you are to have thought of that.'

A timid, dubious look from Bazooka. *I never do*

103

anything right. What kind of parents would lead a little girl to think such a thing?

The more parents there are, thinks Agnes grimly, the more traumas there are, too. Why don't they make you take a parental competence exam, in the children's best interest? Why is it only outsiders such as herself who seem to be prepared to take children seriously, who don't regard them as little creatures who only need to know one thing: who calls the shots around here?

The little boy slips down off his chair, picks up the mouse and places it on the table. Silently he pokes the animal in the side with a short, stubby finger, so that it rolls onto its back, legs sticking up in the air.

That shakes Agnes out of her musings. 'We'll give it a lovely funeral, don't you think?' They'll mark the grave with a chunk of painted rock, there will be flowers and maybe even some singing. She knows the ritual by heart: in Port na Bà, every one of her little kids has had to bury some small creature at some time or another. There should be enough room for Ivatuq's mouse between Dennis's hedgehog and Effie's seagull.

2

When Muriel comes over to chop wood, she has a message for Agnes from the elder Mrs Flynt, inviting her to the farm for tea this afternoon. They've already made a chocolate cake for the bairns, she says. She issues the invitation in a manner that's as offhand as it is matter-of-fact. And why not? After all, everything is exactly the way it has always been in years past, as far as Muriel can tell, anyway. Her ugly, friendly face. Her enormous wellingtons. Her muffins. 'We'll be expecting you at four,' she concludes.

'We'd love to,' Agnes replies, with the distinct sense that the chocolate cake sanctions, in some way or other, the children's presence here. As if the gods had chosen Muriel Flynt's cake-making hands as the means to convey their approval and consent.

Muriel says, 'Gran's fair excited about it.'

'So am I,' says Agnes. From their very first encounter fifty years ago, she has had a soft spot for the elder Mrs Flynt, who back then was still the only Mrs Flynt, and held sway over the whole farm, where she energetically ran a bed and breakfast as a sideline. She fried eggs on a gigantic wood-fired Aga. She pumped water, she scoured her floors with sand. She churned and spun and darned socks at night by the light of an oil lamp. She wore two skirts and two jerseys on top of each other and she washed her hair with water from the rain barrel.

Agnes thought her life romantic.

You, said Benjamin pityingly, you think everything is romantic – even that stinking *Weinstube* last year in Vienna, and that street organist with the mangy monkey: how many times must we drag you around the world in order to knock some sense of discrimination into you?

Oh, many times, said Agnes, many times.

Agnes at twenty, right after the war: hair in braids wound round her head, immersed in the writings of Rudolf Steiner. But did it make all that much sense, really, to declare that children should never be conveyed anywhere at a speed greater than that of a horse and carriage? She thought, I am too modern for such views. This discovery gave her immense satisfaction. She wasn't about to go through life half asleep. Avidly she tried to copy her brothers in that department, who all had such a head start on her.

Only Benjamin was still studying, or at least was still enrolled at the University of Leiden. He called himself a 'free-thinker' and held smoke-filled gatherings in his rooms overlooking one of Leiden's canals. Immensely popular he was; spoilt and lazy. Agnes feared his intelligence would prove too much for him; he'd have to look after himself better if he ever wanted to be able to harness his brainpower adequately. Every weekend she brought him his clean laundry, stoically looking the other way while he swept the feminine lingerie off the only armchair for her. Did she want that kind of bohemian existence for herself? Agnes Stam, free-thinker.

Or should she take Justus, her eldest brother, as her model? The warm atmosphere of a house with a well-stocked china cabinet and sparkling window panes. The drawings of little Gemma, aged four, on the walls and the building blocks of Joost, aged two, all over the floor. Seated in the bay window with a pipe stuck in the corner of his mouth, Justus corrected his students' Greek homework, grinning with delight if a paper deserved high marks. His wife Nora rattling pans in the kitchen. The buzz of children's voices. That, too, rather appealed to Agnes, for herself, for the future.

Or else to live like Frank. Wildly creative Frank. Absent-minded Frank! At dinner his elegant hands would sometimes stay dangling for over a minute in the salad bowl, without seeming in the least out of place there. His hair stank of turpentine, there was paint on his sweater, but his eyes shone. Found a bulb shed with m-marvellous northern light, Aggie. If the bank goes along with it I'll have the perfect studio!

To have a special talent: what a privilege, she thought, while brushing out her braids. Did she have a talent? She wasn't bad at the piano, and she had a nice voice. But Robert, for example, played the saxophone incredibly well. Languid Charlie Parker melodies, seeming to spiral lazily through the air. Except that he had little time these days for his music. A vet worked long days, calves and lambs decided to be born when it suited *them*. Robert in a filthy jacket with leather elbow patches, muddy knee-boots. His wife Elise would have much preferred a practice for domestic animals, pet poodles and long-haired cats.

How busy they all were, and Agnes herself no less so, what with college, the liberal hiking club and her piano lessons. Before you knew it, there was never any time to see each other any more. That may have been why, the night Frank showed them his new studio, they made a spur-of-the-moment decision to go off somewhere together for a week, just the five of them. To catch up, to reminisce about their childhood, to be a Stam amongst other Stams.

None of them had done much travelling, but Justus had fond memories of his honeymoon in Vienna. Agnes didn't own a suitcase; she packed her clothes in Benjamin's laundry bag, her shoes in a shopping net. She was teased about her bag-lady gear for the duration of the train ride. In Austria her brothers bought her a leather case, and a fur hat.

It snowed incessantly all that week in Vienna, a blur of powdery snow that necessitated visiting one *Konditorei* after another and drinking lots of *schnapps* and eating sachertorte. 'Perhaps next time,' said Frank on the journey home, prostrate, visibly bloated, 'we ought to try to get a little more exercise. Climb a m-mountain, or something.'

The next time?

Indeed, not for nothing did Justus's wife Nora often sigh to Frank's Mathilde, 'In this family you only need to do something once for it to turn into a tradition.'

That year the trip took them to Mull, for no other reason than that Robert had read an article about the Scottish island in a magazine. They could just as easily have taken a trip up the Rhine, except that nobody happened to read an article about it.

But visiting Mull, back then! With tent poles that weighed at least a kilo apiece, but no fuchsia-red rain gear, no Velcro fastenings or vinyl map sleeves. They managed to climb Ben More the very first day notwithstanding. When they reached the top the fog was so thick that enjoying the view was out of the question. Agnes brewed a pot of tea on the camping stove. Benjamin took snapshots of the invisible landscape. He said that by the time the roll was developed, the fog would have lifted.

The second day they followed the sandy footpath to Croig, where they ate sandwiches on the dock, their feet dangling in the water, and one by one they fell asleep in the sun. After that no-one was much in the mood for putting up the tent. But Robert had spotted a farm with a B & B sign. They sauntered over there intending to stay one night and stayed the remainder of the week.

Narrow beds, hard as concrete, with surprisingly comfortable straw pallets. To wake up without hearing a clock ticking anywhere. To splash ice-cold water from the washbasin onto your face to the constant *kakaka* of the indefatigable seagulls outside. The pleasant, stomach-churning response to the mouth-watering smells wafting up from downstairs. To think that you'd never realized you were capable of putting away so much food in a single day! Fried eggs and bacon for starters. A hearty leek and buckwheat soup for lunch. High teas without beginning or end. A mid-afternoon snack of dripping honeycomb, a coarse hunk of bread. Haggis, made of sheep's intestines, if anyone was still hungry at night. Briny whisky, which the Flynts distilled themselves.

'We seem to be slipping b-back into the same old bad habit,' Frank remarked.

'But we'll walk it off again,' said Agnes.

On long rambles in the surrounding countryside she felt happier than she could ever remember being. Was it the warm, fragrant breeze? Was it the lovely beach strewn with seashells and stones? The old cattle port in the distance, with the picturesque tumble-down cottage that was missing its roof? It wasn't until the fourth morning that it hit her: it was the breadth, the grandeur of the landscape. There were simply so many breathtaking vistas here that it gave even Agnes, with only one good eye, a boundless sense of space, width and depth.

'It just feels as if I can see more clearly here than anywhere else,' she told Robert, elated. She tossed her head back and laughed out loud. 'It's just so amazing!'

Perhaps that was what did it. Or else it may have been the inclination for repetition, which ran through the Stams' temperament like a red thread; what was excellent had to be continued. And so, a few hours before the departure of the ferry that was to take them back to the train station in Oban, Robert had bought the ruin at Port na Bà.

The honeysuckle boughs are bent low by the weight of the rain, the front path is strewn with snapped fuchsia buds and the display of homemade jam on the stone wall is covered with a piece of plastic flapping dismally in the wind. Muddy boots in the porch, dripping oilskins under the overhang by the barn. It's windy as hell in the courtyard of the farmstead inhabited by the Flynts and their irreconcilable womenfolk, and the gusts lash the rain in all directions.

But inside, in the kitchen, the colossal Aga glows just like in the old days. The kettle is singing on the stove, steaming laundry hangs to dry overhead. Some things never change, thank goodness.

'Will ye mind the bairns dinnae gae near the stove, Agnes?' asks the younger Mrs Flynt as she sets the table for tea, her deeply grooved face perspiring beneath the unkempt grey hair. Chocolate cake, paper-thin finger sandwiches, hard-boiled eggs with mayonnaise, fruit, jam rolls. Then she resumes her monologue.

The younger Mrs Flynt can talk like a steam engine, in an insistent, even tempo, the way women talk who do not labour under any illusion that they are necessarily being heard. They pin their hopes on repetition, on the inexhaustible variation on the same theme, the drip-drip of water onto a stone. Over the years, the younger Mrs Flynt has developed an intonation hovering somewhere between resignation and indignation, truly a great accomplishment in the art of discourse.

'And does Muriel ever so much as lift a finger for my poor mother-in-law? Of course not. Never. It's a' up to me. Day in, day out. I do it with love, that's no' it, I'm no' griping, but that's what the young are like, I always say, they canna conceive of what it means to be bedridden, relying on others to take care of you, madam doesn't even gi' it a moment's thought, she likes to put her own needs first, so I'm not exaggerating when I tell you that it's a' up to me, but ye ken, we each have our cross to bear, and it makes us the stronger for it, what say you, Agnes, true or no?'

'Oh, true,' says Agnes.

The younger Mrs Flynt inspects the feast with her usual scorn: it doesn't come up to scratch and never will, either. Then she pours water into the pot, pops the tea cosy on top, pours boiling water into one pitcher, milk in another.

'Why don't you fetch the teacups,' Agnes says to Bazooka. 'Quick, over there, on the dresser.'

With an angelic expression Bazooka accomplishes her task.

'Aye, you can surely tell she's a true Stam, that one, so well brought up. What I was wanting to say to you, Agnes, I'm no' getting any younger mysel' mean-while . . .'

'Oh,' Agnes demurs. She never really has the sense that people do grow old; people may at most become a

112

little more well-rounded, but mentally, most people remain forever sixteen: brimming with hopes and dreams. Take herself, for example. She suspects that in the past seventy years she has probably never allowed herself to be robbed of an important illusion; not once.

'Aye, and I'm ready to start taking it easy,' says the younger Mrs Flynt. She pulls up a chair and sits down with a pained expression on her face. 'It's time Muriel took over caring for Mother. And at sixty it's about time for me to have my own roof over my head at last.'

It's too warm in the kitchen and the heat, combined with the humidity, is starting to make Agnes feel she's in a sauna. The way she imagines a sauna might feel, that is. She unbuttons her cardigan. It's a thick Arran wool knit, in an ingenious brown-and-white pattern. She's had it, oh, probably at least twenty-five years. She wishes the younger Mrs Flynt would not stare at her like that, an expectant look on her permanently exhausted face. Bloodshot eyes lined with dark shadows, starkly prominent cheekbones, a puckered upper lip. Nobody would claim that this Mrs Flynt has had an easy life.

Suddenly she blurts out, in an entreating tone, 'So will ye no' be talking it over with your sister-in-law, Agnes? What good is Port na Bà to Elise now, now that she's decided to start renting it out to the tourists? I mean, now that you yourselves willna' be using it any more? She wrote to us as soon as Robert—'

'Dear heaven,' Agnes exclaims. So there's no point going to Island Rentals with her complaint about that brochure! It's not as if there's been a mistake or a misunderstanding. Flustered, she says, 'I'll get in touch with her right away to tell her—'

'Thank you, oh, I truly do appreciate that.'

'But we'll never sell the house, you can be sure of that, so—'

'Well now, how lovely,' the younger Mrs Flynt interrupts her loudly, a guilty blush turning her cheeks nearly purple, 'here's Mother!'

In a wheelchair that is a triumph of island technology – cobbled together from the carcass of an old armchair and the wheels of a pram – the elder Mrs Flynt is wheeled into the kitchen, pushed by Muriel-who-never-lifts-a-finger.

She's listing sideways in the cushions, more brittle and frail than Agnes has ever seen her, a tartan blanket over her knees, a wool wrap round her shoulders. Her mouth is puckered, there are long white hairs growing from her chin. 'Agnes, dear lass!' she cries. Her voice is shaky with age, but her watery eyes are beaming. 'There you are! How lovely! And which of your many bairns have you brought along this year to keep you company? Do introduce us!'

Agnes kisses the wrinkled cheeks, shakes the feeble hands which used to slam the Aga's hotplate covers back into place with a thundering crash, which once spun wool and churned and darned and pumped water – and with that, she finds herself catapulted through a hole in time, all the cells of her body stop dividing, her skin turns smooth and tight again, her fingers remember the feeling of pliable tresses that had to be braided and then wound round her head, her scalp can sense the hairpins. And with a friendly, mild ache, her skull remembers how it felt when he'd pull her braids out, to tease her, sometimes. And she thinks, he never knew, I never gave him any hint. She has every reason to be proud of herself. And every reason to be sorry, of course. But that last thought is just a fleeting one, and

114

anyhow, she's having tea at her neighbours', what can she be thinking of, standing there daydreaming, and she smiles at the elder Mrs Flynt, sits down again and takes another piece of cake.

Oh, to be Agnes Stam.
So, what of it?
There are much greater tragedies in the world.

To be Bazooka for instance (further particulars unknown): to be dragged along to see some old carcass in a fucking wheelchair. She just can't get over it. She isn't even over it by night-time. 'I just about wet myself when that witch rolled in. That was mean of you, Agnes, really wicked.' There's an excited, querulous undertone to her voice: she must be over-tired. Her eyes are set even deeper in their sockets than this morning, when she was playing her mirthless game on the beach. That one needs very little more to send her completely over the edge. There's going to be trouble if I'm not careful, thinks Agnes, although of course a display of temper like this is also an indication that the child has begun to feel a little more at home.

'Mrs Flynt is just very old,' she says soothingly, as she stacks a few logs in the fireplace in the living room, which is growing dark. 'And she didn't have her dentures in, because they hurt her.'

'Christ, wouldn't it be better to just give someone like her an injection to put her out of her misery?'

'But my love,' says Agnes, struggling to her feet again to look for matches, 'there's plenty of room in this world, even for old people, you know.'

Bazooka sniffs disapprovingly. There's a limit, her

face implies. 'I don't get it, why they don't just stick that old bag of bones in a home.'

'They love her,' says Agnes and wonders if that's true.

The matches are on the mantelpiece, of course. She tries to light the fire, but she hasn't used enough newspaper and has to get down on her hands and knees to puff at it. Where can those bellows have gone?

When she has finally got the fire going, she flops down on the couch, out of breath. The little boy shyly sidles up against her knee, sucking his thumb. 'Want to sit on my lap?' she asks. To her surprise, he nods his head. She wipes her sooty hands on her dress and pulls him to her.

Bazooka's expression turns twice as sour. 'I *could* write a letter to the Queen, you know,' she threatens. 'Agnes! You listening to me?'

It suddenly occurs to Agnes that for about a hundred thousand years insistent children's voices have been demanding her attention. 'Go ahead, write a letter to the Queen, then. Go ahead, lodge a persuasive complaint against revolting old people. Maybe they'll be banned.'

'You bet I will,' says Bazooka, jumping to her feet. In less than a minute she's found pen and paper in the desk by the window, as if she's in her own home.

You bet, Agnes thinks cynically. When her ship docks at Rotterdam in a few weeks' time, people in white lab coats may very well be waiting for her on the quay. Time for a nursing home, madam. Or, worse: time for your injection, to put you out of your misery. How convenient, really, that Joyce of the black nail varnish is already looking after her fish, that way she can at least go to heaven with an easy mind. She'd

116

never have expected it of Joyce, actually, such a helpful offer. But perhaps Joyce's mother Gemma had nagged her: 'Why don't you offer to do something for Aunt Agnes, for once. She's more than earned it, I should think.'

'Esteemed Majesty,' Bazooka reads aloud.

'That's a good beginning, anyway,' says Agnes.

The girl glares at her. Then she goes back to her passionate scribbling, putting pen to paper in big, shaky letters; fierce, slanted words. What can possibly be *that* terrible? Surely not the continued existence of the elder Mrs Flynt! Just look at that face: the mouth pinched shut, the eyebrows, so blonde they're nearly invisible, two razor-sharp triangles.

When she notices Agnes's eyes on her, she jeers, 'You're an old corpse yourself, actually. You're probably going to die very soon.'

'Is that so?' says Agnes, disconcerted. She's got a nerve, that one. But she is not about to let an overwrought child send her into a tailspin.

Bazooka stands up and with a furious jerk of the arm sweeps aside her important letter. 'And once you're dead, the jellyfish will gobble you up, your insides and your muscles and everything, and only your bones will be left. *So* gross!'

'Oh,' says Agnes, thinking that last night's bedtime story, about the Spanish galleon in Tobermory Bay, may have been just a little too gruesome after all, 'that's news to me. I'd always hoped that when my life was over I'd be an angel at God's throne.'

'*No!*' the child screams. Her hand flies up and the next moment the pen hits Agnes in the temple.

'Hey!' she bursts out indignantly, only to check herself when she sees Bazooka's face: pale as a sheet, but gleaming with secret glee because she's finally made Agnes mad. And suddenly she understands that this little girl *wants* to be yelled at and punished. How come you've been acting as if nothing's the matter, Agnes? How come you gave me hot tea and dry clothes, how come you took me on a visit to the neighbours? Can't we please, after twenty-four hours, finally get to the point: did I run away from home, or didn't I? Are you going to do something about it, or is running away no big deal, in your book?

Nevertheless, Agnes cajoles, 'Don't you think it's time you went to bed? You're worn out, I think.' There's no reasoning with an exhausted child, after all, it's hopeless, and tomorrow is another day. The Nobel Peace Prize goes to Agnes Stam.

'I'm not going to bed!' snaps the girl. 'I'm never going to bed ever again!'

'Why not? Do you have bad dreams?'

Bazooka bares her teeth. 'Is it any of your business?'

'Well,' she says. 'If I were you I'd probably have nightmares too, so far away from home.'

'Silly old bitch,' says Bazooka. 'You're *not* me.' She waits for a reaction. Those thin lips.

'Get out!' Agnes shouts, losing it.

Bazooka jumps up. She tugs her clothes straight. 'I'll sit in the kitchen,' she snarls, with visible satisfaction. 'I'll stay in the kitchen all by myself all night long, that way you won't have to look at me, anyhow.'

There are breathing exercises to calm you down. Agnes tries as best she can, while wondering if this is what Bazooka is used to at home: being sent out of the room.

It's lucky that Ivatuq, on her lap, has slept right through the whole commotion, sated with cake

118

and hard-boiled eggs. His eyelashes don't flicker, his breathing is deep and regular. Oh, to be able to sleep like that in the arms of a total stranger. Is that normal, actually, for a little boy?

'Well, of course it is,' she immediately imagines her great-niece Joyce saying cattily, seeing that everyone seems to have it in for her today, 'the ability to fall asleep in a stranger's arms is a talent they're *all* born with, absolutely typical male behaviour.' A pitying look: Aunt Agnes wouldn't know about such things. She only knows about the sun and the moon and the names of the birds. That certainly makes for an easy life. Seventy and still a virgin! Let's put Aunt Agnes in a museum – they don't make them like her any more.

Agnes pictures herself behind glass. It's an uncannily clear picture: she can count the stitches of her Arran cardigan, the threads of the spider web stretching from her head to her left shoulder, the liver spots on her hands, her varicose veins. Her sturdy shoes all smeared with mud, the torn skirt. People press their noses against the glass, shuddering. Mothers tell small children: 'Do *you* want to end up like that?' Pointing to the brass plate underneath that says: OLD MAID.

Now that Justus, Frank, Robert and Benjamin are no longer there to break people's legs or to smack the sly grins off their faces, now they're all laughing at her. And who knows what else they may be up to, behind her back. 'Say, Joyce,' Gemma may have remarked with motherly foresight, 'what if you staked a claim to that flat of Aunt Agnes's? Doesn't that boyfriend of yours know someone in the squatters' movement? Those people can tell you how you go about it. All you have to do, I understand, is move in your own furniture, and they can never throw you out – and the apartment is in such a great location, so central. Aunt Agnes won't be able to live on her own much longer anyway, and we wouldn't want a stranger to make off with that great flat of hers, would we?'

Joyce, eager but somewhat guilty, to her great-aunt Elise: 'Couldn't she just stay in Mull?'

Elise, alarmed, to her nephew Joost, a solicitor: 'I've got this feeling Agnes might be intending to stay in Port na Bà. Can't I, how do you call it, evict her? And besides, shouldn't we have her declared non compos mentis, while we're at it?'

Heads are shaken with compassion, hands push forms across the desk. Now that Robert isn't with us any more. Now that Justus isn't with us any more. Now that Frank and Benjamin aren't with us any more, we don't have to keep up the pretence either. Their widows huddled in a tête-à-tête: Elise, Nora, Mathilde and Kshema. Kshema is a sannyasi; she was Benjamin's third wife. A sannyasi is simply a seeker. I'm a spiritual seeker, Agnes. I am searching for a certain path through life. The path of patience, of acceptance, of compassion.

Nora, Mathilde, Elise and Kshema: wasn't it a life-long scandal, a crime, to think that in Justus's, Frank's, Robert's and Benjamin's eyes, Agnes always came first? Agnes, the little princess. Yeah, that's what *she* thinks! Poor, silly Agnes. The widows have always understood perfectly well what the story was. But that's ancient history, and they don't have any use for it now. They don't owe Agnes a thing. It's about time they laid their cards on the table.

Ivatuq, on her lap, mutters something in his sleep and Agnes is startled out of her musings. The nonsense a person will get into her head. Hadn't Kshema sent her a lovely fern for Christmas?

She whispers into the sleeping child's ear, 'Hey, little man, I'm going to put you to bed.'

Promptly he opens his eyes and whispers back, 'I want some Smarties.'

'Tomorrow. Come, it's time for bed.' She smoothes the hair away from his face, and wipes a smudge of dirt from his brow. A quick shower would be a good idea, but on the other hand, there's always more mud tomorrow.

She steers the little boy up the stairs. Off with those clothes. On with those pyjamas. Go have a pee. Brush those teeth. Wash those hands. At the end of all that, naturally, Ivatuq is wide awake again. OK then, a hundred laps up and down the hall: let's see if you can do it. He works up a sweat. His short little legs toil and scamper. 'A hundred!' Agnes cries. Everyone's happy. Now, let's tuck Ivatuq into the bottom bunk, quick, the bed countless young Stams have slept in.

She holds up the covers, he hops in. His beaming face suddenly turns distressed. 'It's still wet,' he says, crestfallen.

Agnes suppresses a sigh. Couldn't you have told me this morning? 'OK, get out, I'll make up another bed for you.'

Mortified, he lowers his bare feet onto the linoleum, snatching something from beneath his pillow.

'Now what do you have there?' she asks in disbelief.

He opens his little fist.

'Since when do we take dead mice to bed?'

Ivatuq's face clouds over, his lips bulge.

'Just hand it over, I'll keep it for you.'

No, no, no, he shakes his head. He hides the mouse under his pyjama top as if to protect it from her.

Agnes thinks, oh, damn, I forgot to clean out that kitchen cupboard as well.

The piercing gaze of her sister-in-law Elise, the reproachful voice: mice, Agnes? Mice, and you haven't done a thing about it? Any tourist would take better care of the cottage than you do.

Agnes peremptorily holds out her hand. 'Here, hand over that mouse.'

Perched on the bed, the little boy glares at her threateningly.

She thinks, I could throw you out into the street in a heartbeat, what do you expect, if I hadn't been so kind, so good-natured, to take you in here, if I hadn't, then you wouldn't, I'm the one who's in control here, do you hear me, you're the guest, you'd better abide by my rules.

'No-o,' Ivatuq cries shrilly, and shoots past her like an arrow, out of the bedroom.

Agnes wipes her hot brow. She takes the soaked sheets off the bed, carries them into the bathroom, stuffs them into the washing machine, pours in some washing powder, turns it to the main cycle. Back in the bedroom she puts her hand on the wet mattress. She has seen worse. She'll sprinkle some salt on it, tomorrow she'll brush it off and that'll be that. Practical problems are simple to take care of. In the bedroom opposite she makes up two new beds.

Now there are two angry faces at the long old table that was so lovingly sanded and waxed over and over again fifty years ago.

'Why isn't he allowed to keep that mouse? The way it

is now, at least, he can pet it because it won't run away,' Bazooka bellows at her.

Ivatuq's flashing eyes. He sucks noisily on his thumb, keeping the little corpse pressed to his round cheek with his other hand.

'It's filthy,' Agnes answers shortly. 'You yourself were the one going on about that mouse disease.'

'Bullshit,' says Bazooka. 'They aren't contagious once they're dead, trust me. And he always goes to bed with a teddy. He's got to have something to cuddle in bed.'

The boy nods with trembling lips. It's true, you know.

In *my* bed, Agnes thinks – but it isn't her bed, it belongs to Elise. It's always been Elise's bed. From the word go.

'He's crying,' says the girl indignantly. 'You're always making him cry.'

'Not true,' says Agnes. Might as well be childish herself.

'OK, quiet now,' Bazooka croons, pulling the sobbing child close. 'Nobody's going to take your mouse from you, I'll make sure of it.'

'Fine with me,' she snaps. 'Fine with me. Just do whatever you like. See if I care. Sort it out for your-selves.'

She turns her back on the children, opens the cupboard under the sink and begins cleaning it out. She throws out any remaining chewed-open packages, sweeps up flour and sugar and mouse droppings, and scrubs the shelves clean, all in one great burst of energy. Will that do, Elise? Or is there any other way I can be of service? Excuse me, what did you say? Oh certainly, that hole in the wall through which the rascal got in, I'll take care of that next. Here, I'll stuff it with a big wad of crumpled-up newspaper. There, now that's taken care of as well. Yes of course, I still need to fix it on the outside. But would it be all right with you if I put on my coat and boots first? It's pouring outside, you may not be aware of that over there in Wassenaar, but here it's raining cats and dogs. Just look at how wet the grass is, look at the puddles and pooling water all round the house. Right over there: smack under the kitchen window, that's where it's got to be. A fistful of gravel in the hole for starters, then we'll slop on a generous layer of mud, and to finish it off a couple of heavy rocks in front of it. It will have to be an extraordinarily clever mouse to find its way into this fortress. My beleaguered fortress.

The nerve, Elise, the nerve!

Robert's ashes are still warm, in a manner of speaking, and you've already come up with a use for his cottage that he'd never have agreed to. Signing up with a rental agent! How dare you! Robert would never have stood for it, throwing me out for a bunch of *tourists*! Don't think that I'll ever let it happen.

Agnes lifts her burning face to let the rain cool her off. Through half-closed lashes she sees that the sky over the sea is growing lighter, tinged with innumerable shades of grey and old rose. The outlines of the mountains in the distance are faint and hazy, and in the dusky light the rock outcrops in the bay look like ship owners, immobile, silent, searching the horizon for their fleet.

The ship owners have stood watch over the bay of Port na Bà since time began, they are as old as the world itself, millions of years older than Elise with her blasphemous plans, millions of years wiser. They have survived storms and ice ages, spring floods, lava, hail. Nothing has ever roused them from their slumber. Lurking inside their stone hearts must be the conviction – we belong in this place – and nowhere else.

I'll be just as obstinate as the ship owners, just as immovable as those rocks, thinks Agnes, and just as impervious. That way nothing bad can happen to me. She puts up her wet collar. She feels wonderfully heartened. She is in Port na Bà, and there's no way on earth she won't be here again next year. It's a law of nature, it's written in stone, and that's that.

'Agnes!' Bazooka shouts. 'Agnes, where are you?' She comes running out of the house, onto the beach, with no coat on. In the twilight her blonde hair seems almost to be ablaze. Her little brother comes running after her in his pyjamas.

'There's water everywhere! Come quick, the whole house is getting flooded!'

Four

And God said: let there be lights in the firmament of the heaven to divide the day from the night; and let them be for signs, and for seasons, and for days and years; and let them be for lights in the firmament of the heaven to give light upon the earth.

Genesis 1

1

First thing in the morning, traffic on the narrow road to Tobermory is severely hampered by bad weather. The caravans have trouble negotiating the hairpin bends in the driving rain, and traffic is almost at a standstill. Tired as she is, Agnes has to force herself every few minutes or so to sit up straight and stay alert. Her windscreen wipers are hardly a match for the rain, the water cascades in broad rivulets down the windscreen, blurring and distorting visibility. It's as if she were in a diving bell, slowly sinking to the ocean floor – which is littered with dead bodies, according to Bazooka.

Agnes racks her brains about the washing machine. Did she push the wrong knobs last night? What could have made the bloody thing overflow? Or was there something wrong with it even before she turned it on? Has this appliance, like the telephone, merely succumbed to overlong neglect, to a lack of human touch? Can objects take revenge when they feel ignored? Look at me – pay attention to me – or else – or else I'll write a letter to the Queen.

Agnes stretches her back, stiff from mopping floors half the night. And little rest for the weary after that, as well. She found Bazooka sitting straight up in bed no less than three times, in a white T-shirt much too big for her, the sleeves flapping at her flailing arms, eyes bulging wide, sweaty and frightened. Not a trace left of the recalcitrance, of the bravura: a scared little girl.

Agnes on her feet, rushing round with glasses of water and soothing words, 'It isn't your fault, really it isn't.' It had shocked her, to see that Bazooka seemed to expect to be blamed for the defective washer. As if as a matter of course she'd be made to pay for something that had nothing to do with her. Could it be that at home, any excuse will do to . . . to do *what* to Bazooka? To beat her up?

Sitting behind the wheel, suddenly wide awake, it hits her: yes, because what other reason would a child her age have for running away from home? And more than that, for not wanting to go back to her mother? If that isn't grounds for suspicion, nothing is. She steps on the brake abruptly, screeches to a halt, her head spinning. The rain clatters on the roof of the car.

Tense, unpredictable Bazooka, and the taciturn little brother who wets his bed and is always so close to tears. She should have known. She should have figured out immediately what was going on with those two. After all, in her long years in the classroom she has seen this sort of thing often enough. She could kick herself.

Behind her comes impatient honking. In automatic response, she starts the car again. What she'd most like to do is turn round this minute and drive back to Port na Bà, where she has left Bazooka and Ivatuq with a pile of Little Golden Books. She pictures them on the couch in their socks, nervously flipping through the books. 'Agnes will be back soon,' they tell each other. 'She will.'

132

She jumps, just in time to slam on the brakes: a sheep on the road. She toots the horn. The drenched, filthy animal throws her a doleful look, bleats pathetically, and then, stumbling in its panic, flees up the bank.

Call it a coincidence if you like, those two climbing into her car on the ferry. But fate itself must have had a hand in it. As if it had been decreed in heaven, as if a luminous finger had pointed them towards her Volkswagen and a mellifluous voice had murmured, 'Go, shelter under Agnes's wing. Agnes is an old hand at this.'

Tobermory is swarming with people. All the tourists are looking for some sort of distraction in town, now that there's so little to enjoy outdoors.

After fifteen minutes of trying to find a parking space, Agnes gives up, irked, and leaves her car up on the pavement. She makes a dash through the pouring rain for the household appliance shop. There she explains her problem as succinctly as possible to an indifferent young man whose hair has been gummed into a sort of helmet with hair gel. The serviceman, he informs her, while gazing over her head at the parade of umbrellas out on the street, is at present holidaying on the Riviera and will not be available until two weeks hence.

When you live on an island, patience is often advised. But today the path of patience is not Agnes's path.

To give herself some sense of control over the situation, she buys a new washing machine hose, an astonishingly pricey purchase, and writes down on the back of the sales slip the installation instructions which the salesman reluctantly imparts to her. Let's hope there's still a monkey wrench in the house somewhere. Plumbing has never been her strong suit. That used to be Robert's department.

Sadness and yearning bring unexpected tears to her eyes and, nearly tripping over her own feet, she walks out of the shop. I've bought a splendid hose for the washing machine, Robert. A first-rate hose. Only, I'm not sure if there was really anything wrong with the old one. Help me. Stay with me. Don't ever leave me.

Outside, under the awning, she blows her nose. Silly of her to get so upset about a stupid little mishap. The floors are nice and clean now, anyway, and it was getting to be time to replace the living room's worn grey carpet. Even Elise would agree about that. Finicky Elise. Telling Mathilde, with pursed lips: 'And now she's managed to flood the whole house too, on top of everything!' And Mathilde, sympathizing indignantly: 'Oh no! How *does* she do it!'

Why couldn't her brothers have married other wives, instead of this judgemental bunch, this tribunal that won't give her a moment's peace, day or night?

Agnes crosses the busy street and hurries to the supermarket. She grabs a shopping trolley, gets out her shopping list. In the towns of Wassenaar, Haarlem, Enkhuizen and Dalfsen, Elise, Nora, Mathilde and Kshema are probably doing the exact same thing, except that they've probably managed to get hold of a trolley whose wheels don't suffer from some wobbly deviation necessitating constant adjustment in the steering. Calmly and with dignity they push their trolleys along, filled with a half-loaf of wholewheat bread, a single veal chop, and a box of cherry liqueur chocolates for the long, empty hours that await them when they get home with their meagre purchases and put them away in the refrigerator that's much too big for one. Out loud they sigh, 'Now for a nice cup of tea,' and they are startled by the sound of their own voices, or perhaps by the ineradicable longing to hear someone answer, 'Yes, that *would* be nice.' The kind of commonplace remark that upholsters a marriage. But the sad fact is that Elise, Nora, Mathilde and Kshema have never had much experience of loneliness, and from the grim set of their mouths one can see that they resent it bitterly that, at this late stage, they're being forced to develop a whole new skill. Oh, the silent rage of widows!

And at night, when, despite half a sleeping pill, sleep refuses to come, they rewrite their marriages, they edit out the rotten parts, they scratch out the unbearable irritations, the misunderstandings, the fights, the moments of pure hatred and murderous thoughts – and what's left they polish up until it's so glossy that it fairly sparkles, and they tell themselves contentedly, 'That's how perfect it was.'

Now that Justus, Frank, Robert and Benjamin are dead, their widows have complete sway over them at last, that is their meagre consolation. In the grave the men are more docile than they ever were when alive, at last they allow themselves to be improved upon and recast as the men they always could have and should have been; nor, for the time being, do Elise, Mathilde, Nora and Kshema have any use for an eyewitness who might provide their version of the truth with her own footnotes. It used to be painful enough for them that Agnes always seemed to be present at every crisis. The examples she could give of this are legion. Take that one time, for instance, with Frank.

*   *   *

It wasn't Mathilde's fault, Mathilde was a consistently easy-going, cheerful and competent woman. She could turn two onions and a potato into a gourmet meal, she'd take cast-off furniture she found in the rubbish and restore it with bright paint, in an hour and a half she could whip up a dress out of a piece of leftover fabric. Always busy, always ready with a laugh, always reasonable: how do you expect me to pose for you now, Frank, with three days' washing-up in the sink? With the children home from school at any moment? With not a single clean sock to be found in the entire house? Come on, Frankie-oh, you tell me! And there's also that pile of bills to pay. Mathilde always knew how to accompany that sort of remark with such a sweet caress, a conciliatory pat, a fond squeeze.

'She's right, my boy,' said Agnes, who was crazy about her spirited sister-in-law.

'She's a-always right,' Frank answered shortly.

One evening he'd unexpectedly shown up at her door, without a hat or scarf, an ominous set to his jaw. 'Do you have anything to drink?' he asked.

She hadn't lived all that long in the spacious apartment she had decorated with Mathilde's help; she loved being able to entertain guests in her own home without any meddling from nosy landladies. She poured her brother a large glass of gin from the bottle left over from her birthday. The vase of white roses, from Robert, was still on the table; Elise had asked her, 'Wouldn't you rather have had some pretty napkins instead?' To be twenty-five, and still the youngest. Sometimes she had the vague feeling that nobody took her seriously. Nobody ever came to her for advice. Her counsel was never sought.

She handed Frank his glass. 'Help me, Agnes,' he said dully.

Alarmed, she sat down across the table from him.

Did she realize how frustrating it was to be married to someone like Mathilde? To be married to someone without flaws? To have a wife who rubbed it in every day what a f-failure you were?

'Oh, come on,' cried Agnes, but the comforting words died on her lips when she saw his face.

'She's destroying me,' said her brother. 'She undermines my self-confidence. Save me f-from that harpy, Agnes, before I'm completely crushed by her.'

Dazed, Agnes said, 'But you'll never find anyone like Mathilde.'

'That's certainly to b-be hoped,' Frank replied.

She made up the bed in the guest room for him. She phoned Mathilde and lied that Frank had had too much to drink. Her sister-in-law laughed. 'Oh, then please keep him there.' But twenty-four hours later she wasn't laughing any more. Her cool, commanding voice: 'I want my husband back, Agnes.'

'I think he needs a little space, to pull himself together,' said Agnes awkwardly. It seemed needlessly cruel to tell Mathilde that Frank wouldn't under any circumstances come to the phone to have a word with his wife. But what *did* Frank want? He lolled on her wicker couch all day long, unshaven, sunk deep in thought, smoking one cigarette after another. She felt hopelessly inadequate, spying on him surreptitiously while pretending to correct arithmetic homework. How could she help him? It seemed to her that he was becoming more lethargic by the day, more listless, more vacant. Where was his usual animation, his enthusiasm, his zest for life? Frank of the thousand and one projects, Frank who used to take her along to exhibitions and museums when she was young, Frank who had enthralled her so often with his ideas, his theories: Frank seemed to be disintegrating before her very eyes.

'Do something,' she told him in despair. 'Make a decision. You can't stay here on the couch the rest of your life.'

He looked at her dully. 'But can't you get it through your head that I c-can't make any decisions? She's got me exactly where she's always wanted me.'

Pity swept over her. He is so sensitive, she thought. He always was, too. He doesn't have any armour, he only has his ideals and dreams, he has to have peace and quiet, otherwise he can't paint. She went to make him a cup of tea, which he let grow cold.

After three days Mathilde simply came over to take him home. 'But first, would you please be so kind as to tell me, Agnes,' she hissed aggressively as soon as she'd stepped inside, 'what I've done to deserve this? You should have taken my side. You've known Frank longer than I have. You know he's a weakling. He needs guidance. The one thing you mustn't ever do is let him have his way. You should have sent him home at once. There are three little children there who are waiting for their father.' Then she went into the living room, shutting the door behind her.

Agnes stood dispossessed in her own hallway, while a monstrous feeling of doubt took hold of her. She thought of her brother sleeping on her couch for hours at a time, an aggrieved expression on his face. Frank, a weakling? Was what she'd always taken as her brother's sensitivity in fact a lack of spine? Was he the kind of person who was unwilling to shoulder any responsibility for his own life? But that wasn't the man she knew at all.

She was still leaning against the wall, motionless, hands pressed behind her back against the modern striped wallpaper she'd picked out with her sister-in-law, when the door of the living room opened and Frank and Mathilde followed each other out. Frank looked a little sheepish, but also unmistakably relieved; no longer rudderless, left to his own devices, but, quite simply, safe and sound under Mathilde's thumb again. Not one of the three said a word. From the look on her sister-in-law's face, Agnes suspected that their lips were to remain sealed not only now, but forever. Frank's escapade would be added to the other family secrets, and thereby erased. Every family has its secrets and its hidden failings. Intimacy has a price.

'I brought along a scarf for you,' Mathilde told her husband. 'It's a little chilly out this morning.'

Agnes saved the bottle of gin for a long time, in case her brother might need her solace and support again some day.

2

Tobermory has only one supermarket, which in the high season has to supply thousands of tourists with their daily needs. The shop is a tossing sea of damp wet weather gear, so that Agnes very soon starts to feel dizzy. Hastily she loads her trolley with bread, fruit and cheese, Smarties for Ivatuq, chewing gum for Bazooka, pudding mix for the fish mould. And she mustn't forget the new *Hello!* at the checkout counter for the elder Mrs Flynt, who likes to keep up with the trials and tribulations of the various European royal families.

Impatient arms reach across her for jars of peanut butter and marmalade. She's got the feeling she's in everyone's way. You'd better not stand there dithering, people get so annoyed. You've got to be quick, nimble, decisive.

She pushes off again. Hot dogs. Salt. Milk. Coke. The obligatory crisps. She notices that she's trundling her trolley against the traffic, but it's so crowded that she doesn't have a chance to turn round. Steering a course through the crush, she suddenly remembers she's forgotten the meat. Am I feeling all right? she asks herself. Is it just me, or is it awfully stuffy in here?

Muttering apologies, she forges her way back to the rear of the store. Chicken? Mince? She is leaning over the meat section when she feels herself getting light-headed. The floor begins to tilt beneath her feet. Promptly her knees give way. Then, a sensation of infinite slow motion as she falls, falls, keeps falling, while with sluggish certainty she knows she can count on outstretched arms to catch her, arms that have always been there for her. Unable to find anything to grab on to, her hands slide down along the smooth wall of the refrigerated meat display. Somewhere, someone starts to scream.

When she opens her eyes, strangers' faces are leaning over her. It only takes a few seconds to realize that she has landed on her back, on the floor of the supermarket. Alarmed, she tries to sit up.

A shop girl in a red apron pushes her way through the bystanders, sinks to her knees. 'Madam? Madam? Are you hurt? Can you get up?'

'I'm all right now. If you could just . . .'

Helpful hands are held out, with pooled strength they pull her to her feet.

'Wouldn't you like to sit in the office for a tic, to recover from the shock?'

'My shopping . . .'

A second apron comes into view, a man this time. The manager? 'Come with me.' The professional smile doesn't quite manage to mask a trace of irritation. An old biddy sprawled all over the floor. How is anyone going to get to the boneless fillets?

Agnes willingly allows herself to be led off to a messy little office, to be offered a chair and a cup of tea, still only vaguely comprehending what has just happened to her. Never before in her life has she passed out. It's not like her. Always fit as a fiddle. She should have taken the time this morning to eat a decent breakfast, of course. Haste, fatigue and an empty stomach have all combined to play tricks on her.

'Can't we ring someone for you? Should we . . . ?'

She shakes her head, burning with embarrassment. 'I do apologize for the inconvenience,' she says as she gets to her feet again.

'Don't you want to sit a few more minutes?' the shop girl insists. She rests a hand with long, blood-red nails on Agnes's sleeve. Maybe she's glad to be away from that seething cauldron out there for a bit, and was just looking forward to having a nice peaceful smoke.

'There are children waiting for me,' Agnes explains.

'Oh, then you're right, you'd better get along as soon as possible. You should never leave children alone too long. What a terrible thing, don't you agree, about those two missing . . .'

The manager clears his throat impatiently, and the shop girl shuts up.

'I'm on my way,' Agnes quickly reassures him. 'Again, my apologies, and I do thank you for your concern.'

Suddenly a change comes over the man's face. 'It's only just this second struck me,' he says, 'you're from Port na Bà, are you not? I *thought* I recognized you. Mrs . . .'

'Stam. Agnes Stam,' she says gratefully. How nice to be treated like an old acquaintance; she isn't just an anonymous face.

'Of course, Mrs Stam.' He lowers his eyelids a moment. 'May I offer you my condolences over the

142

passing of your brother? I heard it from Ben Flynt a few weeks ago.'

'Thank you,' says Agnes, shaking the proffered hand. Nothing stays a secret on Mull. Nothing.

'I'll just bring your purchases to the till for you, so that you won't have to wait in the queue.'

'How very kind.'

'No trouble at all. And I'll have someone carry your bags to the car.'

Agnes shakes hands with him again, blushing with pleasure at so much solicitude.

In no time at all she's out of the shop with her groceries. A parking ticket adorns her VW's windscreen, but, well, that's life: for every piece of good luck, there's inevitably a price to pay, in the form of a piece of bad luck. That way everything stays on an even balance.

She loads her shopping and washing machine hose into the car. She'll swing by the Flynts on her way home to ask for some old newspapers: she can spread those over the soaked carpeting to absorb the worst of the moisture. She's got everything under control, there's nothing to get excited about.

3

At home she finds Bazooka with an old net curtain tied round her waist and the checked tablecloth from the kitchen draped over her shoulders; Ivatuq is wearing yellow boots several sizes too large, and a colander on his head. Standing stiffly at attention, he smartly presents his weapon: Justus's air rifle to be precise, which always hangs from a hook at the very back of the scullery. The children look at Agnes expectantly as she enters.

She puts down her shopping bag. Stay calm now, she mustn't dash over there in a panic. Is that thing loaded?

The girl sashays closer with trailing net-curtain train, and solemnly intones, 'I am the Duchess of Hungary. Have you seen my Mrs Jansen, by any chance?'

Agnes shakes her head in wonder. What next! The girl must have been all ears, then, on their walk over to the Flynts' farm when Agnes was describing the Stam family game. Lowering her voice, Agnes can't help whispering the familiar, magical words: 'Mrs Jansen has gone to market.'

The Duchess stamps her foot. 'That woman, it's always the same story with her! Soldier! Go fetch Mrs Jansen and bring her to me at once!'

With an expression of pure bliss on his face, Ivatuq starts wheeling round the room like a spinning top. Water splashes up from the carpeting with every step.

'And you there, underling! Prepare the bonfire. We're going to burn him alive at the stake if he doesn't find Mrs Jansen.'

Agnes says gently, 'That isn't the way it goes.'

Bazooka hoists up her train with a haughty flounce; then steps out of character: 'But didn't you say anything goes?'

'You're not supposed to *find* Mrs Jansen, you have to try and *become* her.'

A cryptic smile flashes across the pinched little face, as if she's found new inspiration: aha. Got it! Why couldn't you say so in the first place!

It gives Agnes so much pleasure to see her cheerful and relaxed at last that she forgets her own tiredness. 'Hey,' she remarks, 'I understand that in Hungary there's always a lot of snow on the ground. Shall we use the old newspapers I just picked up from Muriel for the snow?'

'Yo,' says Bazooka. 'Soldier! There's work to be done.'

'Surrender your weapons,' calls Agnes, touching two fingers to an imaginary cap and clicking her heels.

While the children go to fetch the newspapers from the car, she runs up to her bedroom with the gun and shoves it under her bed as far back as it will go. Sits down on the mattress for a spell to catch her breath. Sees in her mind's eye the way Justus used to crack open the barrel and cock it. His rather hoarse, dry voice. Are you paying attention? Pistons. Suction. I don't want anything happening to you when you're here alone. And watch out for the recoil.

Thoughtful Justus. Straight-shooting Justus.

It had started oh, so innocently, a long, long time ago. With a phone call. Aggie, do you still take piano lessons on Tuesday nights? You never give up, do you! Tell me, what time do you go again? Oh, right. May I use your house for those two hours? Yes, I do have a key.

The strange thing was that that very day she'd been asking herself, why am I still continuing with the piano? Plugging away at it week after week in the old man's musty parlour – she'd been counting the whiskers in his ear since she was twelve years old, and there was always a cup of weak tea for her. Tonight there'd be a ginger biscuit on the side, on account of the holiday season. When she was little he used to let her put out her shoe by the hearth for St Nicholas when she had her lesson. He was unquestionably very fond of her. But was anyone waiting to hear her play, exactly? In the classroom, 'Frère Jacques' and 'Now I know my ABCs' was about the long and the short of it. Was that worth continuing her piano lessons for until doomsday? She had a craving for something new. A course in Spanish, or something else exotic.

It wasn't like her to feel so dissatisfied, and as she rode home on her bike that evening after the lesson, the cup of tea and the spice cookie, she was in some foolish way relieved that there was going to be someone waiting for her at home for a change. Justus would be there, chortling over the silly St Nicholas rhymes he'd been composing, surrounded by half-wrapped presents, paper and ribbons.

But the house was empty and there was nothing to show that her brother had been. Apparently he'd found some other way to take care of his gift-wrapping in secret. She swallowed her disappointment and went to bed with a hot water bottle.

She celebrated St Nicholas Eve with Robert and his family. She arrived early, to help Benjamin into his St Nick costume. His rented red bishop's gown was too short for him, his long white beard wouldn't stay on, and they kept clutching each other with smothered laughter. Robert's dogs ran in and out, greeting the good saint like a cherished old acquaintance, wagging their tails. 'It's going to be one of those nights,' muttered the saint, just before sweeping into the room filled with hushed children.

In a corner, cradling a cup of steaming chocolate in her hands, her head still reeling from laughing so much, Agnes almost melted with contentment. The adults all witty and affectionate, the little ones touchingly grave, belting out songs at the top of their lungs, handsome in their Sunday best, full of potential and promise, everyone happy and healthy. Robert's youngest son came and leaned against her knee, whispering, 'St Nicholas has the same shoes as Uncle Benjamin.' As she hugged him to her, she thought fervently, don't stop believing yet. You still have the rest of your life to be blasé. Allow yourself a few illusions!

A few days later, engrossed in the course catalogue of the Open University, she suddenly heard a key turning in her front door lock. The sound of wrestling, Justus's voice saying something she couldn't catch, followed by a girl's laugh. Gemma! thought Agnes, eagerly pricking up her ears. Justus's daughter always liked to come and show her aunt the presents St Nicholas had brought her. She put the catalogue away, straightened the table-cloth, took two teacups from the dresser. Three, in case Justus's wife Nora had come along as well.

More commotion in the hallway. Then, suddenly, nothing.

Surprised, Agnes got up after a pause, to reconnoitre. Not a sign of anyone. Down the corridor, the door to her bedroom was open a crack. She sidled up to it.

The girl on the bed wasn't Gemma. Except for a demure childish vest, she was naked. All that Justus had on was his shirt and his socks. 'Justus,' said Agnes. She didn't recognize her own voice.

The girl uttered a little scream. Her brother turned round. He gave Agnes a glassy stare. After what seemed like an eternity, he said, 'I didn't realize you were home.'

'The light was on, wasn't it?'

'But you left it on the last time as well, when you were out. And weren't you supposed to be at piano?'

'I have a cold,' Agnes clarified. She went into the living room. Robot-like, she opened the catalogue again. Monday night: bridge. Tuesday night: first aid. Wednesday night: Esperanto. Thursday night: 'Minor repairs around the house anyone can learn.' Friday night: life drawing.

'Agnes?' said Justus from the doorway. He had his trousers on again.

'I'm going to go to Esperanto,' said Agnes without looking up.

'There wasn't anywhere else we could go.'

'From seven to nine p.m. on Wednesdays. Will that suit you?'

'Oh, Aggie. It's not what it looks like.'

'No, it was a Latin tutorial. I could tell.'

148

He sat down and buried his face in his hands. 'I should have told you, of course . . .'

'And then what?' asked Agnes, shaking. 'What do you think I'd have done in that case? Left you some clean sheets?'

'Let me explain . . .'

'What's there to explain? A horny old goat with a tasty young lamb. All perfectly clear. In *my* bed. You seduce your students in *my* bed. You vile pervert. You walking cliché.'

'I'm sorry,' said Justus. 'I'm so very sorry, Aggie. But she is so special! She makes me feel that I—'

Agnes ran to the bedroom, ripped the blankets and sheets off the bed, and hurled them off the balcony. 'How dare you pollute me with this filth?' she screamed when Justus tried to stop her.

He grabbed her by the arms, shook her roughly. 'These things happen! Oh, grow up, Agnes, won't you!'

She felt the blood drain from her face. 'And what, exactly,' she managed, 'do you mean by that?'

'That maybe you're not the best person to be acting all high and mighty about things you haven't any clue about . . .'

She yanked her arm loose and stormed into the kitchen, where she gulped down three glasses of water one after the other. Panting, she gasped, 'So I only have the right to speak my mind if I come down to your level?'

Justus stood in the doorway, suddenly sheepish again. 'Let's not say things we'll regret later.'

But enough had been said. And enough, certainly, had happened. Little Gemma didn't come over that week, as she always used to do, to show off her presents. And on Sunday morning when Agnes had everyone over for coffee as usual, Justus and his family stayed away. Seething, she thought to herself, he's simply afraid I'll tell on him, that I'll let the cat out of the bag in front of Nora. She pictured him slowly but surely getting himself all tangled up in a web of lies, fabrications and excuses. She hoped it would strangle him.

Then, late one evening, the telephone rang: Nora. From the smothered way she said her name, Agnes instantly knew that Justus had made a clean breast of it to his wife. She pressed the receiver to her ear, sat down, took a fraction of a second to brace herself for a lengthy talk in which she would be called on to console, understand, sympathize. But she never got the chance. Nora said just two things before hanging up on her.

She said, 'To think that you provided him with the *opportunity*, Agnes.'

She said, 'To think that you've been *covering* for him all this time.'

'You narrow-minded bitch,' Agnes said into the phone, which had gone dead. 'These things happen.' Then she too slammed the phone down.

That night she turned her wardrobe upside down to find the old teddy bear that Justus had given her as a child. It was a bear with only one eye: Justus had dug the other one out and stuck a plaster over the empty cavity, as proof that she wasn't any different from anybody else. OK, only one eye: so what? Nobody's perfect.

She clutched the animal to her chest. So Justus wasn't infallible. So now she knew. People who loved each other accepted these things about each other.

She took the bear to bed with her, astonished at its

puny dimensions. She remembered it as being much larger. But then it did date from the time when she herself could fit in a potato crate and her brothers were giants who slayed dragons and monsters for her, a time when the whole world was still endowed with mythological proportions.

The next morning she took herself to the hairdresser's and had her braids cut off. About time, too: she was almost thirty. The perm made her face look vapid, feminine. Grown-up. As it turned out, she would forgive Justus for his infidelity ten times sooner than Nora did. But then, Nora wasn't family. She was only related to them by marriage.

4

In the kitchen she softly hums 'The Ballad of Loch Lomond' to herself as she goes through the familiar motions of measuring milk into a bowl and then adding the pudding mix. She stirs and beats, pours the pink mixture into the fish mould and sets it aside to cool. Then she opens a tin of frankfurters and pricks them onto skewers. It will give the Duchess of Hungary the greatest of pleasure, she is certain, to grill these over an open fire for her midday repast. As she arranges the skewers on a platter, she looks forward with eager anticipation to the next episode of Mrs-Jansen-goes-to-market: the intrigues, the role switches, the subplots and unexpected twists and turns. She hears the children banging around upstairs, busy getting ready, it seems. She is certain they'll come up with some pretty unusual characters. All their fantasies can come into play, they can be whatever they want to be. Except Mrs Jansen; never Mrs Jansen. Those are the rules.

When she enters the living room, the newspapers spread over the floor rustle under her feet. Dark footprints mark the spots where the paper has been trampled into the wet carpet. She'll have to fetch stacks more newspapers. She stirs up the fire, puts down the plate of sausages, and just as she's about to sit down, the door is flung open.

Bazooka in the doorway. Triumphant face beneath a headscarf. 'Well, well, old thing, are you taking it easy, for a change?'

Agnes quickly starts clicking imaginary knitting needles, as she gives the girl the once-over. This is not the Duchess of Hungary; the headscarf means she's a new character, worth five points. 'Are we acquainted? I don't believe I have had the honour,' she says, amused.

'I am Mrs Jansen's nanny,' Bazooka replies. She rolls her eyes up to the ceiling while holding up five fingers to claim her points. 'Oh, what a precious little thing, that kid! It's not often you come across such a sweet, obedient child. Most of them are horrible little brats, you know.'

'But shouldn't you be watching the precious little thing, Nanny?'

Bazooka tilts her head back round the door, snaps her fingers, and now the precious little thing enters the room. The straight black hair has been tied with bright blue ribbons in two little tufts high up on the head; a faded summer dress is stretched over the rotund belly.

'Oh!' Agnes exclaims; to think that with such limited means one can contrive such a metamorphosis. 'What a darling little girl.' She stretches out her arms to Ivatuq, who is bashfully toying with the hem of his dress.

Nanny continues, 'As long as you're just sitting there knitting, old woman, you might as well babysit her for me. I have to go to the dentist, unfortunately.'

'But of course.'

Bazooka's face lights up. She pulls the knot of her

headscarf a little tighter under her chin and reveals her trump card: 'Mrs Jansen will be along in a minute to pick her up from you.'

'Oh crikey,' mutters Agnes, unexpectedly out-manoeuvred. This is going too fast. But all is not yet lost. Over the course of the years, false passports have been produced, the dead have been exhumed from their graves, there's hardly a trick in the book that hasn't been tried; and yet there was always some Stam who was able to step in and stop the game from being over. And who should be sitting here but a Stam: Agnes herself, who promptly comes up with the solution. If Bazooka, when she comes back, finds Agnes wearing a white coat and holding a pair of pliers, then Bazooka cannot, alas, be Mrs Jansen; she'll still be the nanny, arriving right on time at the dentist's for her annual check-up. Those are the rules.

She installs the little boy dressed as a girl next to the frankfurters and grabs Elise's beige raincoat from the coat rack – Elise has never been one for oilskins. She puts the coat on back to front, buttons at the back, she tucks in the collar and rolls up the sleeves, exposing a pair of pink, naked arms similar to those of her own dentist. She's just taking a pair of pliers from the cupboard below the stairs when someone knocks at the front door.

She dashes down the hall and opens the door. 'The *dentist* is ready for you now,' she growls triumphantly.

There's a man outside. Her dramatic appearance causes him to step back hastily.

'Good afternoon,' Agnes manages. She slips the pliers furtively into her pocket.

'Detective Inspector Miller, CID,' says the man.

Her eyes travel from his identity card to his face. It's

rare to see such an excellent likeness in a passport photo.

'Are you Mrs Stam? Could I come in a minute?'

'But what . . . oh, that parking ticket, of course! Yes, well, you see, I didn't have time this morning, but sometime this week I will . . .'

He shakes his head. 'That's not our department, madam. That is something you will have to straighten out with the local uniformed police.' His eyes behind his spectacle lenses are dull and bloodshot, as if he's been working far too late.

He reminds her of Robert, after delivering a stillborn calf. Or of the teenage Robert, wiped out after a game of hockey. When he'd come home with muddy thighs under his black shorts, sweaty hair flopping into his eyes. She never pushed that hair back, she never said, 'Look at me. Take notice of me.' A thousand times she let the opportunity pass her by.

She struggles out of Elise's coat. 'Come on in,' she says.

The detective steps over the threshold. 'You've been coming here with your family for years, haven't you?' he asks, following her down the corridor.

'Yes, for fifty years.'

How is one supposed to address someone like that? Inspector? Detective? *Commander?*

'Do your nieces and nephews ever play with other children?'

She stands still in the dark corridor, only now struck by an alarming hunch. 'Well, they don't know any English yet, of course, so they don't have that much . . .'

'But how about Dutch children? There are plenty of Dutch tourists here, such as yourself. We are looking for these two children.' With those words he hands her a couple of photos.

The blood is hammering in her ears. Ivatuq and Bazooka at Efteling amusement park, next to one of those refuse bins in the form of an ogre with his mouth wide open crying, 'Rubbish here!' An enlargement of the same snapshot: Ivatuq leering at the camera beneath his hood, mouth open wide; Bazooka looking bored.

'We have reason to believe these children have been kidnapped.'

She has to bite her tongue to stop herself saying, 'Of course they haven't. They're here of their own free will. It was they who decided to come with me.'

'Agnes!' Ivatuq yells from the living room. 'The hot dogs's all gone! Agnes!'

'Your presence is required, I believe,' says the detective. She has no choice but to lead him inside.

At the sight of a stranger Ivatuq stops yelling. With a bashful look on his face he starts plucking at the short puff sleeves of his dress.

'Hello, little girl,' says the inspector. Then he looks down at the wet newspaper that's making squelching sounds under his feet. His eyebrows shoot up.

Instinctively Agnes pulls Ivatuq close and presses his little face into the folds of her cardigan as she tries to come up with the right words. But the inspector is rattling on enough for two, tapping the photographs with his index finger: these two, a sister and brother, boarded the ferry in Oban with their mother, but upon arrival in Mull they seem to have disappeared without a trace. If one were dealing with teenagers, one might conceivably come up with some different kind of explanation, but in the case of such young children,

156

this immediately takes on a more sinister aspect. Especially if there has been no ransom request in the first twenty-four hours. In that case, one is forced to suspect that . . . The inspector fixes his scrutinizing gaze on the beamed ceiling, he clears his throat. In the case of little kids – it's a scandal of global proportions – well, how to put this – there's a lively trade in child-trafficking going on. *All over the world*. Does she see what he's getting at? Kids forced into prostitution. Child pornography.

'Good heavens,' says Agnes breathlessly.

'A thorough search of the ferry came up with no clues. Theoretically, of course, those two children could have been carried off to a private yacht, but we've been keeping a close watch on all the moorings. We're still holding out the hope that they are being held somewhere on the island, waiting to be smuggled out. In any case, we've published these pictures in all the papers.' Again he shows her the two snapshots. 'I was just at your neighbours', the Flynts, and they are convinced they've seen these children somewhere, quite recently. Unfortunately they don't recall where it was that they saw them. But considering they don't get about much, it must have been in these parts.' He pushes his glasses firmly up against his nose and looks her straight in the eye. 'And you? Have you seen them?'

With an unsteady hand Agnes takes the photos from him. She coughs a few times.

'Or might the children that are with you have seen them perhaps? When they were running around playing outside? My guess is that these kids find all kinds of places to explore which the grown-ups don't necessarily think of. They may have heard something out of the ordinary, or—'

At which moment Bazooka darts into the room, confident of victory. She is a glorious Mrs Jansen: she's put her hair up and painted her face, presumably with felt-tips. Eyes rimmed with blue. A mouth as big and red as a cow's backside, out of which Robert used to pull his calves. Eyebrows like two bolts of lightning. A flowered dress that reaches nearly to her ankles. Stiletto heels. Startlingly grown-up.

Her eyes zoom in on the photos Agnes is holding in her hand. Under the war paint she turns white as a sheet. Her face takes on its night-time mask, the face of the scared little kid hounded by nasty dreams. Wide-eyed, she stares at Agnes. Don't give me away.

Agnes stares back. Actually, she's never seen herself as such a pillar of righteousness. Honesty may be the best policy, but it does depend on the circumstances, doesn't it. The mother of these children may be putting on a great show of worry and anxiety for the authorities, but if she really had been such a loving maternal animal, her daughter wouldn't be waking up screaming in the middle of the night. Agnes comes to a hasty and reckless decision. 'My great-niece,' she says, indicating Bazooka. She has the sense, vague yet unequivocal, that she's just gone and put her head in a noose.

At the sight of Bazooka, the expression on the inspector's face has grown even more drawn and tired. 'I have one like that at home myself,' he tells Agnes. 'God help us, they're impossible at that age!'

'It's not easy being young,' she answers brusquely, giving him back the pictures. Ivatuq is struggling to free himself from her arm lock.

'Or being a father.' He pushes the photos at the boy's face.

Ivatuq looks at them with great interest. 'That was in Efteling,' he lisps.

'What did she say?'

'Efteling,' Agnes translates. 'It's a well-known amusement park in the Netherlands. She recognizes that ogre there.' One of Ivatuq's blue hair bows has started to droop, and instinctively Agnes tightens it.

The man turns to Bazooka, who is still nailed to the floor in the doorway, in her stiletto heels, her face too pale, her eyelids too blue, and shows her the pictures.

'Would you like a frankfurter?' Agnes asks nervously. 'I mean, we were about to eat.'

'No thank you.' He looks at the silent girl, gives an almost imperceptible shrug, sticks the snapshots back in his breast pocket and takes out his card, which he gives to Agnes. 'Please call me if you remember anything, or if you see something that might be of interest.'

'Our telephone doesn't work,' she says, realizing with a shock that she'd meant to take care of it this morning in Tobermory. Never mind, flash him a nonchalant smile, quick.

'Right, those things tend to take forever in a place like Mull,' says Inspector Miller. 'At home on the mainland they've got everything much better organized.'

A city dweller, thinks Agnes contemptuously, someone from Edinburgh or Glasgow, someone accustomed to exhaust fumes. 'I'll see you out,' she says evenly.

Even though Bazooka couldn't follow the conversation in English, she has understood enough. With trembling red-painted lips she declares, 'That was a policeman, wasn't it?'

'Yes,' says Agnes crossly. She sinks to her knees and begins flipping haphazardly through the wet newspapers. ANNUAL MARKET IN SALEN HUGE SUCCESS. BREAKTHROUGH IN CANCER RESEARCH. YOUTH FOUND DEAD IN OBAN HARBOUR. Well now, a dead body in Oban: why doesn't Inspector Miller occupy himself with that, instead of with a couple of innocent children? Her gaze lingers a moment on the article. Crushed skull. Identity unknown. She turns the page, leafs through the rest of the paper, picks up a new one. Here, in yesterday's paper. The pictures are printed on page three. Above them in big fat letters, it says, ABDUCTED?

Bazooka snatches the sodden paper out of her hands so suddenly that it almost rips in two. When she sees the pictures, she begins to moan softly. Her brother stares at her, bewildered, his thumb in his mouth.

'What does it mean, abducted?' she asks miserably.

'Kidnapped. They think you've been kidnapped. To be sold as sex slaves, no less.'

The girl jerks her head up. 'Stop it, Agnes! I only made that up, in case you went to the police!'

'Don't the stories you make up come true, sometimes?'

Bazooka blushes unexpectedly. She looks away and starts picking at the heel of her shoe. 'Kidnapped!' she says. 'Is that why we're in the newspaper?'

'Yes,' snaps Agnes. 'And that's why that man was here.'

To her astonishment Bazooka suddenly starts laughing nervously.

'I don't find it that funny. They're looking for you. And it won't be long before they find you. The Flynts are already suspicious. Do you understand the risk I'm taking?'

The child hugs the newspaper to her skinny chest. 'It's your own bloody fault! You shouldn't have made us come along when you went to visit them!'

In the ensuing silence they can hear that it's raining buckets outside. Inspector Miller is driving round out there in that foul weather, with Bazooka and Ivatuq's pictures in his breast pocket. Oh, but Inspector, this afternoon didn't you yourself assume the little one was a girl, and the other one at least sixteen? How should I have known they were the children in the photographs?

I'm going to hang, Agnes thinks.

Worn-out Inspector Miller, half hypnotized by the swish of his windscreen wipers, toiling his way over unfamiliar, unlit, unpaved roads, over muddy cart tracks without markings or signposts; every hairpin turn might well turn out to be his last. Except that Agnes knows Providence all too well. Whenever someone dies, it's always one of her dear ones, never an enemy who has it in for her. But perhaps she never had to confront enough enemies in her life to be so opinionated on the subject now. They always shielded me far too much, she thinks, and now that I have to cope all by myself, I don't know what to do.

She goes to the window, wipes a small section of the fogged-up pane clean and gazes out at the beach, which is getting a hammering from the rain. Robert's ashes must long have been washed away, claimed by the elements. She leans her forehead against the glass and pictures herself in a cramped interrogation room, the kind in a detective story. A lamp directed at her face. Sitting across from her is a man wearing a fedora, a smouldering cigarette dangling from the corner of his mouth. 'But Mrs Stam, how did you happen to come by these kids?' And behind him, a little over to the side, Inspector Miller, in a voice dripping with fake sympathy: 'Didn't it upset you just a little that your own family wouldn't trust you with their children any more? Didn't you want to prove to them you were still quite capable of taking care of small children?' And now the other one again: 'You lured them away, didn't you!' Whereupon Inspector Miller, who is trying to win her trust: 'Don't be so hard on her. She only wanted to play a game of Mrs-Jansen-Goes-To-Market with them. That isn't a crime.'

'Oh, don't cry, Agnes!' exclaims Bazooka. 'Crying gives you wrinkles, it does!'

'Haven't I looked after you well?' Agnes stutters, through her tears. 'I even made you a pudding. Look in the kitchen, I made you a pudding just this afternoon.'

'So, aren't we having the best time here?' Bazooka yammers. 'We are! That's why we want to stay with you.'

'You simply turned up, out of the blue,' Agnes chokes. 'What else was I to do?'

Outside it's raining. God, how it's pouring out there.

'We'll think of something,' says Bazooka feverishly.

Agnes shakes her head.

'That old fart didn't recognize us, did he? Agnes, listen! We'll just stay in disguise. That's simple enough. And then you'll take my brother over to those Flynt people again dressed like a little girl, so that they won't make the connection between us and the kids in the pictures. I *know* they'll fall for it.'

Agnes is feeling very tired. 'And how did *you* get to be so smart?'

'I just have to,' says Bazooka. She's sitting cross-legged on the floor. The childish pose contrasts sharply with her dramatic make-up and adult outfit.

'What did you say?' asks Agnes.

The pale little face is suddenly quite expressionless.

'I just have to?' Agnes repeats.

In a shrill voice Bazooka says, 'And we'll call him Barbie.'

'How about if instead of all the jiggery-pokery you told me why it's so important for you to lie low.'

The child is silent. Head bent, she begins to count the buttons on the dress that's far too big for her. From top to bottom and back up again. Then she turns her back on Agnes. 'None of your business,' she says to the wall.

'Oh yes it is,' says Agnes angrily. She grabs Bazooka by the shoulder and yanks her close. Immediately the girl cringes, as if she's been slapped. Agnes swallows the rest of her angry retort as her earlier suspicions come flooding back. It's true that she has got herself in a fix by taking these kids in, but surely she's old and wise enough to get herself out of trouble too, one way or another. At least *she* isn't a little child, at the mercy of someone else's cruel whims.

She might as well strike while the iron's hot. Quietly she says, 'Shall I just try and guess what's the matter? When children run away, they usually do so for some good reason. For example, they might be running away because there are things that are happening at home that aren't right. Things that shouldn't be happening at all.' She hesitates briefly.

Bazooka has suddenly turned bright red. She seems overcome with confusion. She chews on her lip, pulls at a strand of hair that's worked its way loose. She's avoiding Agnes's gaze.

Don't abused children almost always think it's their own fault, that they deserve every hiding? It breaks your heart. Reassurance, that's the key. Heartened by the thought, Agnes continues, 'If you ever decide you

163

want to tell me about it, I'd very much like to hear it. Together I'm sure we can—'

Ivatuq pulls at her sleeve. 'The hot dogs's all gone,' he says timidly.

'I'll get some more for you in a minute, sweetie. But right now—'

His sister jumps up. 'Can we stay, then? You won't turn us in?'

Trust, thinks Agnes, everything hangs on trust. 'No, I won't turn you in.'

'Cross your heart and hope to die?'

'Of course,' she says resolutely.

'Because if you do they'll make us go home.'

'No,' says Agnes, 'I won't let them make you go home.'

In the evening, as she's gathering up the soaked newspapers, she comes across her two stowaways again. MISSING: THOMAS (4) AND CHRISTINE (10) JANSEN, FROM HOLLAND.

Thomas, thinks Agnes to herself, Christine. She feels a little let down.

In one of the newspapers there is a photograph of the family in happier times. With her frail looks, Christine takes after her mother, a somewhat too thin young woman wearing a slightly surprised expression: Sonja Jansen. Next to her a much younger dark-haired man smiling lazily at the camera, a hand resting in Sonja's neck: Jaap Geuzenaar. The couple is at present staying at the Western Isles Hotel in Tobermory, awaiting the outcome of the police investigation.

Agnes has a hard time deciphering the print, which has bled. The family travelled to Oban from . . . and spent a few nights camping there. This past Monday

. . . over to Mull with their two youngest . . . while eldest son Waldo (16) left the same day for Skye, to climb the Cuillins.

A big brother! How could that boy just abandon the little ones to their lot? But that's the way it works, in that kind of family: everyone out for himself. She studies the picture some more. Waldo must have been the one to take it, since he's not in it. The mother and her boyfriend look like your average, ordinary people. But that's the problem. Child abusers tend to look like everyone else. God help Thomas and Christine Jansen.

And suddenly Agnes has to smile, in spite of herself. No wonder Bazooka is so good at Mrs-Jansen-goes-to-market: she's a mini Mrs Jansen herself. Then the smile dies on her lips. For what's the most distinctive thing about Mrs Jansen? The fact that she is pure fiction, a complete invention. She doesn't really exist, not even during the game itself. She is more insubstantial than the air and as obdurate as a lie: she is the power of the unbridled imagination personified.

The moment she's acknowledged the thought, she is ashamed of doubting Christine. After all, no-one likes to believe that nice-looking adults could be child-beaters. That's the very crux of this problem they call child abuse. But Agnes isn't about to make *that* mistake.

Five

And God said: Let the waters swarm with swarms of living creatures, and let fowl fly above the earth in the open firmament of heaven.

Genesis 1

1

Foamy white clouds drift in the clear blue sky, mists steam off the mountain tops and the ocean glitters as if any moment now she'll surrender all the jewels she has ever seized. A morning that makes one say, 'Ah!' like a sip of champagne. A morning like a clarion call.

Agnes blinks her eyes against the light as she throws off the covers and gets out of bed on creaky legs. At last she'll be able to put on a summery blouse, and slip her bare old feet into a pair of sandals. First she'll make some sandwiches, and then it's out into the sun.

But when she gets downstairs it appears that Bazooka, whose real name is Christine Jansen, is in the process of setting the kitchen table. Knives, forks, teaspoons, even checked red napkins: she's thought of everything. 'Would you prefer coffee or tea?' she asks Agnes solicitiously as she slaps down a basket of bread on the table. The water is already on the boil. Both the teapot and the coffee pot stand ready on the sunny counter.

'Well now. Tea, please,' says Agnes. She has always taken the position that children should not be pushed to do household chores. There'll be plenty of table-setting and washing-up for them to do later on.

Standing on tiptoe at the counter, Christine pours water into the teapot. She is wearing a clean, light blue tracksuit that she must have found in one of the wardrobes. She has washed her hair and tied it back, still dripping wet, into a neat ponytail. Her cheeks gleam as if they've been thoroughly scrubbed. 'Shall I put a slice of bread in the toaster for you?'

You really don't have to be little miss perfect all of a sudden, thinks Agnes, her mood plummeting abruptly. I won't send you away, honest. She says, 'Yes please, that's great.' She sits down.

'Tommy!' yells Christine. 'Come and eat!'

The little boy comes storming in, throws himself into a chair and immediately snatches up a piece of bread.

'Say grace first,' orders his sister.

'What?' he says, baffled. For him, a gingham dress with a smocked bodice has been produced from somewhere. A single bow in the sleek black hair today.

'Jesus, dummy!' the girl exclaims. 'God *does* exist, you know! And say good morning to Agnes.'

'Good morning,' mumbles Tommy, formerly known as Ivatuq.

'Good morning,' answers Agnes. 'How lovely you look today! That dress used to be Willemijn's. It's just beautiful. Do you like it?'

He stuffs a hunk of bread into his mouth.

'There aren't enough clothes for him here,' says his sister, taking two slices of bread out of the toaster and handing one to Agnes. 'You're going to have to buy him a couple of skirts.'

'I think we should ask him for his opinion first.'

'He does what I say.'

'Well then, let's hope you always know what's best for him, Christine.'

172

The girl's eyes darken. 'My name is Chris.'

'OK, Chris,' says Agnes.

Tommy explains in a clear voice. 'Christine is a *girl's* name. Chris is much tougher. Chris is much more dangerous. Chris has—'

'Oh shut up, you snot,' the girl bursts out.

'No name-calling,' says Agnes. 'I really have a problem with that.' She hastily goes on in a conciliatory tone, 'And what are we going to do on such a beautiful day? You choose. Your wish is my command.'

'Oh, come on, just act normal,' says Chris sullenly. 'No need to sweat it.'

Agnes sips her tea. Perhaps she's right. Perhaps it's she herself who is trying overly hard to please.

'Agnes,' says Tommy, gravely looking up from his bread, 'why don't you have a father, anyway?'

His sister sniffs. She says, 'He means why aren't you married.'

Agnes, taken aback, says, 'Just because.'

'Everyone has a father, don't they?' Tommy establishes.

'Well, I don't.'

'So you prob-bab-bly don't have any kids either,' says Tommy, breaking up 'probably' into separate syllables.

'Exactly,' says Agnes.

'Old people *can't* have children any more,' Chris tells her little brother. 'For babies you've got to have supercharged hormones, you know.' She sends Agnes a pitying look.

Agnes puts down her piece of toast. Rather curtly, she says, 'Speaking of fathers, you each have one, and I should like to know why you haven't ever told *them* about your problems.'

Chris's baffled face. 'My father? How would I know where he lives?'

'Doesn't your mother have his address?'

'My mother has plenty of other things to worry about, you know!'

Agnes thinks of Sonja Jansen, in the newspaper; she's gazing with downright amazement at Jaap Geuzenaar at her side. Are the Sonja Jansens of this world *so* happy to have a new man that they don't have time for anything else? But surely there must be *someone* in those two kids' periphery who isn't totally blind?

'Haven't you ever told your teacher either?'

Icily: 'About what?'

'About what you told me yesterday.'

'I never told a thing!'

A light bulb goes on in Agnes's brain. 'No, you didn't tell me a thing. I just guessed. Of course, you're not allowed to tell, are you? That kind of thing is always supposed to remain secret.'

Chris puts three sugars in her tea. 'Actually, a secret also means someone trusts you, you know,' she says with tremulous pride.

'How do you mean?'

'You wouldn't understand anyway, Agnes.'

'Then explain it to me.'

Chris shakes her head. 'I won't ever tell. Not even if you torture me.'

'Dear me, as if I was planning to do any such thing!' says Agnes. She gets up, takes the orange juice out of the fridge. It's quite enough for her that at least Chris's secret has now officially been confirmed. We're beginning to make some headway. As she puts down a glass of juice in front of the girl, she touches her shoulder briefly. She gazes at the dimple in the frail little neck. Such pale skin. The kind of skin that probably bruises easily. Then she changes the subject, to take the pressure off her. 'We'd better hurry up and go outside, now that the sun's finally come out.'

'Can we go swimming?' asks Tommy.

'Of course,' begins Agnes, when suddenly she notices he's taken out his dead mouse and is dragging it by the tail round the rim of his plate. 'But first let's go over to the Flynts and ask them if they have a nice little bunny rabbit for you. You'd like that, wouldn't you?'

The little boy gazes at her with glassy eyes.

'So, what do you think of that idea?' asks Agnes hopefully. 'And you know what we'll do next? Next we'll give your mouse a proper seafarer's burial, we'll have a ceremony and fling him into the waves from the rocks, you'll see, there'll be a huge splash, and then we'll—'

Chris leaps to her feet. Plates and utensils rattle, the butter dish falls on the floor. She's practically shrieking, 'Stop being so morbid! That's much too scary for him. It'll give him the creeps!'

'But child,' Agnes begins, flummoxed.

Chris clasps her hands over her ears and races out of the kitchen. When, ten minutes later, to make amends, Agnes stands outside her room with a cup of tea, she finds the door locked.

She has blown it again.

A walk with a toddler is a time-consuming business: on the way to the Flynts, Tommy Jansen halts every other minute on the rock-strewn grass, he picks up an unremarkable twig and stows it securely into the pocket of Willemijn's dress, or he squats down for a long time with a pensive frown on his face: what kind of stone is this? A piece of marble? Basalt? Gneist? Granite? Sandstone? Gravel?

'Schist,' prompts Agnes, picking up the stone from the grass. Scattered here and there among the blooming bluebells are seashells that have been carried here on the wind: whelks, Baltic clams, mussels, horn shells, limpets, soft-shell clams, piddocks, wedge shells, cockles. There are so *many*, she thinks, stunned, there are so many *things*.

She picks up a large necklace shell, lovely and intact, as a peace offering to Chris, for later. Throws it away again. Can already hear it: 'A stupid old seashell for me, and a bunny rabbit for that dodo?' It's going to have to be two rabbits, then. Or maybe for the girl a chicken. A fresh-laid egg every morning, specially for her.

'Look, Agnes, a boat!' cries Tommy, pointing to a sailing boat with billowing sails gliding along out in the bay.

'Yes, a beauty, isn't it?'

'I want to go sailing too.'

'And where would you sail to?'

He picks out one of the many islands visible on the horizon. 'There!'

'Oh, that's Skye,' says Agnes. But hang on: Skye? 'Well, I'll be . . . There are who knows how many islands out there, and here *you* go pointing out the very one your brother is on right now, mountain-climbing.'

The boy freezes. His eyes are as round as bullets suddenly.

'You did know that, didn't you? That Waldo went to Skye the day you came to Mull?'

He shakes his head, half astonished, half disbelieving. His hand seeks hers. 'Can he see us?' he asks, holding his breath.

'We could wave.'

But Tommy doesn't move a muscle.

'Isn't it nice to know that he's over there?'

'Does Chrissie know?'

'We'll show her where Skye is later.'

'She pushed him.'

'Did she, the little devil!'

He looks down and sticks his thumb in his mouth.

'I used to have four big brothers,' says Agnes. 'So I've had to fight off a few myself in my time. Come, lets walk on. We'll take the binoculars next time, so you'll be able to see the mountains of Skye for yourself. And if the weather stays nice, maybe we'll rent a boat one of these days, and we'll sail over there.' She thinks, a little motorboat, I could still manage that, God knows I've made the crossing often enough. Heavens, I used to cruise over to Skye way back in the days of *Agnes I*.

The *Agnes I*: an old barge used by a lobsterman to set his traps out at Croig. It was on their third or fourth summer on Mull that she and Benjamin had noticed the small vessel for sale at the docks. The owner was soon found, a man as gnarled as an old tree, and about as talkative, too. Upon accepting their cheque, he waved them off with a surly, 'All right, gae along wi' ye.' As far as he was concerned, they could take their barge and push off for Port na Bà immediately.

Benjamin at the helm, Agnes inside the dilapidated deckhouse, daydreaming about the curtains they'd put up, as well as other projects too numerous to mention. She was going to learn to recognize the fish from their silhouette in the water, from the colour of their scales. Cod. Herring. Tuna. Red mullet. Sardine. Thornback ray. She'd finally find out what a bowsprit was and

177

she'd take a knot-tying class. Agnes Stam, ordinary seaman first class.

When they were halfway home, the engine died. Her brother went below deck to cast an inexpert glance at the boiler, which was leaking oil. Neither of them knew what to do, and they could only look on helplessly as the tide swept their ship aground in a deserted cove.

'Stams at sea,' said Benjamin as they waded to shore. 'I told you nothing good would ever come of it.'

'We'll rent one of those trailers, for the car,' said Agnes firmly. A boat, she said, was exactly what Benjamin needed. Something to call his own, an activity where he wouldn't be overshadowed by his older brothers who always had all the answers. What she was really thinking was: why can't you ever get excited about anything, Benjamin? Come on, get fired up about *something*.

They found a trailer to tow the barge home. But just before they reached Port na Bà, it capsized on the bumpy basalt flats.

Hands thrust in his pockets, Benjamin paced around the shipwreck. 'Right here is the ideal resting place for it,' he finally observed. 'Our nieces and nephews can play pirates in it.'

'It'll be at least another two years before this place is ready for the children,' Agnes pointed out reasonably. Her sisters-in-law were increasingly inclined to complain, 'What are the five of you getting up to on that island? Why isn't the house ready yet? Why don't you hire some help!'

But Agnes and her brothers weren't in any hurry. They plastered and painted, certainly, they restored door frames and hung doors from them; it's just that one generally gets only one chance in a lifetime to build a house with one's own two hands, so it had to embody every one of their dreams. The mantelpiece not such, but so. That window not over here, but over there. They had no problem ripping out work that had taken them days to complete if on second thoughts one of them came up with a better idea. They went around in dirty overalls, left beer in the surf to chill, and chased after each other with hammers and saws.

'But Aggie,' said Benjamin, leaning over the boat, 'there's a hole in the keel. Them's heavy odds, as they say in Las Vegas. This thing is dead in the water.'

'But didn't you want to go sailing in this thing?'

He shrugged.

'Frank will repair it,' she said quickly. Frank could work wonders with two old planks and a crooked nail.

And indeed, 'I'll have it fixed in a jiffy,' Frank said. 'As long as Robert gives me a hand.'

Sitting in the grass, Agnes looked on as the restoration began. Her irritation at Benjamin's apathy had already evaporated. She could never stay mad long at any of her brothers. She picked a daisy and stuck it through the buttonhole of her dress. She scratched at the scab on her knee. She thought, I've got such infantile knees, always a welter of bumps and bruises; and looked at her brothers' legs, which were equally beaten up, and smiled. She had no reason to suspect that her life would change radically in just a matter of seconds. Everything seemed so normal.

She sat in the grass absent-mindedly pulling up grass stalks, which she wound round her fingers before tossing them away again. Frank called for more nails and Robert, chewing idly on a piece of straw, was banging his hammer on the ship's keel. He was wearing a pair of grey shorts that had been washed a hundred times, and a striped vest. The contour of his strong, lean body was visible through the fabric. And as she looked at him through half-closed eyes, her heart took on the rhythm of his hammer, and she sat quiet as a mouse, letting it sink in how inexplicably but consummately happy she felt all of a sudden. It was a joy that needed to be shouted to the wind right this very minute, it was the supreme kick of knowing that she was alive, it was a heightening of all her senses. 'Oh, Robert,' she wanted to ask him, 'does that happen to you too sometimes, that out of the blue you . . .'

'I'm going for some more wood,' he was telling Frank. He threw his hammer down in the grass, stretched his back a little and, whistling, disappeared into the old barn where they kept their supplies.

'What *are* you up to, sitting here beaming to yourself, Agnes?' said Justus, who came trundling up with Benjamin, a crate of beer between them.

'Oh Justus, does it happen to you too sometimes, that you—'

'You're actually radiant, you're giving off light! Look at her, Ben. Is that normal?'

'What's this, Aggie?' said Benjamin. 'That look can mean only one thing. You can't fool me.'

'What do I hear?' asked Frank, abandoning ship a moment in order to grab a bottle of beer from Justus. 'Is our Aggie in l-love?'

'She is young,' said Justus in a paternal tone. 'It may pass.'

'Oh my God,' Benjamin exclaimed. 'She has finally found her true destiny!'

'And we didn't have a clue,' said Frank. 'Who's the happy man? Do we know him?'

180

'Robbie!' cried Justus. 'Where are you? Come and have a beer.'

'To Agnes's happiness,' said Benjamin, raising his beer at her.

'Are you going to fill us in on the details, or what?' asked Frank. 'About how the lightning suddenly struck, how your whole life was suddenly a wondrous thing and you were just kn-knocked off your socks and didn't understand what the hell was happening to you?'

'Come on, out with it,' Benjamin ordered, 'tell us why you love him so much. And be quick about it.'

'As if a heart needs a reason to love,' Justus interceded. 'True love doesn't need a reason why. It just hits you over the head without any warning, right, Agnes?'

She turned away from their teasing faces. She thought: but this can't be, this can't be true at all. Nervously she jumped to her feet. 'I'm going for a swim,' she blurted out.

'Oh, how cruel,' Benjamin groaned.

Robert came walking up carrying a plank on his shoulder. 'Did you say a swim, Agnes?' he shouted. 'Good idea. I'd like to cool off a bit myself.'

'Oh, no,' said Agnes, 'I . . .'

He leaned the plank against the ship's keel and, laughing, caught hold of her protesting hands.

On the beach she pretended she couldn't undo the buttons of her dress. She was appalled at the thought of the old blue bathing suit she had been wearing under her clothes since the beginning of the holiday, and she was appalled that she'd never even given it a thought before. She was self-conscious about her stomach, her breasts, her thighs. 'You go ahead,' she said awkwardly.

Robert pulled off his vest and flung it down on rocks strewn with spiny cockles. Agnes stopped fumbling with her buttons. It was as if over the calm whooshing of the sea she could hear the sucking sound of the snails inside their shells clinging tightly to the rock as Robert's vest smothered them. He tossed his shorts on top. His swimming trunks were slightly twisted round his narrow hips, and he pulled the cord a little tighter.

Her heart was hammering. She could feel every single grain of sand separately under the soles of her feet.

'Can't you manage?' said Robert. 'Wait, let me.' He came closer, warm and sweaty. His fingers brushed her skin as he began unbuttoning her dress. 'You've got the goosebumps,' he said. 'It isn't cold, surely? Or has all the hammering made me sweat?'

With a start she realized she couldn't look at him. The blood was throbbing all through her body. Everything inside her seemed to be reaching out to him. You. Stay with me. Never leave me.

'What's the matter?' he asked. 'Agnes! Are you coming down with something?' He took her chin in his hand and his worried eyes bored into hers. Blue eyes flecked with grey. She saw herself mirrored in them. She thought: he sees me. Which immediately made her feel inconceivably beautiful, invincible, capable of anything. Her arms flew up of their own accord, her heels came up off the ground, she was standing on tiptoe, it was incontestable, it was the way it had to be, him, her: Robert and Agnes. She was no longer somebody who simply deserved compassion, because of her glass eye. She was a very special, enviable young woman.

'It might be best, ducks,' said Robert, 'if you didn't go swimming today.' He freed himself from her embrace, draped her dress over her shoulders again and patted her on the back. Then he sauntered, taking his time, down to the surf.

After a few moments' hesitation, she scrambled after him blindly, and tripped, landing on her tattered knees on top of the shingle. Her fall made her come to her senses somewhat, she blinked and shook her head, dazed. Rubbing her bare arms, she looked about for something familiar, something safe, to hold on to. The rocks bristling with cockles. The slimy strands of seaweed on the white sand. The indignant screeching of a seagull. The beach lay deserted under the low grey sky. It was an ill-defined day, neither sunny nor rainy, one of those days that could swing either way but can't seem to make up its mind. The air felt the way it does just before a thunderstorm, when there's an atmosphere of hesitation, of temporary suspension. And suddenly it was as if she could see far into the future: this was what her life would be, if she didn't get a grip on herself – a hiatus, a waiting that would never be rewarded. She clenched her fists.

She scrambled to her feet. Without another glance at her brother in the water, she strode back to the cottage. She would learn the names of the fish, she would buy a special fish notebook and paste a neat label on the cover, and every day she'd peer out of the porthole of Benjamin's boat and call out, 'Sardines!' She would put all this other ridiculous nonsense out of her head. There was absolutely no reason for it. Justus was right – what was it Justus had said, exactly?

2

The Flynts' farmhouse is deserted. No Muriel, no younger Mrs Flynt, no husbands; everyone is always hard at work in the morning, and perhaps that's because the midday meal consists of potatoes swimming in fat, tons of potatoes, literally, digestible only after thorough exertion. Agnes guesses that Muriel packs away at least a kilo per day.

'Hello!' she calls in the direction of the kitchen where the cooker is always sizzling, just to make sure. No sign of life. Up the stairs, then. She knocks loudly at the bedroom door of the elder Mrs Flynt; pokes her head round the door. The smell of lavender, of camphor, of unwashed clothing.

'Agnes!' says Mrs Flynt from the bed, startled out of the grogginess in which she often finds herself these days, neither fully awake nor asleep, a somnambulist state in which powers mightier than her are in control of her life, her death, and everything else. 'Agnes! Dear lass!'

Agnes can't say she isn't an old softy at heart. Indeed, this warm welcome does her a world of good. 'I've brought you a magazine.'

'How very kind of you.' Up pops the toothless,

bird-like head. The ancient eyes blink at the child clutching Agnes's hand. 'And how lovely of you to bring *him* along again as well.'

'Her.'

'I wasna wearing my specs. Tell me, Agnes, whose wee one is he, again?'

The point-blank, unexpected question sucks all the air out of her lungs.

'We keep telling each other, we ken his face, but we can't quite place him.'

'Her,' stammers Agnes.

Mrs Flynt waves this interjection away. 'Aye, it's so hard to tell with wee ones that age.'

Agnes is still trying to recover her breath.

'Whose is she then?' Mrs Flynt insists. 'Which ones are her parents?' Again she gives Tommy a keen once-over. 'That other bairn you have with you is Alice's sister, that's plain. But this wee lass? Is she Ada's or Ida's? We never could tell those two apart either, here.'

The relief almost knocks Agnes off her feet. 'You've just seen too many Stams in your lifetime, that's all. Shall I freshen up your bed a little for you, by the way?'

'Oh, yes please, if it's not too much trouble.'

'There, that's better, isn't it?'

Mrs Flynt groans with well-being as she lets herself sink back in the plumped-up pillows.

'And shall I read to you a little?'

Mrs Flynt puts her frail hand on Agnes's arm. 'What an angel you are, lass.'

She hastily opens *Hello!*, then pulls Tommy onto her lap so that he can look at the pictures too. 'Well, what will it be? Film stars or royalty?'

Mrs Flynt raises her handkerchief to her face. Grooves deep as gutters run from the corners of her mouth to her chin. She dabs at some spittle, casually and calmly, the way one might pin a stray lock of hair back in place. 'Film stars,' she replies. Her eyes twinkle. 'Did you read about the one, last week, what's his name again, who had to use a bicycle pump if he wanted to have sex? They had given him this thing, you know, an implant, and now he pumps himself up whenever he . . . but you're blushing, Agnes!'

'You ought to be ashamed of yourself. At your age!'

Mrs Flynt's corrugated mouth is set in an expression of downright astonishment. 'If you have to keep your trap shut about certain subjects even at my age, then when *can* you speak about them? What have I got to lose? All I have left to pay for it with is my life.' She says it in a way that's neither plaintive nor resigned; on the contrary, she sounds very content.

'Go on, have a look and see if there's anything about that bicycle pump, I think it was Sylvester Stallone.' She nods at the magazine in Agnes's hands, which is filled from the first page to the last with the trials and tribulations of the rich, the famous, the blessed, the mighty, the celebrated; all those unfortunate beings who have so much more to lose than the elder Mrs Flynt: their reputation, their wealth, their beauty, their success, their youth, their fans.

Agnes feels an itch behind her glass eye as she makes a show of leafing through the magazine looking for Sylvester Stallone. She presses her chin to the top of Tommy's head, beside the silly tuft of hair his sister tied up in a ribbon. Aren't her most important losses, like Mrs Flynt's, far behind her? Why hasn't that made her as detached as she is, then? Why is the smell of unwashed child's hair enough to make her want to keep clinging on, suddenly? Because she'd still like to have something to lose. Because she wants to feel she's alive.

She starts reading out loud, at random.

Within a few minutes, Tommy, on her lap, grows fidgety. He stretches his plump little legs and starts telling his knees, softly, 'I'm gonna get a bunny soon, a white bunny or a brown bunny, that's right, Missus Flynt gonna give me a bunny.'

The old woman remarks amiably, 'That wean of yours has had enough. What's his name again?'

'Her. Barbie. Barbara,' says Agnes, all in a tizzy again.

'Barbara, come here, child.' One nearly transparent hand beckons, the other gropes around the bedding for her glasses. 'Tell her to come closer, Agnes.'

But Tommy has already deciphered the international hand signal by himself. He slides down from Agnes's knees and makes for the bed, as if expecting a rabbit to be produced from the bedsheets by magic.

Mrs Flynt studies him through her glasses. 'Still, I dinna see a trace of any Stam.'

'No,' Agnes quickly equivocates, 'but we have Sennemi and Mi Ying too, don't we?'

'You mean it's another one of those poor adoption lambs? Why did ye no' tell us before?'

'Well, we tend to forget it ourselves.'

'And you, always so good to every Tom, Dick and Harry. You'll tell us, will ye no' lass, if you need any help, if we can do anything for you? You know you can always count on us.'

Agnes gazes into the warm, cloudy eyes. For fifty years they have taken each other at their word. Isn't it terrible how lies produce new lies? As if the lie cloned itself spontaneously. Troubled, she thinks, Mrs Flynt is my friend, and now I'm hoodwinking her.

'Oh dearie me,' says the old woman, 'I can see from your face there's something you're wanting for but no' asking. Come on, out with it, lassie, dinnae hold it in! Agnes, hen, I can understand more than anyone else can how you must be feeling, all alone in that house you fixed up with your brothers . . . and now Robbie too . . . Aye, he was dear to me. A terrible loss. Terrible. But still, I think you know our hearts are wi' you, and we do think of him often.'

Agnes stammers, 'He was very fond of all of you, too.'

'Salt of the earth, he was. Reliable, forbye. Like yourself, in fact.'

Oh, the temptation to sink to her knees by the bed. To make a clean breast of it. And why not? Wouldn't Mrs Flynt be the first to agree she has done the right thing?

'Lass,' says the old woman, 'you're no' alone. You may feel you're alone, but we're still here for you, you know. What is it troubling you, Agnes? How can I help you?'

She opens her mouth. Hears herself say, 'Actually, I was hoping I could ask you for a couple of animals as pets for the children. I mean, I'll pay for them, of course.'

'Dinnae insult me!' Mrs Flynt cries. She breaks into a coughing fit. Still sputtering, she says, 'Go find Muriel right this minute, and tell her she'd best let you pick out something bonny for the bairns.'

'Thank you,' Agnes replies, burning with shame.

She stands up, fumbles for Tommy's hand. 'Come on, we're going to go find your rabbit. Hurry up and say goodbye to Mrs Flynt.'

*   *   *

Muriel and the younger Mrs Flynt are seated together at the kitchen table in sisterly fashion. It's such an unusual sight that Agnes hesitates a moment in the doorway. Have they finally buried the hatchet, then? Or is each simply gathering her strength for the next round of never-ending internecine warfare? Muriel's rough face is set in a hard, hostile scowl. Her tight muscles show dangerously through her overalls. The younger Mrs Flynt's neck is blotched red and her fists are clenched, making the sinews in her arms stand out.

'Am I interrupting something?' asks Agnes.

'On the contrary,' says the younger Mrs Flynt stiffly. 'We were waiting for you. We heard you upstairs, with Mother.'

Was the younger Mrs Flynt ever really young? Was she ever carefree? Did anyone ever buy her a leather suitcase and a fur hat, did anyone ever scale Ben More with her, has she ever known passion? Agnes feels herself growing weak-kneed. The richness of her own life.

Tommy whispers timidly, 'Am I getting my bunny now?'

Muriel is the first to explode. 'I'm fair disgusted with you, Agnes! You owe us an explanation! To think that you've been flat out keeping it from us all this time!'

'Aye, and stringing me along, forbye! Pretending you were going to phone Elise!' complains the younger Mrs Flynt.

'Phone Elise?' stammers Agnes, who has no idea what they are talking about. 'But my telephone isn't working and I haven't had a chance—'

'As if you couldna' use our phone! What kind of daft excuse is that? You knew, and you didna tell us, on purpose.'

'Hang on a minute now. I—'

'And I was going to chop firewood for you today, too,' Muriel says bitterly. 'But you'd better ask your estate agent to do it from now on.'

Agnes grasps the edge of the table with both hands. She chokes, 'What has Elise done now?'

'Do we have to tell you?'

'I don't know a thing! Believe me! What has she done?'

Muriel and the younger Mrs Flynt exchange glances. Then Muriel takes a letter out of the bib pocket of her overalls and places it on the table.

Agnes recognizes Elise's neat handwriting. Quickly her eyes scan the lines. Regarding the renting of the house at Port na Bà. Elise regrets to have to inform them of a new development: it appears that the agency charged with renting the house has a policy of never doing business with local caretakers. Total in-house control of the holiday home is the sole guarantee of excellence. Now that Robert's house is no longer a family destination but a rental property, it is to be hoped that the Flynts will understand that they . . . with many thanks, of course . . . it's always been a pleasure . . . and as of today, seeing that the house has been unexpectedly rented from 10 August.

'Quality!' rasps the younger Mrs Flynt. 'There's a vile insult to our family, is it no'? We who've been slaving away for generations to make sure everything's to your liking.'

'We demand compensation,' Muriel chimes in. 'Did you think we could just get by without the extra income? Did you think this place was such a gold mine?' She wrings her large hands in agitation.

'Not to mention the fact that it's now good riddance

to our chances of taking over the house ourselves . . .'
The younger Mrs Flynt is massaging her temples with a
stricken look on her face. She and her despised house-
mate glare at each other: here we are again, then,
foisted on each other for all eternity.

Open-mouthed, Agnes stares from one to the other.
How can she have been so blind to Elise's machi-
nations? Was it because she was so occupied with the
children? Or did she simply assume that there wasn't
any hurry because Elise would never actually be able to
bring herself to rent out Robert's house? An ad in a
brochure doesn't have to mean anything, in and of
itself. Her sister-in-law could just as easily have been
trying to determine if at some future date, sometime,
there might be any interest in Port na Bà. She bangs her
fist on the table. 'But this is dreadful! That's next
weekend! I'll still be here!'

'Nice of you to be so sympathetic,' says Muriel
sarcastically.

'Oh, hell,' Agnes cries out, 'this comes as a complete
shock to me, I knew nothing of this, I'm hearing it for
the first time myself, I'm sorry, but I—'

'Well,' says the younger Mrs Flynt, 'then it must
come as a nasty surprise, seeing that you've always
gone around acting as if all Port na Bà belonged to you,
just because you come here a week or two out of the
year.'

'Meanwhile, who's been looking after the house year
in, year out? Who's been looking after the gutters, the
roof, the chimneys, the grounds?' Muriel's face speaks
volumes: your problem is just a spoilt little rich lass's
setback, Agnes!

'We should have known,' says Mrs Flynt, closing
ranks. 'We shoulda had a word with Elise ourselves,

instead of leaving it up to you. Even if you *had* phoned her, although it *was* asking a bit much, I'll grant ye that—'

'Oh, stop it,' Agnes interrupts. 'Please! I know you must be disappointed, but—'

'She knows we must be disap*poin*ted,' Muriel sneers at the younger Mrs Flynt. Muriel, of the muffins and the firewood, Muriel, who chugged over to Port na Bà on her mini tractor. *That* Muriel? And the younger Mrs Flynt – oh dearie me, if I'da only known you were coming, I'da cleaned the house and brought over some food – that same Mrs Flynt now says: 'Even if you had phoned Elise, you wouldna have accomplished a thing! Elise doesn't give a damn about you! That's perfectly clear now, is it no'? And didn't we always know it? Because what kind of weight did you ever pull, in your family?'

'D'you ken what they call you?' asks Muriel, almost dreamily. 'Barmy Aunt Agnes.'

'Nora always says, every family has one.'

'Mathilde always says, if you miss the boat – oh well, that's what you get, do you no'.'

'Kshema always says – no, I mean Benjamin's previous wife, the red-haired one, she used to say . . . what did that one used to say, again?'

'And Gemma and Joost told us just last year—'

'But Robbie,' minces the younger Mrs Flynt, 'may he rest in peace, *such* an admirable, patient man, your brother Robbie used to say, "My sister has so little in her life, Mrs Flynt, can I count on you to make her stay here as pleasant as possible?"' A gesture of the gnarled fingers that's impossible to misinterpret: crisp bank notes exchanging hands, a hefty tip to make up for the burden of Agnes's presence.

The sun is shining as she leaves the farm, a tepid wind wafts in from the east, bees are buzzing over the heather in bloom, a sheep bleats in the distance. The world has not come to a standstill; the world is indifferent to the question of whether a human being named Agnes Stam is weeping or laughing. There are much more terrible disasters than a heart stung by hateful words, and even in the case of those much more terrible disasters, the world, as we know, never stands still.

As if Robert would ever have done anything as humiliating as the Flynts just insinuated! They must simply have misunderstood, those two, that's it, their petty little minds can't grasp that a person might do something like that out of love and concern, out of a sincere desire to make someone else happy.

She walks on, robotically putting one foot in front of the other.

From far away comes the peal of Dervaig's church bells sounding the midday hour, and here comes Ben Flynt walking through the fields, a scythe over his shoulder, as is his wont at this time of day: the world keeps turning, and that's all there is to it.

'Hello, Agnes,' says Muriel's husband, the son of the younger Mrs Flynt. He has a large, self-satisfied face; he gazes at her neutrally, with no inkling of the earful awaiting him at home.

'Ben.' Agnes nods. The absolute certainty she'll snap in half if she finds herself having to have a friendly conversation with him.

But Ben Flynt isn't aware of her mood; after a long morning in the fields, he himself wouldn't mind a little chat. He is one of those men who like to hear their own voice and who supply life with a confident running commentary. Is that no' a bonny dress your wee lamb has on there, Agnes. Followed by some agricultural and horticultural updates, a recapitulation of the latest news, a final summing-up, and no beating about the bush, either.

Agnes stands there like a pillar of salt. Next to her, Tommy's anxious jabbering: 'It doesn't have to be a big bunny, a little bunny is probably better, because little bunnies don't eat as much.'

'Ye ken that murdered tourist, that they discovered this week at the bottom of Oban harbour?' Ben Flynt continues his soliloquy. 'For my part I'd no' be surprised if there wasna' a link between that and the kidnapping of those two Dutch bairns; nothing ever happens in these parts, so when ye do get two cases like that in a single week, nae doot they're connected. It's organized crime that's behind it, mark my words.'

'Yes, who knows?' Agnes blurts out wildly.

He broaches a new subject. 'See that rental agency of yours, d'you no' think it'll be wanting to put a new roof on the hoose as soon as possible? I was saying to Muriel, I says to her, I'll have a bonny new roof up there in three weeks.'

Agnes clenches her teeth.

'It shoulda been done years ago,' Ben continues, shaking his head. 'Me and Robbie, we discussed it many a time. But his heart wasn't in it any more. He said to me, he says, "Ben, lad, that house is a millstone round my neck."'

'Well, Ben, I'll be seeing you,' says Agnes abruptly. 'I must—'

'Come to think on it, that was the last time I spoke to him.' He scratches his neck. 'Five year ago, mebbe six.

194

No, hell, seven year, aye, we'd just bought the new combine. He niver came back after that, did he?'

'He had . . .' says Agnes with burning cheeks. 'I mean, he was – well, what's a few years?'

Ben Flynt hoists his scythe back on his shoulder. He says, 'Aye, ye're right, he'd simply had enough. He wanted to be rid of the house. An eternal shame, really, that Muriel and I didna' take it off his hands right then and there. Aye, well, the rental agency will be needing to have it fixed up this winter, so there'll be something in it for us in any case. Will ye no' agree, Agnes, your brother did let the house get a wee bit rundown.'

3

And what do you know, there's a letter with a Netherlands postage stamp waiting for her too. 'Dear Agnes, I hadn't wanted to bother you with this earlier because I did so want you to have one last carefree holiday at Port na Bà, but now I do have to let you know that I . . .'

Agnes smothers a profanity, then resumes reading.

'. . . hadn't counted on being able to rent it out so soon . . . that I can't let this opportunity pass . . . do understand that I'm inconveniencing you, seeing that you were to stay on Mull until 1 September, and therefore would be happy to offer you a stay in the Western Isles Hotel in Tobermory, at my expense. I'm so sorry to have to tell you in this letter that it's already a fait accompli, but I couldn't reach you by telephone. Would you make sure that by 11 a.m. on the tenth, the house has been cleaned and vacated? You can expect an estate agent from the agency to come by one of these days, to check if everything is in order. Yours, Elise.'

Agnes slaps the letter down on the kitchen table. She wants to be incensed, but suddenly all the cups of coffee and tea she has been offered by Elise in her lifetime come to her mind. She thinks of the billions of words that have been exchanged between them, of the countless kisses they have planted on each other's cheeks by way of greeting or leave-taking. It may be that those gallons of coffee and tea were dictated largely by common decency, that their conversations were conducted mainly out of routine courtesy and that they kissed each other merely for form's sake, but even so, Elise and she share a long, long history. Stretching back to time immemorial. She can't help seeing before her her sister-in-law as a bride, her dress a perfection, a fitted damask bodice and an endlessly long tulle train which in the evening she impatiently wound up into a knot for the dancing: Elise laughing, happy, blushing. Her clear young skin. Her pitch-black hair, fastened on top of her head with haircombs.

What a wedding!

A yellow and white striped tent, the garden of their parental home strung with Chinese lanterns, the lavender in bloom, a nearly full moon, long trestle tables at which to sit and eat and drink, Benjamin showing off his latest conquest, the rowdy brides-maids and ring-bearers, and Agnes, seventeen, no less whipped up with excitement than the younger children. She danced the polka with Frank until they were both ready to drop. She danced the waltz with Justus, who had been Robert's witness in a morning coat and high hat. Twirling around in his arms she suddenly cried out, 'But we completely forgot about the gypsies!'

Was it just a superstition, or could there really be something to that ancient custom? Besides, you could never tell when the gypsies might show up on your doorstep, tomorrow, or the day after, with their knife-sharpeners and tinker's tools, only to find out there had been a wedding and nobody had thought of asking them for their blessing. Oh, no!

Delighted with her brainwave, Agnes ran into the kitchen. A care package for the gypsies! She knew what you were supposed to give them: six eggs, a pound of flour, a side of bacon, half a pound of butter, a salt-glaze bowl. And a gold coin, for good luck for the newlyweds.

She yanked open drawers, grabbed stuff out of cupboards. When she was halfway through she was interrupted by Elise storming in. 'Ah, here you are, Agnes! Listen, in a little while, I'm going to toss the bouquet in your direction. Keep your eyes peeled, you've got to catch it, all right?'

'But I've still got to take care of the gypsies' . . .' said Agnes, but they were already starting to play the departure music in the garden. Everyone was ready with rice and confetti. 'Come on!' cried Elise, grabbing her hand.

Outside, festive chaos reigned.

There were no steps for Elise to stand on, no sweeping marble staircase; she came out through the kitchen's back door. She was nevertheless greeted with delirious applause. Congratulations were shouted out. Off-colour jokes. A great clamouring for the bridal bouquet to be thrown. 'Go and stand in front,' whispered Elise. 'I'm going to toss it right at you.'

Because otherwise, thinks Agnes bitterly, zipping back through time to Port na Bà where Elise's letter is lying on the table, because otherwise we won't ever get rid of you. Something along those lines must have crossed Elise's mind. Elise, always so generous. Right! She just didn't want Agnes constantly getting underfoot.

She slides the letter back inside the envelope, irked by the sharp little voice telling her she's doing the youthful Elise an injustice. Because surely Elise did have a warm spot for her back then, and when Agnes herself, in her pink organza party dress, had gone hunting for a salt-glaze pot and a side of bacon, she had been just as sincere in wishing her sister-in-law a long and happy marriage.

Waving her bouquet, Elise had climbed onto Robert's shoulders to loud acclaim, her eyes searching the crowd for her sister-in-law. Her dress had risen up and you could see Robert's hand holding a shapely leg by the ankle, his face disappearing under the frothy skirts; he had tossed them aside, he had looked up at his bride amorously, he had smiled, and he'd let his hand slide up hungrily towards the hollow of her knee.

4

Children keep life going: they have to eat, they have to drink, they need clean clothes, and above all else they need to be entertained. So at lunchtime she takes the young Jansens to the beach. Tommy is lugging the picnic basket. Chris is silent and tense.

Agnes spreads the checked picnic blanket in a sheltered spot among the rocks, she takes out cups and plates, lemonade, bread and fruit.

'Hey, Agnes?' says the girl sullenly. 'This morning someone came to the door, when you were out with Tommy.'

'Now you tell me! Was it that Inspector Miller again?'

'I don't know. I didn't open. And then he slid this under the door.' She extracts a crumpled business card from the pocket of her trousers. *Island Rentals*.

They certainly don't let the grass grow under their feet, Agnes thinks, startled.

'Was that another cop?' asks Chris anxiously.

'No, not that.'

'What was he then?'

'Oh, don't fret. It was just someone coming to look at the house.'

'But why?'

'Oh, well, you know, we're going to have to get out of there soon.'

Chris sits up in alarm. 'When?'

'By next Saturday.' And now that she's said it out loud, it's a reality. Real and unavoidable.

'Then where will we go?'

'Well, I don't know. But we'll think of something. You just go and play, now.'

'Aren't we going to eat?'

'No,' says Agnes. 'I mean, just go and play for a bit. Leave me alone for five minutes.'

The child jumps up, kicks over the picnic basket with a defiant scowl, and runs to the water's edge.

Tommy scrambles hastily to his feet. 'Chrissie,' he shouts. 'Chrissie, do you want to have my banana later?' He trots after her as fast as his little legs will carry him.

Agnes starts painstakingly picking up the food that has landed in the sand. Sandwich. Sandapple. But why bother? Let it start raining sand, see if she cares. A vision flashes through her mind of her old bones, picked clean, lying next to a cactus, a vulture hovering above. She can't bring herself to laugh. But then she's never claimed to be a humorist. All she's ever done is try to lead a decent life. She's never even cheated on her taxes. Other people chase after pleasure, fame or fortune, other people are ruthless in their desire to leave their mark all over the place. But she has always been more than content with whatever life has had to offer her.

She stretches out on the blanket, shuts her eyes. She simply can't stomach it. Doesn't it just stick in your throat, the thought that you might end up being punished for your very modesty? Is there no justice, then? In all the wide universe, is there no avenging angel to act as her champion? An angel with a double-edged sword, who will demand that she be given Port na Bà as her richly deserved reward for her silent dreams, for a lifetime's yearning, which she has borne so calmly without leaving any victims, without sowing any mayhem or grief?

She thinks, *I* am his widow, not Elise.

She had asked if 'The Ballad of Loch Lomond' could be played at his funeral; he once told her that was what he would like. But Elise preferred a requiem, she thought it was more suitable. Elise never did pay very much attention to Robert's wishes. Makes you wonder if she ever really loved him. She was probably only enamoured of the comfortable life he provided for her, and yet she still always wanted more. And Robert always so giving, Robert always giving in. He hadn't been to Mull for a few years only because Elise no longer liked going to Port na Bà. That was as plain as the nose on her face. If it had been up to Robert – but he hadn't wanted to rock the boat, and that's certainly understandable: after all, a wife does fulfil certain needs in a man's life. A wife entertains your mutual friends, she accompanies you to receptions, she folds shirts, opens the mail and keeps in touch with acquaintances: oh, we're very well, thank you. This year we're going to. We thought we would. We.

We! thinks Agnes derisively. That's what Elise thinks. Her sister-in-law has been living a lie all her life. Because in his heart, Robert was always here, in Port na Bà. Elise believes her husband was devoted to her, while he merely showed her the courtesy of not hurting her feelings. He simply wasn't capable of causing anyone any pain.

Agnes presses the palms of her hands deep down into the sand on which she's strewn his ashes. Without her, Elise's marriage would never have survived. It was thanks only to Agnes's love and support that Robert was ever able to stick it out with that ice queen.

Robert, lifting his fifth glass of whisky to his lips. At least half a bottle every night. He's telling them about the otters he saw today. Their cunning, their strength, their courage. The forts they build.

'I'm going to bed,' says Elise, yawning.

Outside an unseasonable storm lashes Port na Bà. The wind howls and the house groans like a ship on the high seas. In their bunk beds the grandchildren toss and turn, chewing on the ends of their salty hair in fright. 'Grandma!' they cry.

But Elise has already gone to bed.

Agnes and Robert are sitting by the fire. The grandchildren cry out again, and she stands up, she goes upstairs, gives them a glass of water, tucks them in, kisses their cold ears. Her life is good, everything is just as it's supposed to be, in the fort that Robert and she built together.

When she comes downstairs again, he has poured himself another glass. His face is puffy, his gestures elaborate, his voice loud. He repeats what he just said a moment ago about the otters. He never complains about his wife, not a word, not a whisper of reproach, he is too loyal for that.

Agnes looks at him in the flickering light of the open fire. Light, dark, light, like love, smouldering from time to time, yet always flaring up again. The wind rages in the chimney. A fire needs nothing except oxygen. You breathe. You inhale and exhale. That's all.

He talks about the otters.

'Oh, really?' she says. She listens. She nods.

At least he's got Agnes to talk to.

She can't just lie here idly on the beach all day; she's going to have to swing into action. If she doesn't come up with some solution now, there will be a family of strangers holidaying in Robert's house in a few days' time and she'll be breathing the fish-and-chips stench of overcrowded Tobermory, cooped up in the Western Isles Hotel.

The Western Isles Hotel?

Where, according to the newspaper reports, Sonja Jansen is currently staying with Jaap Geuzenaar, waiting for the outcome of the police investigation into the disappearance of her children. What on earth do the gods want from me? wonders Agnes.

She looks at Chris and Tommy playing in the surf. Crawling on hands and knees through the wet sand, they're hard at work digging. Agnes brings her vision into sharper focus. Sees their bare arms and legs. She clutches her chest. And suddenly she knows what it is that doesn't add up; and she's also aware that she's known it all along, but hasn't allowed it to sink in. For from the first moment she peeled those two out of their wet clothes and parked them under a hot shower; from that moment until today, she has never noticed any trace of abuse, anywhere on their bodies.

She gets up.

Chris has dug a network of trenches and pits, which are slowly filling up with sea water. In a sweat, she erects a dyke here, scoops a new canal over there, engaged in an age-old struggle with the elements that she has no hope of winning. She doesn't see Agnes approaching. Tommy does. He turns an unhappy, muddy face towards her. 'I wanted to make a nice little hole for my bunny, but it's filled up with water.'

'Yes, now it's just like a swimming pool, isn't it?' says Agnes.

'You don't even have a rabbit, stupid,' Chris explodes. 'And can't you watch where you're going, Agnes, you're about to step on my dam.'

Tommy asks, 'Do bunnies know how to swim?'

'A little,' Agnes guesses.

'Waldo knows how to swim much better than bunnies, right?'

Chris jumps up, grabs her little brother by the shoulders and shakes him violently. 'Shut your mouth! Did you forget what I told you? Did you forget what the deal was?'

Before Agnes knows what she's doing, her hand shoots out. She smacks Chris on the ear; it sounds like the crack of a whip. 'Stop it, you!'

With eyes like red-hot coals the child feels her cheek.

'Sorry,' says Agnes contritely. 'I *am* sorry, I shouldn't have done that.'

'You criminal,' hisses Chris, 'you're just a no-good low-down criminal, you are!'

'I really am sorry. Come here, I'll kiss it better.'

'Oh yeah, and take a bite out of my cheek, I suppose!'

'Now you listen to me for a change. It's clear you don't want to talk about Waldo, but that's no reason to fly into such a rage at—'

Before the girl can throw another tantrum, her brother points at the islands in the endless sea. 'Waldo is over there,' he says, full of awe. 'He's swum all the way over there, hasn't he, Agnes?'

Chris stares at her open-mouthed. The expression on

her face switches quick as a flash from alarm to incredulity. 'How do you know?'

'Well, I don't know about swimming,' says Agnes. 'But it did say in the newspaper that he's on Skye. Over there. That island with those big mountains.'

'Oh,' says Chris. She starts swinging her arms self-consciously, as if she suddenly doesn't know what to do with herself. Her face runs the gamut of conflicting emotions: horror, disbelief, fear, relief. 'Was it really in the newspaper? Was Waldo in the newspaper?'

'Absolutely,' says Agnes, 'I can show you the article.'

A wave comes rolling in, and Chris has to jump aside. Hissing froth engulfs a good portion of her dams and dykes. Within minutes there will be nothing left of her earthworks. And in the morning the beach will be pristine once more, as if no child had ever touched it. It will be as virginal as her own flesh. Who said everything must necessarily leave some indelible mark behind?

The girl bends down to scratch some flakes of seashell off her drenched left foot. When she looks up again her eyes are suddenly sparkling with inexplicable joy. She flings her ponytail over her shoulder and on spindly legs does a few wild dance steps, then leaps high in the air, arms raised, twice, three times, as if the greatest piece of luck in the world has suddenly come her way.

Six

And God said: Let us make man in our image, after our likeness. And God created man in His own image; in the image of God created He him; male and female created He them.

Genesis 1

1

In the middle of the night Chris is jolted awake by a hand on her thigh, hot breath on her neck. She wants to turn round, but the bed is too narrow. The sheets are damp with perspiration; her legs are all tangled up in them. She braces herself and thrusts her bottom out. A scream in the dark, and then the thud of her little brother crashing onto the floor.

She climbs down from the upper bunk. 'Silly goose!' she whispers. 'Did you break anything? Serves you right, you should have stayed in your own bed.'

Tommy howls.

She feels his arms, his legs. She hugs him tight, pats the convulsing shoulders. If only Mister Ed would come galloping up from the beach right now, his mane flowing, his hooves glittering in the light of the moon and the stars. Because now that she's awake again, she remembers just how happy she is. She could – she could just burst into song! I had such an ama-ma-ma-mazing dream. Except that this time it's real, it's the truth. It was in the newspaper.

As soon as she remembers that, she can't stay still any longer. She jumps up and, with Tommy clinging to her leg, limps over to the window, pulls open the curtain and presses her nose eagerly against the glass. There's a whole lot of night out there, and no sound except the calm sighing of the sea. In the indistinguishable distance, on the island called Skye, Waldo is probably listening to it as well, if he's awake of course. How tired out he must have been, after swimming all that way – it must have taken him a day and a night at the very least, she thinks. In her mind's eye she sees him slicing through the waves like a knife, and, shaking Tommy off, she hoists herself onto the wide window ledge, pulling her T-shirt down over her knees. A whole day's swimming is just about doable. But if you aren't asleep, the night lasts about ten times as long as the day, so at night one mile will *feel* like ten. You have to work these things out scientifically. Numbers create order.

Is he mad at her? she wonders.

She worms her elbows inside the sleeves of her T-shirt and clasps her arms round her ribcage. His voice, breaking: 'Chris *pushed* me, and then I had to swim for miles and miles!'

When their mother hears that, she'll be in real trouble. She sits, unable to move.

But maybe he won't tell on her. Hasn't he himself told her plenty of times that adults don't need to know everything? As he's saying it, he's cracking his fingers. His leather wrist strap has rubbed a mark on his skin and his fingernails need trimming. She sees it clearly before her, as if he's sitting right next to her on the windowsill, in his black Diesel jeans torn just above one of the knees.

'Is it morning yet?' asks Tommy. He has sat down on the floor with a glum expression on his face, his legs outstretched.

212

'No,' says Chris.

'Are we going to play?'

'Not now.'

Waldo always says she can trust him blindly. You'd have figured it out long ago, Chrisso, if you couldn't trust me. Because if that were the case, I'd have told your mother over a thousand times what goes on in your room at night. But you can count on me. I can keep a secret. You know why? 'Cause you'd really be in trouble otherwise. I'm just trying to protect you.

There's a pretty good chance he won't tell a soul what happened on the docks in Oban. All of a sudden, she sees the slimy, slippery stones before her again. She feels the rain drizzling on her skin. She smells the stench of dead fish and rotting rope. Waldo jumps high up in the air, his jacket open, he has his U2 T-shirt on underneath, he gives a shout of exultation. 'Yeah!' she yells in turn. It's pretty far out, really.

Waldo thinking she was going to fling her arms round his neck. And falling over backwards. The cracking sound of his head hitting the rocks.

She gulps. Please don't let this be the Waldo she'll always remember, as if his smashed skull were the essential thing about her brother: revolting and creepy! Completely forgetting that she put bars up in front of her eyes a long time ago, she begins to cry.

She pushes her fists into her eye sockets, but the tears keep coming. They roll down her cheeks to the tip of her chin, and then drip onto her neck; there are too many to wipe away, and with every tear her crime grows more heinous: Waldo thinking she was flinging her arms round his neck. 'Oh, shit,' she moans, 'oh shit.'

Startled, Tommy promptly starts bawling in sympathy, with quavering intakes of breath. He's still sitting on the floor, on the worn linoleum, his chubby toes curled in a bit. Through her tears, Chris notices how his feet have grown lately, and realizes he needs new shoes. She sobs, 'Come here, then,' but he stays stiffly where he is – because, after all, wasn't he a witness to what she did in Oban? The weight pressing on her chest gets twice as bad, and, gasping for air, she wails, 'Oh, come *here*!'

She wants to tell him she didn't mean to push him that way, and the tears start coming even faster. She'll make it up to him, she's still got her Mister Ed fund, she's rich enough to treat everyone to ice cream at an outdoor café. A sorbet for Waldo. Red syrup is oozing down his chin: you're bleeding, says Sonja and she starts to scream as she tries pressing her napkin against his face, the face that's splattered in all directions.

But everything's turned out all right in the end after all! Agnes herself read it in the newspaper. Waldo is on Skye. There's no need for tears. Stop it. Stop it at once, Chris!

She sniffs loudly. She rubs her cheeks dry. 'And you, stop your snivelling too,' she says to Tommy. Her voice sounds reedy.

He looks at her uncertainly. Fat tears still cling to his eyelashes.

She slips off the windowsill, sits down next to him on the dusty floor and starts tickling the soles of his feet until he shrieks with laughter. With her mouth all twisted like Lucky Luke's, she asks him (immediately appalled at herself for saying it), 'You do love me, don't you?'

He nods, however.

OK. OK! Brusquely, she says, 'As long as you realize I'm the only one looking out for you around here. Without me you're lost. There are cannibals here, you hear me?'

He opens his eyes wide. 'And crocodiles too?'

'Jesus,' she says, 'it's crawling with them. But I just roll them up like this, see, and then stick them in my pocket. I'm just as awesome as Space Man, you know.'

It's a pity her mother doesn't know these things about her, but her mother doesn't have time for that sort of thing because she has to bring home the bacon, for her children and for Selma. Selma is very expensive. 'But it doesn't matter,' Sonja always says, punching the keys on her calculator furiously, 'because we love her so very much, don't we?'

And all those evenings when her mother is too exhausted to even spare her one thought, Waldo is thinking of her, Waldo of the clammy skin, the searching hands; she never has to beg for *his* attention. He is there for her, always. And that, that's the only thing that matters. She can't believe she's never realized it before.

And at once she misses him so very much that she can hardly stand it, while at the same time she's overcome with homesickness for her whole life, for Selma, who is now forced to watch MTV all by herself, for Jaap, who slaps her on the back and calls her his *misschrissypuckissy* when he's in a good mood, and for her mother, who then will laugh and look all happy. She wants to go *home*.

What's to stop her from going back, anyway, now that everything's all right with Waldo? She bites her lip with excitement. Maybe the newspaper that had their picture in it also says where her mother is now, with Jaap, so people can alert her if they've seen her kids somewhere. So she could simply call her mother up, right now. Except that on her first day here she cut the telephone wire first thing in the morning, to make sure Agnes wouldn't call the police. But Agnes can drive them over to their mother in the morning, of course. She's going to wake Agnes up right this minute, to ask her.

Agnes's room isn't completely dark: she sleeps with the curtains open. Grey, misty moonlight fills the room and makes everything look mysterious. Chris turns her head away politely when she notices a glass with dentures in it on the bedside table.

A chair, piled with clothes. A chest of drawers, with a little vase of bluebells on top. Next to it, some photographs in shiny frames: a boy in an old-fashioned sailor suit holding a fishing rod, someone in black shorts waving a hockey stick, a young man tinkering with plumbing pipes, a man reading a book by the hearth, an old fellow smiling at the camera.

Her eyes swivel from the old man back to the young boy. She picks up both photographs, turns them over. Robert, summer 1919. Robert, February 1995. All the other photographs turn out to be Robert as well. An uneasy feeling comes over her. This must be one of Agnes's dead brothers: she's holding someone's dead brother in her hands. She replaces the pictures so abruptly that she knocks over the little vase of bluebells by accident. It lands with a clatter on the ground, spins around a bit and then rolls, unharmed, under the bed where Agnes gives a sigh and turns over.

Chris sinks to her knees, quiet as a mouse, and feels around the wet linoleum for the vase. Her hand brushes something smooth, something long, a tube or curtain rod, only heavier. She pulls the thing out from under the bed. Only when the butt comes into view does she realize that it's a rifle she's holding by the barrel. Get this: Agnes sleeps with a shotgun under her bed. There's another one just like it hanging in the scullery. Is she afraid of something, then?

The thought alarms Christine. Grown-ups aren't supposed to be afraid. But Agnes isn't a scaredy-cat, or else she'd never have the guts to live in this spooky haunted house, where everything's constantly rattling and creaking. Maybe it's because of that Inspector Miller that she keeps the gun close at hand. If he thinks he can just sneak in here in the middle of the night to do some more snooping around, well then, he doesn't know Agnes. Hands up, Miller! We'll show you who's boss around here.

Her toes curl up with gratitude.

Agnes is like a tree that's good for climbing – irrefutable proof of God's existence. How often do you come across someone who packs a gun specially for your sake? To think that Agnes sets such store by her! Bloody hell, wait till Sonja hears about *this*. Then she can't possibly stay mad about the two of them going missing for a few days.

'Chrissie?' whines her brother. He comes waddling in groggily, still half asleep. 'Are we gonna sleep in here?'

'Yup.'

He flops down on the floor and nestles his head on her knee. He closes his eyes. Within a couple of seconds, she can tell from his breathing that he's nodded off again. She hoists him up and heaves him

217

over into the bed next to Agnes. How that Agnes can sleep! Nothing wakes her up. Agnes has no idea Chris is here, dying to tell her she's going home. Agnes, open your eyes!

Her mother's migraine face, her words a volley of jagged cobblestones: 'But why, Christine, *why* did you get into a complete stranger's car on the ferry? What did you run away for? Well? Will you *please* explain to me what this is all about?'

Her hands grow cold. She clasps them tight. Even if Waldo doesn't tell on her, their mother will keep asking questions until she knows the whole story. Everything's turning out fine, yet she's still going to get punished, you'll see. Unless she can think of something that will make Sonja forget all about her rage, something that will make her forgive her daughter everything.

With an envious glance at Agnes and Tommy, who are sleeping as if they haven't a care in the world, she gets up and trundles back to her own room. She crawls back into bed. Lying on her back, she stares at the bulging damp spots on the ceiling. The worst leak is in the far corner of the room; Agnes has left a bucket under it. The whole house reeks of damp and mould, like a dark forest. Here and there the wallpaper is peeling off the walls, and the paint is flaking all over. The doors are so warped they won't close, and in the wardrobes, rusty clothes hangers tinkle softly in the draught that penetrates every nook and cranny.

It's such a depressing house that it's putting a damper on Chris's own mood. But it's clear she can't leave here before she's pulled off some great feat that will both surpass and cancel out all her other exploits. The kind of deed the Queen awards you a medal for, at the very least.

2

The pan she used for heating the hot chocolate in last night is still sitting caked up in the sink, together with the rest of the dirty dishes from the last few days. Agnes realizes too late she should have left it to soak. She wipes a few ants off the sticky counter. Spilt sugar crunches underfoot. Fortunately today is the day Muriel comes to clean

She looks at her watch. Chris must have chosen to sleep late, so she'll just grab a piece of toast with Tommy. He comes trotting after her wearing just his pyjama top, babbling about this and that, bursting with stories and confidences without any beginning or end. Is this the same little boy who couldn't string three words together just a few short days ago?

'Oh, certainly,' she answers, 'absolutely.' Abandoning her stab at housekeeping, she strokes the smooth hair. It's so touching, that he took it into his head in the middle of the night to get into bed with her. Who cares if the sheets were soaked when she woke up? Muriel will just have to install that new washing machine hose as soon as she gets here, so that the laundry can get done again. What's keeping her, anyway?

'And then Chrissie signed a contract,' Tommy informs her.

'My word,' says Agnes. 'In her own blood, I take it? That sister of yours really is something.'

'But what's a contract?' His grave eyes.

'It means making an agreement. Promising something.'

He thinks it over. 'Is that a good thing?'

'Oh, well,' says Agnes. 'It depends on what the contract says exactly.'

He shakes his hair into his face. He lisps, 'Waldo thought it up.'

'Then it's probably quite all right, I expect.' She gives him an encouraging smack on his bare bottom. 'And now, go and get dressed.' It's already practically too hot for clothes. Even though it's still early, she's sweating, and she's wearing nothing but her dressing gown.

In her bedroom she takes the wet sheets off the bed, carries them with Tommy's pyjama bottoms and her own nightgown into the bathroom, and stuffs everything into the washing machine. Why did she go out and buy an expensive new hose? Not for the sake of a bunch of strangers who think they're going to rent the house! No, sir; after she's finished here, she's getting in her car and driving right over to Island Rentals. Simple as that.

The doorbell rings downstairs, and she's still not dressed: that'll be Muriel, homely and familiar.

'I'm coming!' she shouts, with a hasty glance in the mirror at her dowdy dressing gown, her uncombed hair. And then her blood runs cold: she has lost her eye! Instinctively she covers the empty socket with her hand. For weeks now – no, months – her eye hasn't fitted well. The eye cavity tends to grow more hollow as you grow older, the optician told her only recently, keep a close watch on that glass eye, Mrs Stam, or you could lose it.

She stands stock-still, afraid to move in case she hears the sound of glass crunching underfoot. Her eye must have fallen out of its socket just now, when she was stripping the bed. Let's not panic.

She dashes back to the bedroom, looks round. 'Oh, come on,' she mutters.

When she was little she sometimes fancied that if she wanted to, she could flip her eye with her thumb and index finger and send it skittering along the pavement like an alley marble – that way you could sit on the kerb yet still watch everything rushing by, the tall linden trees, the fences with their spiral railings, the baker's cart; your eye would take in the whole wide world, and you wouldn't have to move a muscle.

For one absurd moment she hopes her eye will reveal its location to her that way. But the renewed peal of the doorbell brings her back to her senses. She should have listened to the optician, that's all there is to it. She hurries downstairs, mortified, to let Muriel in. Let's hope the sight of her doesn't scare the woman out of her wits.

But on the front step stands a young man in an expensive navy blue suit, who hands her his card as soon as she opens the door. Island Rentals. With the hand that's clutching the card she pinches her dressing gown closed round her neck; she keeps the other hand pressed to her face.

'Did I get you out of bed?'

'No,' she says, 'No, I . . .' I was just looking for my eye?

'I've just come to check on the house. I was here

221

earlier in the week, but didn't find you home.' He has a very thin moustache, like someone in a film about the nineteen twenties. A moustache requiring considerable maintenance.

Agnes slams the door shut in his face.

She leans against the wall.

The bell rings again.

A lifetime of good manners immediately gets the better of her. She opens the door again. 'Sorry, the wind.'

He looks at her disapprovingly. 'I left my card here earlier in the week. You were aware we were coming, weren't you?'

'Of course, and of course I should have given you a ring, but our telephone is out of service.'

He makes a wry face. 'I see.' He jots something down on the form on his clipboard. 'Any other problems?'

'I don't think so.' She tries to think, then asks, stalling for time, 'Do you know Port na Bà well?'

'No, I haven't lived on Mull very long.'

She can't come up with a new topic of conversation off the top of her head, and her arm is getting weary. She tries supporting her elbow with her other hand.

'Shall we just . . . ?' He gestures inside. Over his shoulder she can see the lofty blue sky. It's going to be a spectacular day, one of those unusually hot days when you can hear the seaweed on the beach drying in the sun with soft popping sounds, a day for being lazy and feeling happy and for picking black-berries. Lukewarm lemonade in a white enamel jug. A splendid day for an outing, too. We'll drive to Kilninian along Calgary Bay, a cup of coffee in Kilninian, and on to Ballygown, we'll pass through Bruach Mór and Lagganaiha, and just before Loch na Keal, shimmering in the sunlight, we'll take the right turn-off, and drive to where the road dead-ends at a concrete jetty. Across the water lies the idyllic island of Ulva, a wilderness preserve. And now, tell me the names of the other islands! Eorsa! Inch Kenneth! Gometra! Fladda! Staffa! Lunga! Bac Mór!

On the jetty there's a shanty with a simple board nailed to it, one half painted white, the other half red, the colour of ox blood. The red part has a wooden catch at the top. When it is raised, the ferryman, pottering in his garden over on Ulva, sooner or later notices he has some passengers. He puts his spade away, he wipes his hands on his trousers and steps into his boat. There he comes. Aye, it's yourselves again. The rippling water, the unhurried putt-putt of the outboard motor.

Look, Aggie, a greylag goose, see its wings?

Agnes, did you bring the sunscreen?

I say, Stams, pay attention, we've arrived, you can grease that neck of his later.

Next to the jetty the shabby café where you can have fresh mussels on white bread.

Five mussels and white bread please and five glasses of white wine, no, sorry, four, and a soft drink for Agnes.

We seem to be slipping b-back into our same old habits.

The calm crossing on the way back, the drive to Port na Bà in the late summer evening light, the Scottish folk songs they always sang on the way. All five of them liked to sing, and sang well, even when they had not been drinking.

'I'll take the high road and you'll take the low road and I'll be in Scotland afore you; and me and my true

love, we'll niver meet again on the bonny bonny banks of Loch Lomond.'

'More sorrowful!' said Justus, who was sitting in front, next to Robert. 'More plaintive! The song is about death. "Take the high road" means—'

'Right, we know that,' said Benjamin, 'but we're not going to get all morbid now. Come on, give us another tune, Aggie.'

Agnes is about to intone 'Fair love of my heart' when Justus's words suddenly give rise to a new thought. 'I'm going to outlive you all,' she says in alarm.

'As long as you give us a d-decent burial then,' said Frank.

'I'd like "The Ballad of Loch Lomond", you'd better make a note of it, and no eulogies,' said Robert. He honked his horn before taking a blind curve. He always did that.

'Muffled kettle drums are always nice,' said Frank.

'Except that you have to be Churchill to get those,' said Justus.

Benjamin said, 'I don't know if I can trust Agnes with my funeral. I bet she'd forget to serve alcohol.'

'In that case, I propose that you try your utmost to stay alive longer than she does,' said Robert.

'Yet statistically speaking, Benny doesn't stand a chance,' said Justus. 'Men go first, that's just the way it is.'

Benjamin said, 'Right, and it's all because of our having to work so hard for the womenfolk, you know.'

'Oh, right!' Agnes cried.

'Be realistic, Agnes. Who's the one out there making a living, putting the bread on the table?'

'You're not putting any bread on *my* table, actually,'

she said indignantly. 'When have you ever put bread on *my* table?'

Robert lit a cigarette and blew a thin spiral of smoke out of the open window.

She thought, he's proud of me: I look after myself, I'm nothing like Elise.

But it was for Elise's sake he would work himself to death.

In the hall the man from Island Rentals is inspecting the calendar from 1984 with scrutinizing eyes. Then he suggests, 'Shall we start with the living room?'

'Just a moment,' she says. She hurries to the kitchen, where Tommy is still traipsing around with a bare bottom. 'Tommy, the man who wants to look at the house is here again. Will you please warn Chris, and make sure he doesn't see you? And see if you can't find my glass eye lying around anywhere. Perhaps in the bathroom, next to the—' She is interrupted by the estate agent who is calling her from the living room.

She rushes to rejoin him.

He's squatting down, feeling the carpeting. The crease in his trousers. The impeccable parting in his hair. Not the type who'll let the wool be pulled over his eyes.

She says, 'We had a little flood. The washing machine is . . .'

He glares at her. 'We'll have to dry out the carpet. And the washing machine, has it been fixed?'

'Muriel is going to put on a new . . .' and it finally hits her like a bombshell. Muriel isn't just running late; no, of course not, she's never coming here again. Her throat is dry. She can't even amble up to the farm in a little while to tell the Flynts, 'You should have seen the man's face when he realized the carpeting was soaked through!' There's nobody left to share her alarm and indignation with.

The man from the rental agency takes some notes. Not looking up, he says, 'Mrs Stam asked us to put all personal effects in storage for the time being. Could you give me a list of the things that we should arrange to have picked up?'

'No,' she says curtly.

He pulls a pained face. 'But Mrs Stam expressly—'

'*I* am Mrs Stam.'

'The first tenants are arriving on Saturday. So we don't have much time. Even when people rent such a . . . such a basic holiday place, they have the right to expect everything to be in order.'

'You'd better tell Elise,' Agnes begins belligerently, but then bites her tongue. Because if she starts being obstreperous now, she'll burn all her bridges with her sister-in-law. The only way for her to keep Port na Bà is to let the man have his way for now; later, when she's back home, she'll use reasonable arguments to try to cajole Elise into changing her mind. Tersely she says, 'I'll see to it that everything that needs to be removed is ready to be picked up in the morning.'

'Excellent,' he replies. He must be wondering why she's standing there cupping her face in her hand, like someone with a bad toothache, or a migraine. 'Will you please show me the way to the kitchen, in that case?'

The counter piled high with dirty dishes, the grubby floor, and Tommy's mouse on the table sticky with spilt jam. 'The view is lovely from this spot,' she says hastily. 'But what do you think, should that window be enlarged?'

'The house seems to be infested with vermin.' With

unconcealed repugnance he stares at the mouse. He doesn't think she has been taking very good care of Robert's house: it's written all over his forehead, in neon letters.

Swallowing her indignation, she says, 'There are five bedrooms. Shall we get on with it?' Oh Elise, you'll pay for this, for the need to put on this cheery voice, for the humiliation of having to show this impersonal navy-blue tailor-made suit around the house that the Stams built.

He pauses by the children's room.

'No,' Agnes says in alarm. 'I mean, this door is locked. I'll go and look for the key.' Her head is spinning.

The new man in charge of Robert's house palpates his moustache to feel if it's still there.

It's not easy, flashing a winning smile at someone from behind your hand. At her wits' end, she asks him, 'Tell me, are you as fond of nature as I am?'

His face lights up unexpectedly. 'I'm a fuchsia man myself,' he promptly admits.

'You don't say.'

'I have over sixty varieties in my garden. I travel all over the country in search of them.'

'Oh, what a wonderful hobby,' she says fervently.

'I've just obtained a couple of cuttings . . .' Making a circle with his thumb and forefinger, which he raises to his pursed lips, he gives a boyish laugh. 'I have the highest expectations of them, come next spring. May I go into this room?' His hand on the doorknob of her bedroom.

'Be my guest. But tell me, what criteria do you use, when you select your fuchsias?'

'The colour, primarily. But isn't this room supposed

227

to have a washbasin with both hot *and* cold running water? That's what it says here.' He walks from the basin to the bed, and suddenly Agnes's face is flaming: there's only one possible explanation for the unmistakable wet spot on her bare mattress. Hastily she says, 'One of the children had a little accident in the night.' But she sees his expression and she knows what he's thinking: this is no nursery, this is the room of an incontinent old woman.

Suddenly she's made painfully aware of the fact that she still isn't dressed and her hair is not yet combed, and she has an almost irresistible urge to rip off the faded dressing gown and jump into the shower. Perhaps she smells. What must he be thinking of her? But she isn't what the man thinks. She – coincidentally she just happens to be . . . and with a sinking heart she thinks: I'm just barmy Aunt Agnes.

3

'Chrissie, c'mon, look,' Tommy whines.

'Shut up,' Chris hisses. She is sitting on the bottom bunk, her ear pressed to the wall. Vaguely she hears Agnes speaking English to that man Tommy says has come to look at the house. It must be the same bloke who was here before, the man she had just let ring the doorbell, he'd rung and rung, earlier in the week. She doesn't understand why Agnes has let him in, or why she'd ever let someone else come and live here. Where is Agnes supposed to go, then – or the two of them for that matter?

She looks at the faded print hanging next to the washbasin. The little seal seems to be pleading, with its big eyes, do something, Chris! Or else some stranger is going to come waltzing in here and rip me down off the wall.

'C'mon, look,' Tommy whimpers.

'Quiet,' she snarls, giving the hand he's holding up an indifferent glance. A glass marble. Well, good for him.

'Shall I take it to Agnes?'

'Moron,' she hisses. 'Then that bloke will see you. We're in danger.'

'But Agnes told me to herself . . .'

'Go put something on instead.'

'I don't want to wear a dress any more.'

'Then don't. Suit yourself,' says Chris crossly.

Her brother picks up a pair of underpants from the chair that has all his clothes on it. Hopping around on his plump little legs he manages to wriggle into them. The jeans give him a little more trouble. He sits down on the floor, huffing and puffing.

Chris squats down. 'No, silly ass, first you put your feet all the way in. Where are those feet?' She tugs the trousers up, yanks them closed. When she was four, she was perfectly capable of doing that by herself. That's because *she* didn't have a big sister to help her with everything.

And now that Tommy is dressed?

Now there's nothing for it but to just wait in here, like a couple of wimps. Chris hates wimps and goody two-shoes. There are dorks, there are ordinary people, and there are those that are real somebodies. You're a real somebody only when you amount to something. She walks over to the basin and stares into the fly-specked mirror for a long time. Her lips are thin and her nose is straight and narrow. Her teeth are a little too big. On her forehead, close to the hairline, there's a pimple. She touches it with her fingertips, wondering if she amounts to anything.

She feels like stamping her feet so hard it'll make the whole house shake to its foundations. But there's no point, unless the bloke who's now chatting up Agnes realizes that it's Chris who's making the walls tremble. *I am an angel with a double-edged sword. I am the Angel of Justice.* The time will come when everyone will know it, you'd better believe it. Like when the

230

Queen pins that medal on her for . . . for having saved Agnes.

It's simply impossible that Agnes of her own free will would let someone else come and live here, in the house she's constantly going on about, smiling as she touches a stripped door, or the cracked tiles in the bathroom, and saying, in a thrilled sort of way, 'Oh! I'd completely forgotten, but we spent a whole summer on this.' And then that face of hers, lighting up with pleasure. 'Port na Bà' is what Agnes says every other minute, 'it's called Port na Bà, and it's the house I built with my brothers.'

Chris is getting so agitated it's starting to make her sweat. If she had built a house with Tommy or Waldo, she would never give it up, never, even if it was some crummy old rat-hole. Agnes herself had let the man come inside, it's true, but then Sonja too always used to act all polite and nice to the bailiff, and then once he'd gone, she'd burst into tears and wail, 'They're crooks, miserable crooks, every one of them!'

And suddenly, in every sinew in her body, Chris senses that she has stopped being just an ordinary person. She's turning into a real somebody. She's got x-ray vision just like Space Man's, she can see right through the wall all of a sudden, she can see Agnes wringing her hands. And now she gets it, finally she gets it: the man has come to take away Agnes's house, the way their own house was so nearly snatched from them so many times by the bailiff.

She spins on her heels, and then she's off: here comes Chrissie Space Man! She's going to give that bailiff the fright of his life. Oh yeah! She knows exactly what to do. In a few minutes he'll go running out of the house and he won't ever dare come back.

231

*   *   *

Back in the kitchen with the fuchsia man, Agnes can't think of anything else to say. Her creaky brain won't co-operate. Wretchedly she offers, 'I'll leave everything in tip-top shape, of course. The children will help me.'

He clears his throat elaborately. Then he says, 'But what children are you talking about? We were given to understand by Mrs Stam . . . by your sister-in-law, that you were here by yourself.'

Agnes ignores that remark. She certainly isn't going to explain to some stranger why she'll never be alone in Port na Bà. She looks out of the window. Sees herself walking along the beach, with little Alice and Dennis, with Willemijn, Floris and Effie, with Ada and Ida, with Johanneke and Dirk, who are now both doctors.

Then the fuchsia man says, 'I won't keep you any longer, I think I've pretty much seen everything here.' He gives his clipboard a little pat. For a moment there it looks as if he's got something else to say.

Agnes starts. 'You mustn't think I'm trying to be difficult,' she volunteers, stammering. 'It's just that, well, this house has been in the family fifty years, and I . . .'

Without another word he offers her his hand.

'Wait, I'll see you to the door.'

Agnes precedes him down the hall. The linoleum. The calendar from 1984. The boots and children's wellies lined up beneath the coat rack. As she opens the door and feels the nurturing light of Port na Bà on her face, she suddenly hears the rush of powerful wings overhead. Looking up, she lets her hand drop in awe: two greylag geese flap by, the drake in the lead, his neck outstretched.

'Oh!' she exclaims as she steps out into the garden to see them go.

The birds don't notice her, standing by the rhododendrons. For them, Port na Bà will always be Port na Bà, no matter who lives in the house. Generations of geese and gannets will fly from here over to Ulva and back again, noncommittally. Shouldn't one follow their example? Isn't one's task in life merely to endure? What good is resistance, what good is questioning everything? You need only involve yourself with whatever lies right in your path.

The geese disappear behind the house, honking.

Agnes absent-mindedly fumbles with the belt of her dressing gown as she walks back to the front door. She's about to knot it more tightly when she spots the fuchsia man standing in front of the house. He averts his eyes so abruptly that she realizes *he* hasn't been watching the geese, not even for a second; all the time that she was looking up into the sky, he was staring at the empty socket in her face.

'I do beg your pardon,' she says calmly. But then the panic sets in: she is an unwashed, uncombed, unsightly old crone, she's a worthless piece of rubbish, all she is now is a nuisance, just ask Elise, Nora, Mathilde and Kshema, and in her distress she trips over her own two feet while scurrying back to the house.

'Madam,' says the fuchsia man, rushing forward to save her from sprawling onto the gravel, 'madam, you have nothing to apologize for.'

Right in the middle of the front path, she feels her dressing gown fall open. She could weep with shame: her breasts, that have never been caressed, her stomach, her thighs, her body that's never been made love to. Her entire insignificant and worthless life.

She can smell the fuchsia man's aftershave, she sees his navy-blue sleeve, a shiny cufflink, the dazzling whiteness of his shirt. And then suddenly, right behind his impeccable shoulder, in the doorway of the cottage, she catches sight of the scarf of Mrs Jansen's nurse-maid.

Utterly dumbfounded, Agnes sees that the girl has tied the scarf over the lower half of her face like a cowboy and that she's holding Justus's air rifle, the gun Agnes had so carefully hidden away under her bed. Another new character; another five points for Bazooka.

'Don't you worry about a thing now,' the fuchsia man's voice comes at her from somewhere far away. 'I don't think this house is fit to be rented. I'll try to reach your sister-in-law today if I can. You can just stay where you are, as far as I'm concerned.'

A few yards behind him, Bazooka raises the gun. 'Hands up!' she yells.

4

The Western Isles Hotel has a sunny conservatory with a view over Tobermory bay, it has a four-star restaurant, renowned for its local specialties, it has a comfortable lobby with gleaming magazines spread out on all the coffee tables and silver dishes filled with after-dinner mints. In the bar twenty-five brands of single malt whisky are served, and the hall is hung with antlers, hunting scenes and gigantic fish in display cases. It's the kind of establishment where, under normal circumstances, you could really live it up. Especially if the tab's being picked up by someone else.

Jaap can't stand it, he says, hanging about all day with nothing to do, so he's taken the car out again, for a drive around the island; he's going out looking, out hunting for the kids, he claims. But secretly Sonja suspects he's simply had it with being cooped up with her in the Western Isles Hotel, just hanging around waiting for Inspector Miller, who comes three times a day with an update. She imagines her lover perking up as soon as he sets foot outside; he clasps his hands behind his neck, stretches, tosses his jacket onto the back seat, and then goes gadding about.

Flipping through magazines, not taking in even the advertisements, sipping endless cups of coffee provided to her free of charge because her children have been abducted on British soil, puffing on one cigarette after another, getting up and then sitting down again, Sonja Jansen feels as if time has come to a halt and she is imprisoned in the selfsame second for all eternity. After four days of uncertainty and dread, this is what's left of her entire life: this waiting, this helpless waiting for this one second to be over. She must – she will – in future she shall – in future she'll make sure she – God, that's for sure! – and never again – but just – always.

Abruptly she gets to her feet, she walks to the reception desk and asks if there are any messages for her.

Then she goes back into the conservatory. She crosses one leg over the other, she lights another cigarette. She thinks, yes, no – that as well – but maybe – however, it's been in all the papers that Jaap and she are staying in this hotel. Except that Waldo, in a mountain refuge on Skye, won't have seen any newspapers, of course. Otherwise he'd have contacted them by now. She stubs out her cigarette. She goes and sits in the deserted lobby, for a change of scene.

Absent-mindedly she polishes off a dish of mints and starts on the next. Where is that inspector? Just as she's turning her head towards the front door, her lover enters the lobby. Head low, he navigates his way through the flowery Chesterfields towards her. Well, Jaap? Did you manage to score with some cute little floozy, at a pavement café, or on the beach?

Avoiding her eyes, he puts a hand on her shoulder and says, 'Nothing, as usual.'

And then she's taken with a hatred so deep, so

intense, so primeval, that she all but spits out her mint. How dare *he* look ashen, worried, defeated? He's on holiday, isn't he? She snarls accusingly, 'But what about Waldo, were you looking for him, too?'

'Waldo? No, why should I? Once he gets to Mull, he's sure to find the message we left for him at the campsite where we were supposed to meet.'

Unless – but – still – in order to. Spent, she says, 'Maybe he's lost the address.'

'My darling, he can take care of himself. Let's concentrate, rather, on—'

'No need to act so snippy.'

Without another word he perches on the arm of her chair. Folds his hands. Rubs his thumbs together.

'You seem to forget that it isn't *just* that two of my kids have been kidnapped, there's also a murderer on the loose.'

'But Sonny, that was in Oban, not here!'

'Do you really think the murderer will just stick around Oban, cool as can be? I bet he took off long ago, headed for one of the islands!'

'But why should he have it in for Waldo, of all people . . .' He sighs, stands up. 'Well, shall I give the campsite a ring, then, and ask them if by any chance he's arrived?'

'Jesus, Jaap! Surely those people would have been in touch with us if there was any news!' The impatient voice of the manager over the phone: Mrs Jansen, I *told* you as recently as this morning that there's no point in calling here every half-hour.

'In the unlikely event that something has happened to Waldo—'

'He doesn't even have his passport on him! He can't even be identified!'

'Sonja,' says Jaap in a loud voice, 'stop it. Stop it at once.'

Astonishment briefly takes her breath away. And at the same time she thinks, startled by her own indifference: I don't love him any more, it's over. If I ever really loved him in the first place – and why should I? Give me *one* good reason! On the other hand, is there ever a good rationale for love, other than delusion? Does love really ever consist of anything but your own desires, your own projections, your own illusions? Dear God! Love wouldn't even exist without illusions!

She snarls at her lover, 'You should never have dragged us out to this miserable island, never!' Uttering the words she has forbidden herself to say over the past four endless days doesn't afford her the slightest relief, and she grimly racks her brain for something that will sound even worse. 'You snivelling sissy,' she hisses, 'you irresponsible piece of shit.'

'You're really losing it, Sonja.'

'And do you think that's so bizarre?' she pants. She tries to work her way out of the deep armchair, but he pushes her shoulders roughly back down.

'No, I don't think it's bizarre, but we really don't need this right now. Get a hold of yourself, for God's sake, or I'll give you a good hiding.'

He was going to teach her to surf on this holiday; he promised. Weakly she says, 'How dare you! If you think that I—'

He lets go of her. 'Come on, up to bed now, you, and take a Valium.'

'But that man—'

'You mean Inspector Miller?'

'Yes, when he comes . . . shouldn't I . . . I mean I'll . . .' She presses her fingers to her forehead. Inspector

Miller, with his cool gaze, his probing questions – she is secretly a little afraid of Inspector Miller.

'I'll talk to him,' says Jaap.

'And what will the two of you talk about, behind my back?'

'You know perfectly well. I've been telling you for days now that we ought to mention the other possibility to him. The whole idea of a kidnapping is just a little hard to swallow . . .'

'And since when are *you* the expert?'

'I know what Chris and Tommy are like.'

'And I don't, I suppose? I'm their mother!'

'Good morning,' says Inspector Miller in the doorway of the lobby.

'Good morning,' says Sonja, smoothing out her skirt.

'Good morning,' says Jaap.

Then all three fall silent.

'Coffee?' Sonja asks, finally. 'Tea?'

The inspector shakes his head. 'I'm afraid I still have no news for you.'

Jaap says as if it's only just occurred to him it might be worth a mention, 'We were just wondering if it's really right to assume it was a kidnapping. The other option to consider, of course, is that Chris and Tommy may simply have run away.'

'Is that so?' says Inspector Miller. He's standing in the centre of the hushed lobby like some exotic plant. Abruptly he turns to Sonja. 'And what's made you think that all of a sudden?'

She wishes she could just go up in smoke, right here on the spot. Is this how she'll go down in history, as the mother who drove away her own children? She thinks, but where did I go wrong? Didn't Christine get her bike, Tommy his paddling pool? And everything

239

else. Mummy, we need to take in ten guilders tomorrow for the school trip. Mum, where's my Lego, my hat, my green felt-tip pen, my father, Muh-hum, *why* didn't you buy any chocolate spread, Mum, my zipper's broken, my ball has a leak, my jeep doesn't work any more, Mummy, I'm so hungry, so thirsty, so sleepy, I'm so cold, so warm, I'm scared, I can't get to sleep, my ear hurts, I've scraped my knee, my frog is dead, when are we going to, how long do we have to, are we nearly there, Mum, Muh-hum, I don't like it, I don't want any, Mum, come on, listen to me, help me, Mum, I have a pebble in my shoe, Mum, Muh-hum, Mum, Muh-hum, Mummy, Mummy, Mummy! Nappies. Measles. Report cards. Mum!

'Oh,' she says, frazzled, 'you think all sorts of things, first this, then that, isn't that always the way?'

'When children as young as yours run away,' says Miller, 'and I've told you this before, they normally turn up within the first day. Even sooner, usually.'

Sonja gets a hold of herself. Somewhat miffed, she says, 'But Christine is *so* independent! She could easily . . .' And, out of the blue, it's as if she's come home after a long round-the-world voyage and sees her very own slippers next to the radiator – and suddenly she's convinced of it: her life isn't smashed to pieces, it's neither splintered nor broken, but surprisingly whole.

Proudly she says, 'My daughter's a handful, but she's also a very special child. Extremely enterprising. Bubbling with enthusiasm, always making plans. Nothing's too much for her.' She thinks to herself with wonder, and she's inherited it from me, yes, she's just like me, I used to be that way too. She ends, 'And what's more, she's fairly headstrong, and contrary. A

240

rather complicated combination of character traits, I'm afraid.'

Inspector Miller's eyes, behind his spectacle lenses, suddenly take on a different look: they turn small and puffy and red. 'I've got one of those little darlings at home myself,' he says. His face twists in a painful grimace. 'You only want the best for them, but meanwhile they like nothing better than to fight you tooth and nail.'

'Ah,' says Sonja, 'I'm with you there.'

They stare at each other a moment. Then, as if by prior agreement, they both look at Jaap, poor Jaap, who is childless and fancy-free, and they both smile somewhat bitterly. Sonja says it in Dutch, almost distractedly: 'I'm sorry. You were right.'

Her wild little hoyden Christine, with Tommy, eager to please her, tagging along at her side. Just as inseparable as she and Selma used to be. Just as faithful and devoted to each other. Sonja has to bite her lip in order not to burst into tears. Come back! The world is much too big for you yet. Tommy's pudgy knees, dimpled on both sides, his grave face lighting up in a fleeting, dazzling smile, his clumsy little fingers struggling with a paper toffee wrapper, Tommy who can't get to sleep without his stuffed animal, his teddy Bobo – Sonja feels her heart beginning to beat faster: her little boy, out there somewhere, without his Bobo. Thank God Christine is with him. She'll think of something. She always thinks of something. Recalcitrant, resourceful Christine. She should have known better than to wish for a daughter who would play with Barbie dolls, she should have counted herself fortunate to have a tomboy for a daughter, a rough-and-tumble daughter, a daughter who wears basketball shoes, because at least that kind of daughter knows how to get by in a world that's such a big, dangerous place.

Jaap offers her his handkerchief, without a word.

The inspector waits until she has finished blowing her nose. Then he takes out his notebook and pen. 'Let's try and figure out why your children might have wanted to run away,' he says.

'We had – we were keeping Christine on a rather short leash lately – no pocket money, grounded that sort of thing – because she'd been getting into so much trouble.'

'The two of them were on the point of making a run for it back in Oban, if you ask me,' Jaap puts in his two cents. 'They tried to give us the slip when we were boarding the ferry.'

'I see,' Miller replies. He takes off his glasses, polishes the lenses, settles them back on the bridge of his nose. 'In order to avoid any misunderstanding here, I must make it clear to you that my department does not involve itself with runaways. If this were in fact no longer a kidnapping matter, I should be obliged to refer your case to the local uniformed police. I'm not saying it has come to that, of course, but you will understand that in that event, there would be consequences with regard to your stay at this hotel.' He casts a rather embarrassed glance at the expensive magazines on the coffee table.

'Naturally,' says Jaap.

Sonja nods distractedly. Again she sees her children, the way they were trotting all hunched over along the quay in Oban. Maybe they thought, if Waldo's allowed to go off by himself, then so should we. 'It is possible that my eldest gave them the idea,' she says. She restrains herself from indignantly adding what she'd like to say to him: but that's not what I'd call running away. Only unhappy children run away.

Miller taps his pen on his notebook. He says, 'Could it be that they wanted to go after your son? Is that what you're thinking? Are they that close, then, the three of them?'

Sonja is silent a moment.

The smurfs, is what Waldo with a sixteen-year-old's disdain calls the little ones – the shrimps. But for all the bravura, he's crazy about them. Sonja knows perfectly well that, big as he is, Waldo still likes to snuggle in bed with Christine sometimes. And she's also seen him sitting with Tommy on his lap more often of late. He turns beetroot when she catches him at it, for it isn't very 'cool', of course, to be seen cuddling your little brother.

'My children, Inspector,' she says, 'are awfully fond of each other.'

5

With her eyes narrowed against the sunlight, Chris
stands on the doorstep of the cottage, hugging the
gun to her stomach. She wants to yell 'Hands up!'
again, but the words stick in her throat at the sight of
the shocking scene in the garden. The bailiff's knocked
out one of Agnes's eyes, he's nearly pulled her dressing
gown right off her, and now he's gripping her by the
upper arms as her legs flail helplessly, legs so white
and brittle and thin that you wish you'd never caught
sight of them.

Agnes makes her think of the pale dead fish Tommy
had wanted to put in his coat pocket in Oban.

The gun trembles in her hands. She can hardly get
over her revulsion. Is this all that gets left of you, if you
live long enough?

Agnes's one good eye opens wide when she sees
Christine standing there. She moves her mouth as if
she wants to shout something, but the left side of her
lips remains slack and her face suddenly takes on an
almost puzzled expression.

Now the bailiff is looking at her too.

Hands up, thinks Chris, bracing herself. If that bloke
thinks he can just get away with it, beating up a little

old lady and making off with her house, the house she built with her brothers . . .

Alarmed, he raises a hand as if to shield himself as she aims the gun.

Chris stands on the doorstep with her finger on the trigger, her cheek pressed against the rifle butt. I chased the bailiff away, Mum! Just ask Agnes! I scared the living daylights out of him and he ran off as fast as he could!

She hears Tommy's bare feet clattering over the hallway floor behind her, he comes barrelling out of the door at top speed in order not to miss Chrissie Space Man outdoing herself, surpassing all her previous feats, and eagerly he flings himself at her.

And then they are both thrown backwards with immense force as the gun goes off with a blast that's louder than all the thunderclaps and lightning bolts in the world combined.

Seven

And God saw that it was good.

Genesis 1

1

So suddenly does the fuchsia man let go of her that it sets Agnes tottering unsteadily down the path again. Helplessly she tries to regain her balance, but her left leg refuses to serve and she feels herself going into slow-motion freefall, a fall that's like a sigh that implies that everything that was good once is now all over.

As she's falling, she is acutely aware of the gentle, salty breeze, of the arched, radiant blue sky and of the fragrant meadow that seems greener than she has ever seen it, every grass stalk unusually distinct, glistening and fresh. The beach, too, twenty yards on, seems whiter than she's ever seen it before, the mica-hued rocks more impressive, the endless sea more violet: more intense, deeper, truer, lovelier than ever before, a riot of beauty and colour, the flaming yellow of the broom over there, the raucous purple of that single clump of heather, the lavish red that has suddenly blossomed on the spotless shirt of the fuchsia man, and, in the distance, black and stern, the rock formations which take on their true shape only in the evening light, when they turn into the ship owners who watch over the bay of Port na Bà and the house that Robert bought for her fifty years ago.

And at the same moment she feels him plop down beside her; his arm flops over her hip, his head rolls against her shoulder. His lips move in her neck, he's saying somthing, mutely. Agh. Aggie. To think I've made you wait for this all your life long.

Then she smells his aftershave and sees the blood-red corsage on his chest. It isn't Robert, but the one who has taken Robert's place here on earth, as the new person in charge of Robert's house: the fuchsia man. She's almost tempted to shout, 'Leave me be! Let me remain here in peace. That was my brother's wish.'

He should have put it in his will. But he always had so much on his mind. He simply forgot to do it.

The body lying beside her doesn't stir. The arm that's slung over her is limp and heavy. There's an abnormal silence, and for the space of one endless heartbeat, as all of this hits home, she thinks she's suffocating. But almost at once, dismay and horror turn into an unreal calm.

She's lying on the front path beside a dead man.

2

The gun's recoil has hit Chris like a punch in the stomach. It's made her fall on top of Tommy and they're now both sprawled on the front step of the house. Her little brother doesn't budge when she rolls off him. He looks at her wide-eyed, too surprised to start crying. In the deathly stillness she can hear the insects buzzing. It's terribly hot. They should have worn shorts.

Slowly she sits up and pulls the scarf off her face. The sweat prickles in her neck. The gun, which has landed a few yards away on the lawn, flashes in the sunlight. She glances up, just once, apprehensive and reluctant; her heart starts banging like a jackhammer the moment she catches sight of Agnes and the bailiff lying on the front path. Scrambling to her feet, she grabs her little brother by the arm and, pushing and dragging him into the house, slams the door shut and turns the key twice in the lock. Her teeth are chattering. Her arms are covered in goosebumps.

Shrilly she tells Tommy, 'It's no big deal, really it isn't.'

Can she help it if Agnes loaded the gun with real bullets? Who would ever do such a thing? Why would you ever expect it to be loaded? In a sudden fury she kicks over the entire row of boots beneath the coat rack. She falters briefly, shocked at herself. She can feel her heart hammering away. Then she runs into the living room and systematically starts kicking over all the chairs, swiping books off the shelves, dragging cushions off the couches. She won't leave a thing standing in Agnes's house. If it hadn't been for Agnes's house, she'd never have touched the sodding gun.

She yanks the drawers out of the big chest and sends them flying across the room, contents and all. When that's halfway done, she abandons the chest in order to tear the canvases out of their frames, then she drops the paintings to bang the poker on the wooden slats of the benches till they snap and crack. But the hard knot of rage in her stomach just keeps growing bigger and tighter.

Whooping, arms flailing, Tommy runs after her, he crashes into overturned furniture, he slips on broken glass and splintered wood. In the kitchen she tries to yank the refrigerator door off its hinges, but it's too heavy for her. So she smashes a dent in it with the kettle instead. She climbs up on the counter and stamps the crockery in the sink to smithereens. Now for the bedrooms.

The bedside tables are flung to the floor, the linens ripped off the mattresses. Tommy has dragged the poker upstairs with him and starts slashing the pillows with it. Through clouds of whirling down Chris spots the display of Roberts, on Agnes's chest of drawers. She picks one up and with all her might hurls it to the floor so that the glass in the frame shatters. And then all of a sudden she's had enough. 'Stop!' she screams.

Her brother freezes. Feathers cling to his hair, drool

is running down his chin. A large dark stain betrays the fact that he's wet himself.

And then she barks, 'And now we're going to clean up this mess.'

Self-consciously she picks the smashed Robert off the floor. There are glass splinters sticking up out of his face.

'No!' protests Tommy.

'Do as I say!' she shouts. She runs downstairs with the photo in her hand. In one of the compartments of the desk by the window there's a glue stick. There's Sellotape too, thank goodness. Everything's going to turn out all right: she's a wizard at pasting. Everyone will tell you. Chris, would you please stick this together for us? Great gluing job, Chris. Get to work, Chris!

She turns round and then her eyes accidentally stray out of the window. In the glittering sunlight the bailiff and Agnes lie sprawled motionless on the gravel. Hastily she pulls the curtains closed and lets herself slide down to the floor beside the desk under the window ledge.

Banging the poker as he goes, Tommy comes tramping down the stairs. He stops short in the room's unexpected semi-darkness. 'Where are you?' he calls.

Chris remains mum.

'Chrissie, where are you?'

She bites the inside of her cheek. Can't he call for someone else, just once? Why does he always need *her*? Just like that time with Waldo. He should've just called their mother that time, instead of Chrissiechrissiechrissie. If he'd called for their mother, the cat would have been let out of the bag then and there, and she wouldn't have had to push Waldo off the wharf, they wouldn't have had to run away, and none of the rest would've happened either; if only Tommy had called for their mother that time, Agnes wouldn't be lying out there on the front path right now.

'Chrissie?' whimpers her brother in a voice bereft of all hope. The drumming of his bare feet as he trots out of the room. He'll step on a splinter or a piece of broken glass next, you wait and see. Chrissie! Chrissie! Chrissie!

Not! Chrissie thinks crossly. She waits. She plucks a few tiny hairs out of her arm. But he doesn't come back. Which makes her fume even more. Now she'll have to go after him, to make sure he doesn't do anything stupid. She waits a little longer. Then she trudges out of the room. No Tommy in the hall, no noises to show he's upstairs. She goes into the kitchen. The back door is open, squeaking softly on its hinges. Now she's scared. She runs outside, down to the beach. It's deserted, except for some birds pacing back and forth at the water's edge on stilt-like legs. They flap away, scolding loudly, as Chris comes near.

Her brother can't possibly swim a day and a night, he'll never make it to Skye, he isn't even allowed to go in the water without his arm bands. 'Tommy!' she screams, but her voice can't be heard over the drone of the surf. 'Come back!'

Without thinking, she splashes into the water. The current pulls at her legs, it's low tide, the sea must have sucked her brother in. She imagines him spluttering and thrashing, a terrified expression on his face. He hates getting water in his ears. Again she shouts his name as she wades in deeper. Her clothes get heavy. A wave dunks her, and instinctively she starts thrusting out her arms and legs.

All around her the water glitters as if it's littered

256

with millions of little silver coins. Beyond the crashing surf, the water will be calmer. She plunges through the breakers, trying to swim in a straight line. She's got both her A and her B swimming diplomas, she can do it. A minute or so later, treading water as hard as she can, she's looking out over the waves.

An endless, undulating, empty expanse of water surrounds her.

'Tommy!' she screams. 'I was only pretending not to hear you!' She takes in a mouthful of salt water and, choking and coughing, goes under. When she surfaces again, the sea seems even vaster, even emptier. The islands and their mountains, rising mistily from the horizon, seem even further out of reach, more remote than ever. Is she swimming in the right direction? Her hair is plastered over her eyes, she can't see a thing. She flips over on her back and begins kicking her feet, but forgets to keep her stomach up high enough and nearly sinks again.

She should have taken off her shoes.

'Tommy! I was just playing hide and seek!'

A cold current trails past her legs. She bets there are jellyfish. And what if the bones of those Spaniards Agnes was telling them about are lying on the bottom somewhere around here? Pale, gnarled hands slowly rising up out of the water to grab her by the ankle and pull her down into the deep. Shuddering, she looks around again, trying to catch her breath while treading water. There! A beach! And the roof of Agnes's house. As the realization sinks in, she nearly goes under once again; she must have turned around somehow, without knowing it.

Dumber than the dumbest water flea. Dumber than a – dumber than a *dodo*!

'Tommy!' she yells. Tommy, who's convinced she's as strong as the Hulk and as clever as Space Man. Tommy, who's got it into his pudgy little head that he can always count on her to come to the rescue. Like that time with Waldo. If only Tommy had called for their mother that time. But he'd called for *her* instead, just once – a single, abbreviated squawk. And even before jumping out of bed in the pitch darkness, she'd known exactly what was wrong. There had been a sweet scent in the house, wafting all the way upstairs: Jaap had brought home a bunch of flowers for Sonja that day. Strange, to think you'd remember stuff like that. A hundred years from now she'll still remember the way the house smelled that night when she flew to Tommy's room. Her mother had said it was flowering dill.

Waldo had grinned somewhat sheepishly. 'Well, but *you* like it, don't you?' he'd demanded, almost plaintively.

Tommy quivering in his bed.

But what kind of a question was *that*, did *she* like it? She was the reason it happened, every time, simply by existing, by breathing and being, that was all. She bowed her head, bewildered, and studied her toes. Wasn't it enough then, simply to be happy that some-one was paying a little attention to you, which made it a bit hard to confess you'd much sooner, for instance, set off a few good smoke bombs together; were you supposed to *like* it, too?'

Waldo pulled on his jeans again. He rocked back and forth on the balls of his feet while thinking it over. Then he said softly, 'Of course, you'll have to compensate me, to make it up to me, Chrisso.'

'Yeah,' said Chris. She had her arms wrapped tightly round Tommy so she would feel less useless. Brothers

258

were the ones who were ultimately in charge, of course, but that didn't mean that a sister couldn't count for something.

Did she understand what 'compensate' meant, asked Waldo.

'I do,' she said.

He said, 'OK, then let's put it in writing. We'll draw up a contract, you and I.'

In the dark she could tell from his voice that he was happy and excited. 'OK then, write it,' she said.

When he read aloud what he'd written, she felt a bit sick. She put Tommy back in his bed and tucked him in. 'Will you stay here and sleep with me?' he whispered under his breath.

'I'm just going with Waldo for a little while,' she whispered back.

Back in his room, first she had to sign the contract. 'Later, when you get married,' he told her benevolently, 'I'll give it to your husband, at the wedding.' He laughed soundlessly, so he wouldn't wake their mother and Jaap.

There's sand between her teeth and she can still taste the sea water when she hauls herself back up onto the beach, crawling on all fours over the sharp grit of crushed shells. She brushes the wet hair out of her eyes and looks up, and for a split second, she thinks she must be dreaming: a little further on, a small shape is toddling along the path past Agnes's house. It's Tommy.

In her excitement her knees almost give way, but she's nevertheless off like a shot. Her soaked clothes chafe her skin as she tears across the beach and races into the garden.

Her brother has sat down on the gravel with his back to her, beside the motionless bodies of Agnes and the bailiff. He leans forward and pulls at Agnes's arm.

'Don't!' yells Chris, horrified.

Agnes turns her head to the side. The empty eye socket makes her face look as if someone's punched a gaping hole in it. 'Thank God,' she mumbles, 'there you are. At last.'

3

On one leg, leaning on the girl's shoulder, it takes Agnes a good fifteen minutes to hobble inside the house. I'm too old for hopscotch, she thinks, dazed, as she slumps against the wall in the hall. Much too old. She's been lying on the path long enough to consider her predicament from every angle, and it's perfectly clear to her what her predicament is. Her poor old blood vessels.

With the inside of her good arm she wipes the sweat from her brow. The staircase is an impossibility. 'I'll go. Lie. Down on. The couch,' she mumbles. Speech is giving her trouble, the way it feels after you've had novocaine at the dentist's, but by taking an inordinate amount of time over each word, she manages somehow. At least it isn't complete aphasia. She almost says it out loud, out of pure force of habit, 'It could all have been so much worse.'

But when she takes in the havoc in the living room, she nearly loses the unreal composure she has hung on to until now. The sight alone is enough to bring on another stroke.

Chris stammers, 'Shall I – shall I make up a bed for you, with the sofa cushions, Agnes?'

She nods, groaning inwardly.

The child nervously begins shifting things around.

Frank's paintings, their canvas all torn. The bird books scattered on the wet carpet, their spines broken. The smashed leg of the little table that for some reason or other used to be known as Benjamin's Side Table, next to a splintered drawer from the antique chest. The cracked glass of a framed child's drawing: the angels drawn by little Sennemi of the Ivory Coast. Two angels with faces as black as hers, in blue robes. 'Why?' Agnes asks.

Chris turns bright red. She cries, 'We just wanted to make sure nobody else would come and live here! It's *your* house, you know! They're *your* things!' She waves her arms about jerkily. Her voice climbs an octave: 'Why should somebody else come and live in your house and touch your things? It's not fair!'

Agnes, speechless, lowers herself unsteadily onto the cushions in the demolished room. The logic of a ten-year-old. But all things considered, what's not to agree with? Not much.

Chris continues, wailing, 'All we were thinking was, if we wreck everything, then at least nobody else can live here either.' Her brother, rocking back and forth on a broken wicker chair, looks up at her with awe.

And the awe isn't completely unjustified either, thinks Agnes, her head throbbing. Because perhaps this is what she herself should have done, instead of giving the fuchsia man a house tour, like some docile old sheep. Given the chance for once in her life to *do* something, she turns out to be just too chicken, too polite, too – too much Agnes. Poor, beloved Port na Bà, forsaken by her the one and only time she could finally have repaid it for all the wonderful summers she's spent here. Oh, no tears now. Would *she* ever have got up the courage to take an axe to Robert's house in order to keep it the way it was, to keep it hers?

'As far. As. Ideas. Go,' she says, spitting out the words one by one, 'It was. A pretty. Good. One.'

The child catches her breath. She blushes again. Uncertainly, she asks, 'But what are we going to do now, Agnes?'

Agnes doesn't know either. She feels her numb cheek. She'd probably best get herself to a hospital. That her mind is still as clear and lucid as it seems to be – isn't that a miracle? She's never claimed to be all that level-headed. It's probably just that she can't afford to panic right now. Should she send the children to the Flynts for help, with a note? The elder Mrs Flynt surely . . . wouldn't she? If Chris and Tommy hurry, they might just be able to intercept Ben Flynt on his stroll home through the fields for lunch.

In her mind she pictures Muriel's man walking up and choking back a bitter invective when he spots the cottage at Port na Bà. Will he stop and shake his fist, or spit on the ground? In doing so, will he see the fuchsia man stretched out on the front path?

She heaves herself up on her good elbow. 'That man,' she croaks. 'He. Must be. Moved. From. The garden.'

Tommy takes his thumb out of his mouth. 'My sister shot the gun,' he says proudly.

Chris wails, 'I only wanted to help! I wanted to scare him off! I wanted to chase him away! So he wouldn't take away your house! Nobody's allowed to steal your house!'

Agnes nearly bursts into tears at that. Such a brave, impulsive, impossible child. Would Sennemi or little Alice, would Dennis, Jeroen or Willemijn, would any of the adult Stams, Joost, Gemma or Isabel, would Robert Junior, would Nora, Mathilde and Kshema, would any of them have done the same thing as Christine Jansen? Would they have lifted one finger to keep Port na Bà out of the hands of strangers? Come on, Aunt Agnes! Don't make us laugh! Pick blackberries? Look for seashells? Five cents for every oyster we find? Pudding in an old cracked fish mould? At Center Parcs they have a tropical swimming pool, you know, a sauna and a video rentals shop, on Corfu the climate's better and the food more interesting, and in Kenya you can see *real* wild animals. We don't mean to be beastly, Aunt Agnes, but after a thousand visits, we've pretty much had it with Port na Bà by now.

If they had put up a united front, they could easily have persuaded Elise to change her mind. But they simply don't care what happens to Robert's house. Only Agnes and this little girl give a damn.

Ben Flynt could be walking by any minute now, too. As soon as he spots the fuchsia man lying there, the shit will really hit the fan. Maybe he's already home, dialling the police with trembling fingers this very minute.

The officer on duty will tell him that there's a detective from the mainland currently on the island.

It won't take Inspector Miller long to get here. He'll grab Chris and Tommy by the scruff of their necks, the way Ben Flynt picked up her dogs Kawa and Saki that time. The truth will be squeezed out of them like juice from an orange – there's no child on earth that could keep mum about the fuchsia man for very long. And then Christine Jansen, the only one who has ever lifted a finger to save Robert's house, will have to pay for it for the rest of her life.

If Miller finds her here, it's all over for her.

She must disappear immediately.

There isn't time for a well-thought-out plan. At best, there's just barely time to wing it. Agnes orders with numb, dead lips, 'Bring me. A pen. And paper. At once.'

Crestfallen, Chris hands her what she's asked for.

Let's hope her scribbles are legible enough. PLEASE TAKE US TO THE WESTERN ISLES HOTEL IN TOBERMORY. She's panting with the effort when she's finished writing. 'Quick. Outside. Out to the road. Where cars drive by. And then. Hitchhike. Understood?'

'Hitchhike?' says Chris. 'Where to?'

'It's written. Down. On this. Paper.'

'And then?'

She mutters, 'That is. A surprise.'

The child's gaunt face registers astonishment.

'Believe me,' says Agnes. Is she doing the right thing? She has no idea.

'A surprise? What for?'

'Because you. Were such. A great. Help. To me. You are. A very gutsy. Little girl. A heroine. But people. Don't believe. That sort. Of thing. Right, Chris? So. We won't. Tell. Anybody.'

'Oh,' says the girl, wavering.

'Hurry. Or it'll be. Too late.'

'But,' begins Chris. There's colour in her cheeks again. Her movements are more lively now. 'But will you wait for us here, then?'

Agnes manages a crooked smile.

'Do you want a blanket?'

'Muriel,' she lies. 'Coming soon. Just go.'

'OK,' says Chris. 'Except, we do have to disguise ourselves of course, before we go out.'

The child needs dry clothes, she looks as if she's been for a swim. But it's warm out, and there is no time.

'No, just hurry.'

Chris's eyes flit round the ransacked room. 'Are there any sunglasses?'

'In. The kitchen. Windowsill. Quick, then.'

'Man, I'm not a magician,' Chris grouses. She folds the piece of paper over twice and tucks it into her trouser pocket. She jogs to the kitchen, returns with a fistful of sunglasses, then wedges herself into the rickety wicker chair next to Tommy.

Agnes's heart contracts at the thought of what's awaiting these two in Tobermory, at the hands of that mother of theirs, and that boyfriend. Forgive me, she thinks. I wanted to save you from their abuse, but now the only way I can save you is by sending you back to them. You'll feel you've been betrayed, you'll feel you've been tricked, but believe me, if you stayed here the consequences would be far worse. And where else can you go?

'What's this one look like on me?' asks Chris from behind a pair of mirrored lenses. 'Or are these better?'

'Hurry. Up.'

'God, Agnes, that bastard really hammered you, didn't he? You can hardly talk!'

'But. Luckily you. Came to my. Defence.'

'Don't you need a cold facecloth or anything?'

'No. Just go. Right now.'

Chris places a pair of plastic pop-art frames on her brother's nose. They size each other up appraisingly through their dark glasses: Bonnie and Clyde.

Bewildered, Agnes wonders, why were we never Bonnie and Clyde, never Ivanhoe and Rowena, or

Lancelot and Guinevere? We were Sir Galahad and Sir Gawain, Castor and Pollux. We were Marco Polo and Amerigo Vespucci. We were always men in the company of men.

The children are standing by the door, hand in hand. 'OK, bye,' says Chris. 'See you later.'

4

You came to my defence brilliantly, Chris. But in the hallway it hits her again: the dead bloke's still lying out there in the garden. The thought gives her a creepy feeling, and to make it go away she picks up the toppled boots and lines them up neatly under the coat rack once more. What's the deal, is she supposed to drag the bailiff under a bush somewhere or hide him some other way? But if so, she'll have to touch him, and she can't bring herself to do that.

She suddenly has this terrible yearning to be lying cuddled up on the couch under the checked blanket with the stack of old Little Golden Books that Agnes keeps in the house. She used to be crazy about *The Poky Little Puppy*. And later it was *The Lively Little Rabbit*, with the big picture of the hilly landscape across the centre spread. If you peered at it long enough through your eyelashes, at a certain point you'd see yourself and Lively Little Rabbit strolling side by side along the twisty lanes, looking for the angry fox with the big red tail. It made you feel incredibly brave and unafraid.

You're a gutsy little girl, Chris, a real heroine.

She sighs. It's true, she thinks, with resignation.

Reluctantly she unlocks the door and pulls it open a crack. 'You just wait here,' she tells her little brother. 'I've got to take care of something first.'

Tommy cries, 'Me too! Me too!'

'No, shorty,' says Chris. 'It would definitely give you nightmares.'

She steps over the threshold and spits in both hands. It's so warm outside it feels as if her damp clothes are starting to give off steam. She stares hard at her feet on the red and black tiles of the front step, wriggles her toes inside her shoes. What's a person need toes for, anyway? Fingers are so much easier to figure out. Reluctantly she looks up. Her eyes sweep back and forth across the garden like searchlights, from left to right and back again.

The bailiff isn't lying under the rhododendron bushes, limp and drooping in the heat, nor in the flower border, nor on the lawn, nor at the foot of the birch twig birdhouse that is supplied with bread by Agnes every morning.

Not a trace.

Anywhere.

She feels herself starting to tingle from head to foot. The *bullshitter*! He's gone! He had the fright of his life, he only *pretended* to be dead because he was so scared.

She shouts with laughter, wild and hard: he must have waited until the three of them went inside, and then sneaked away as fast as he could, shaking like a leaf; and he was never coming back. Or else he'd have rung the doorbell and started in on Agnes all over again. What a – what a chickenshit.

She inspects the gravel. Here's where he must have been lying: there are some splotches of blood on the pebbles, and lethargic, sticky flies buzzing about. But

Waldo bled too, and yet he managed to swim all the way to Skye. If you look at it scientifically, this is the second time the truth has been confirmed, and in the exact same way, that God really does exist and, when you get right down to it, everyone really is immortal.

It's as true as the sun that shines and the wind that blows and the day that always follows night, it's as true as Mum's bottle of nail varnish and her perfume samples, as true as Selma's milkshakes, it's as true as Tommy wetting his pants and the twelve-times table and the newspapers Waldo delivers daily, as true as a snack from The Sprinter, in summer and winter, as true as a mouse in a kitchen cabinet, as true as the Duchess of Hungary.

Bloody hell, she thinks, elated. We rescued an old lady, Sonja! Ask her yourself! She fills up her lungs and yells, 'Tommy! Come here!'

She spreads her arms wide as he comes running through the garden, and scoops him up. Snivelling, he buries his wet face in her neck. He's still sobbing, or he's started sobbing again.

She says sternly, 'We're on our way to that surprise of Agnes's, remember? Come on, give us a smile!'

Tommy hiccups.

'And after that,' says Christine, feeling terrific suddenly, 'after that we're going to go and see Sonja and Jaap.' She puts Tommy down again.

He gulps, holding his breath. Looks up at her with a face that's all trepidation and hope. Slurps snot and tears back inside. Stammers, 'Can't we go and see Mummy right now?'

'If you'll just hurry up for once. OK then, yes, we can ask Agnes where Mummy is, later.'

His bottom lip pouts forward, quivering. Two big fat tears come rolling down from behind his sunglasses. But he puts his slimy hand in hers.

They cross the wide pasture, run along the path past the Flynts' farm and can see in the distance a white mobile home driving along, as well as two cars towing caravans.

In less than ten minutes they've got a lift. Chris, in the back seat, is so excited she sits up straight as a rail the whole way. You wouldn't know it to look at her, but she is the girl who came to Agnes's defence and chased away the bailiff.

The couple sitting up front are quite young, they have the radio turned up loud and are singing along in cheerful, hoarse voices. Sometimes they'll yell something over their shoulder, to which Chris keeps replying, yes, oh yes, yes. She nods and smiles. She can see that these people like company and that's why they like picking up hitchhikers. It's an incredible mess inside the car, clothes, ropes, hiking boots, maps and plastic carrier bags. They're probably here on holiday like them. Maybe they're Americans. Wait till she tells Selma! She wouldn't mind driving round like this, with your arm out of the window, stopping from time to time to pick up a couple of kids standing by the side of the road waving a piece of paper.

After half an hour's drive they get to a town. The houses are painted all colours of the rainbow, pink, blue, yellow and orange. There are lots of shops and cafés. It's definitely the kind of place that lends itself to surprises; Chris feels it in her bones. Maybe what Agnes wrote down was that as a reward Chris and Tommy were to be dropped off at a penny arcade.

They halt in front of a big red brick building.

'There you are, the Western Isles Hotel,' says the girl behind the wheel. 'Lucky you, to be staying in a place like this.'

Chris jumps out of the car. She can't wait to make a beeline for those shiny gold revolving doors, but remembers her manners. She sticks out her hand through the open car window at the American girl. 'Thank you,' she says, in her best English.

Next to her Tommy lisps, 'Fenk yoo.'

Chris points at him proudly.

'Isn't that cute?' the girl says to her boyfriend. They both smile, they wave, and then they drive away, honking their horn.

'Cool,' says Chris.

'Where are we?' asks Tommy, looking around.

'At the surprise,' she solemnly replies. She grabs him by the shoulder and pushes him ahead of her through the shiny gold revolving doors.

Agnes is lying on her back on the cushions, clutching
her dressing gown closed with her good hand. From
this unfamiliar angle the ransacked room looks strange
to her, alarming even, as if every object had taken on
new significance. It's no longer the room in which she
used to kid around with her brothers, discussing house
renovation plans in thickly laid-on Scottish accents: 'I
kinnae git what ye want with the hoose.'

What did we want, she wonders, what did we have
in mind? Doesn't everybody know you can be truly
happy only if you have no desires or expectations?

The thought evaporates into thin air before it's fully
fleshed out. In its stead, clamouring for attention,
comes the realization that she can't stay here like this.
She has to – what in heaven's name is she supposed to
do? With a body that's only half working, and a dead
man in the garden?

Panic sets in.

She tries her sister-in-law Kshema's breathing
exercises. Have faith in yourself. Have faith that whatever happens, justice, fair and impartial justice, will be
done.

In a daze she thinks of the fuchsias, which will

now bloom in vain. Is there someone waiting for the fuchsia man at home, someone longing for his return? If nothing else, the people in the Island Rentals office will be wondering what's keeping him. 'He was going to visit that lady who won't get out of her sister-in-law's house. Shouldn't someone go over there and have a look, in case he's run into a problem?'

It's indisputable: sooner or later someone will come over.

Senseless thoughts flit through her brain. Never knew you could kill someone with an air rifle. And with ammunition that must be a thousand years old, too. But it doesn't make any difference really, because there's a body in the garden, and the murder weapon's lying a dozen feet from it; those are the facts.

The facts are simple.

The gun is lying in the garden.

The gun is still in the garden. With Chris's finger-prints all over it – and little Tommy's too: he held the gun while they were playing Mrs Jansen.

It's a risk she cannot take. After all, a murder is always thoroughly investigated. Clenching her teeth, she turns onto her side. By pushing off with her good leg, she manages to drag herself a few feet across the floor. Luckily the children left the door to the living room open. But when she gets to the threshold her spirits sink as she gauges the distance to the front door. The corridor appears endless. She's mopped it a thousand times, swept it, hoovered it, but never noticed how long it was. So many things you never notice. Until you have to. Propped up on her elbow, she pushes herself forward. Here, in this corner, Robert used to keep the empties.

'Aren't you overdoing it a little on the alcohol?' asked Agnes.

'Bitch,' said Robert.

Somewhere in the hallway the reverberations of that one word have been lingering all this time, hiding behind a skirting board, waiting for the time when she'd come crawling past, clawing her way along with bleeding fingertips. But it's just one memory, and she has so many other memories.

Together with Robert on the beach, Kawa and Saki merrily darting round them, snapping at their whipping coat-tails. His resigned voice: 'Elise has never liked dogs.'

'But I do,' says Agnes out loud to the linoleum, just before she remembers that Robert never actually made Kawa and Saki's acquaintance. It alarms her: she absolutely must keep a clear head.

She can hardly push her own weight off the floor, she has to gather all her strength to reach for the door handle. It opens inward, which is a problem when you're lying on the doormat. She inches backwards a couple of precious feet, until she's within reach of the umbrella stand beneath the coat rack. Black spots dance before her eyes as she grabs a walking stick. After a number of tries she finally manages to pull the door open with it.

The light, the smells – and Agnes on hands and knees painfully crawling over the front step's tiles, over the gravel on the path. She cannot lift her head, and toils forward blindly, inch by inch, slower than the lowest of God's creatures. Ant. Woodlouse. Cockroach. Spider. Daddy-long-legs. Centipede. Water bug. Cockchafer. Stag beetle. Bumblebee, honeybee and wasp. She grabs the rifle by the barrel and pulls it close to her, across the grass.

She allows herself a few moments' rest as she

inhales the summer scents of earth and grass.

Careful now: the gun is loaded. First the safety. That's it. Then, lying on her side, using the lining of her dressing gown, she rubs off the children's fingerprints. Butt, barrel, cock. Every muscle that's still functioning trembles with the effort. OK, that's that. Now she needs to recoup her strength a little, for the return journey.

It must be just about the hottest day of the year. She has visions of elderflower cordial in an enamel jug. It gives her such an indescribable thirst that she yanks a handful of grass out of the earth, stuffs it into her parched mouth and starts chewing on it. If Elise could see her now. Count your blessings, Agnes: Elise isn't expected in Port na Bà any time soon. You can lie here all you want and eat as much grass as you like, in your soiled dressing gown. This is all that's left of your life. Crawling on all fours is all you're still capable of. You couldn't even draw yourself a glass of water. It's the end of your independence. You're ready for a home for the decrepit now. Nurses the same age as your great-niece Joyce will talk to you in cheery voices while wiping the drool from your chin. Joost will come and visit you once, bearing a bunch of grapes, Gemma will bring some magazines. Kshema will send along a plant. And then everything will grow very quiet. As quiet as the grave. Imprisoned inside your useless body, you'll sit there waiting in vain for a child to come and draw angels for you, a child you can make a pudding for, or help into a cardigan.

Agnes thinks, dear Alice, your pink cardigan is still waiting for you here.

Or did Bazooka take it?

*   *   *

276

She must have nodded off in the warm grass. On waking up, she has the sensation, sharp and raw, that Joyce is wiping the spit from the corners of her mouth, and she thinks, without much bitterness, I don't have anything left to lose.

She clamps her fingers round the gun. Now that she's done with it, Inspector Miller can come and get it.

6

The brass door spins Chris and Tommy round at such a speed that it makes them squeal. *'Wheeee! Wheeee!'*

On the other side there's a carpet so thick that it makes the soles of your shoes squeak. Food smells. Muffled clinking of glasses, far off. And right across from the entrance, a desk with a lady behind it who's looking at them with raised eyebrows. 'Are you guests?' she asks suspiciously.

'Yes!' says Chris, looking around eagerly. No sign of a pinball machine.

'What's your room number?'

'Yes,' Chris repeats in her most emphatic English.

Tommy whines, 'I have to go. I have to go right now. I have to wee.'

'Idiot,' she snaps at him. She makes an apologetic gesture at the lady, who is rising to her feet. In a far corner of the hall she spots a sign that says WC. Sighing with annoyance she drags her brother over there.

When she pulls his trousers down, she notices that his last little accident left a large stain, now dried up. No wonder that lady was looking at them so oddly.

Can't really blame her, can you – a kid that's pissed in his pants tramping over your expensive carpet.

'Wash your hands,' she tells him crossly.

In the mirror over the sink she sees what she herself looks like: the sea water has left white rings on her T-shirt, and her matted hair is plastered to her face. Quickly she tries to smooth down the straggly wisps a little. Then she wriggles out of her T-shirt and turns it inside out, in the hope that the inside is more presentable. As she's doing so, the door opens. Startled, she looks round.

The lady from before enters the tiled space, accompanied by a man wearing a blue uniform with red epaulets. 'It's all right,' she says, smiling, 'don't be afraid.'

Chris gets goosebumps all over her bare chest: they've been recognised, in spite of their sunglasses, and that witch immediately called in the pigs. She stands there paralysed while they confer in low voices.

'To think I almost kicked them out! But then the little one started talking in Dutch. I'm sure it was Dutch. And they're the right age, aren't they? It must be them.'

The man scratches his chin. 'Are the parents in?'

'No, they went out a little while ago.'

Chris isn't going to wait around until they've finished their incomprehensible jabbering. She drops her T-shirt, grabs Tommy by the wrist, dives between the two adults, slips out of the toilets and runs. In the front hall she flings herself at the gold revolving door.

The door spits Tommy and Chris out onto the street. They collide full tilt with two people who were on their way in.

It's Jaap and Sonja.

*   *   *

279

Someone has fetched her T-shirt from the lavatory and brought it out to the lobby. She tries to pull it on again, but every time she does so, Sonja grabs her in another bear hug and then she smells her mother's smell, she feels what her mother feels like, and her whole body begins to quiver, to tingle almost, with pleasure. Boy, oh boy, that Agnes certainly knows about surprises.

'Mum!' she says. 'Listen, I—'

'I will,' her mother is saying, 'really Christine, from now on I will, I shall, I mean that I'll . . . You hear me?'

All sorts of smiling faces encircle them. The only one Chris recognizes is Jaap. Jaap, who keeps putting his hand up in the air: hey, Chrissiemissypuckissy, and then his whole face crumples up. He has this appealing habit of blinking rapidly when he's very happy.

'Jaap!' cries Chris. 'Jaap, listen!'

He comes nearer, taps her on the nose. 'First I have to make an urgent phone call.'

'And never again, I mean, I'll . . .' her mother continues. She's laughing and she's crying, she's saying, 'As long as you promise to stay right here with me from now on.'

The lady from the lobby is taking round a tray with glasses. Chris hears her ask someone, 'Was there a reward?'

Her mother takes a glass, she tosses it down in one gulp.

'Sonja!' Chris insists, when she's finally managed to get her T-shirt on. 'Sonja, I have to tell you something!'

'Oh sweetie,' says her mother, 'go ahead, tell me.'

'Waldo is on Skye!'

'Yes, of course he is, but we expect him back any moment.' And yet her mother isn't saying it with her

280

Waldo face, she cups Chris's cheeks in her hands and plants a big kiss on her forehead.

From sheer relief Chris rattles on, 'And on the boat, you know, when we were coming here on the boat? Well, Tommy and I met an old lady. She asked us to go with her, to help her. It's true. Just ask—'

'My little girl,' says her mother. 'I'm so happy to have both of you back.'

'We couldn't call you,' Chris continues, 'because the phone was out of order. But we—'

'My little pet,' murmurs her mother, stroking Tommy's head. 'Don't you have anything to say?'

'Can I have some crisps?' he asks.

Suddenly Chris realizes how hungry she is. She's famished. 'Do they have chips here?' she cries greedily.

'I'll order something for you,' says Sonja. She still can't really think straight, she's a little light-headed with joy and relief. She puts her hand up to call over a waiter. But her daughter has already jumped to her feet. With a lump in her throat Sonja sees the child energetically weaving her way through the crowd. So big, so independent. To think that entire days have gone by without this little girl – she doesn't want to miss another minute of her, not another second.

'Our Inspector Miller can't be reached,' says Jaap, squatting down beside her.

'Oh,' she says. She can't take her eyes off Christine, who has now buttonholed a waiter on the far side of the lobby.

'He's in the hospital, with a man who was found lying by the side of the road with a bullet wound. At the police station they couldn't tell me how long it will take, because he has to wait for the victim to regain consciousness, and then take a statement.'

'Oh well,' says Sonja, 'we don't really need him any more, do we?' She realizes there's only one thing she wants to do, and that is to return home with her children and forget this ever happened, as quickly as possible. 'Wasn't he ready to give up on us anyway? And now apparently he's got a real crime to solve.'

Jaap doesn't look very convinced. 'He'll most certainly want to have a word with Chris and Tommy, after all the trouble they've put everyone through.'

'But runaway kids aren't his department, he told us so himself.' She folds her hands over Tommy's belly, the most delicious belly in the world, and pulls him close. Her kids have come back to her, of their own accord. That's all she needs to know. It was just children being children.

With a worried set to his mouth, Jaap looks at her little boy. 'Where were you hiding all this time, munchkin? Where were you?'

'With Agnes,' Tommy replies promptly.

'Agnes?'

'Jaap, not now. Not here,' says Sonja brusquely. She doesn't even want to know that there's someone called Agnes, someone who's been looking after her children for days, someone they apparently preferred being with. Someone to whom they've confided all her shortcomings. She thinks, beseechingly, for God's sake, can't we just get on with our lives?

Her lover doesn't pay any attention to her. 'Those super trousers you're wearing, did Agnes give them to you, Tommy?'

'Cut it out,' hisses Sonja.

'Hadn't you noticed they aren't wearing their own clothes?' He sounds indignant. He turns back to Tommy. 'Tell me, big boy—'

Sonja squeezes the child tightly against her. 'He is *not* a big boy. Have you lost your marbles? I won't have it, you're not giving him the third degree! Don't make such a big deal out of everything! Just be glad they're back!' She lowers her voice: people are looking at her strangely. Why is she sitting here in public anyway? She should have declined the champagne and taken her children up to her room immediately.

'Christine!' she calls to her daughter, who, gesticulating with hands and feet, is still trying to communicate with the patient waiter. Clutching Tommy to her hip, she jumps up out of the armchair. Let's hope the hotel staff haven't alerted the newspaper. All she needs now is a bunch of journalists asking her children a lot of questions.

'Come,' she tells Jaap, 'we're going upstairs. I'll call room service and ask them to bring up something.'

'But how did Chris and Tommy find us here? Did someone drive them? Shouldn't we at the very least—'

'We hitchhiked,' Tommy interrupts him.

'Hitchhiked?'

'I can't believe he knows that word,' says Sonja, astonished.

Her daughter comes skipping through the lobby. 'Mum! How do you say chips with mayo and onions in English?'

'The chips come with tomato ketchup here,' says Sonja. 'But first you're coming with me. I've had to do without you for far too long.'

'Tell me, Chris,' Jaap begins. He's grabbed her daughter by the arm. Who does he think he is, anyway? Her dad? 'What's this about hitchhiking? And why did you stay away all this time? What was wrong?'

'I just told Sonja,' she replies. 'Didn't I, Mum? I told you.'

Jaap sends Sonja a quizzical, only semi-reassured look.

'We had to help Agnes.'

Still he doesn't drop it. 'Would you be able to find the way to Agnes's house? I'd really like to talk to her.'

'OK,' says Chris, beaming, 'then she can tell you herself what I did for her! She has a house, Jaap, that she built all by herself, together with her brothers. But then a bailiff came and—'

'Where is this house?'

'In Port na Bà. And then, to save Agnes, I just—'

'Port what?' says Jaap, on edge. 'Wait, I have a map in the car. I'll just look it up, and we'll drive over there right now.'

'Why should we?' Sonja snaps.

Confused, he looks at her. 'We want to get to the bottom of this, don't we?'

'I don't,' Sonja would like to say, but she bites her lip.

Someone passing by touches her arm. 'You must be *so* happy.'

'Yes, I am,' she says. 'Oh yes, I am.'

Agnes has no idea how long it's taken her to make her way back as, finally, with bloodied knees and elbows, she reaches the front step of the house. Groaning, she slumps down onto the warm tiles. The sun burns her shoulders and her thirst has grown even more acute. With her last remaining strength she pushes the gun into the hall through the open doorway. And then she's struck with the feeling she's forgotten something. That something isn't right, that something is *missing*.

By pulling herself up by the doorpost, she manages to work herself into a semi-reclining position on the front step. In vain, she tries moistening her parched lips. Her head is throbbing, her vision is cloudy. She has trouble making out the shape of the rhododendron bushes in the garden.

She remembers planting those rhododendrons, long ago: it was an unusually misty morning, the fog didn't seem to be coming from the sky but rising like smoke from the ground, so dense and impenetrable that the trees loomed like spectres. She'd thought there was something magical about the landscape.

You, said Benjamin, you think everything's magical.

Perhaps that was true. But isn't it to be expected, when your brothers have always rushed in to slay giants and dragons for you?

Frank said that as far as he was concerned, this sort of fog made him feel he'd landed in the underworld before his time. Just watch out for hungry g-ghosts, he said.

What do you mean, hungry? asked Justus, being a stickler.

Because their needs would now never be satisfied, said Robert.

But what could they possibly still need? asked Agnes.

She has the feeling that her breathing has become extremely slow, as if her whole life were winding down. She doesn't seem to be able to follow the thread of her thoughts. The rhododendrons. The fog. Orpheus and Eurydice. She doesn't remember what happened next, that morning. Tears of regret well up in her eyes: she's lost one of her memories.

All those years of nursing her memories, rearranging them, preserving them – and now they're going to start giving her the slip, like skittish beasts slinking off to find a safe refuge for the coming night. Her interior universe will be stripped and plundered. All her riches will desert her, every snippet of conversation, a look, a hand on her cheek, every strand of the tapestry that was her life will be pulled out, and in its place will come mist – a dry white fog.

She pictures herself in a barren, foggy landscape. There's not a breath of wind, there's total silence. Even her own footsteps don't make a sound on the stony ground. She's rushing about with rasping breath, searching for her memories. Come back. Don't leave me. Stay with me always.

286

Suddenly she's startled by a loud racket. It's a noise from the world of unhappy mortals who still have a thousand deaths to die: it's Muriel Flynt's mini tractor.

Muriel stops at the garden gate. Hesitantly, she sticks up a hand in greeting. She pulls her baseball cap low over her eyes, dismounts, fumbles about a bit in the roomy plastic crate on the back of her vehicle and then steps into the garden bearing a plate of muffins.

'Agnes,' she says, shuffling her big feet on the ground, 'I've come to offer our apologies . . . Agnes!' She snaps out of her penitent role. Her voice is shrill with worry. 'What ails ye? Are you no' well?'

Hanging sideways against the doorpost, Agnes, out of the habit of a lifetime, tries to smile reassuringly, attempting as best she can to pull her stained dressing gown over her bare legs. 'A minor. Stroke. I think.'

'God in heaven! Why did you no' call? What are neighbours for, woman!'

'Telephone,' Agnes rasps.

Muriel slaps herself on the forehead. 'Aye, of course, your telephone is on the blink. But what am I doing, wasting time. We'll look after you fine, dinna worry. I'm taking you home with me. Is your car unlocked?'

She nods, speechless.

The youngest Mrs Flynt deposits the muffins on the step and without further ado picks her up in her arms as if she were a stray lamb.

She grouses, 'You shoulda sent the bairns over, instead of biding there outside for someone to pass by. There's a good chance you'd still have been sitting

287

there three days from now. There's never a soul passes by here.'

Agnes thinks, *the fuchsia man!* Where did he go? She utters a stifled moan.

'Dinna excite yourself now,' says Muriel. Deftly she pops open the VW's door and lowers Agnes onto the seat cushions. 'Granny has had herself at least three strokes, and she's pulled herself out again, every time. Rest, rest, and more rest, and you'll be your old self again in no time at all. But you shouldna have crawled to the front door. You didna do anything else too strenuous, did you? Oh, jings, where are your bairns? They'll have to come with us too, of course.'

The fuchsia man, wounded and all, is staggering about somewhere, looking for someone to tell he saw Bazooka coming out of the house with the rifle. Agnes stares straight ahead, in a fog. So none of her precautions will do any good.

'Dinnae gie up the ghost on me now, Agnes,' says Muriel urgently. 'Can you hear me, Agnes?'

She's trying to recall the moments leading up to the gun being fired. The way her memory plays it back for her, the entire situation makes her think, for some reason, of an episode of Mrs-Jansen-goes-to-market. Befuddled, she thinks, was it only a game, then? Was a shot ever really fired at all?

'Agnes! Come on, Agnes, where are your bairns?'

'With. Their. Mother,' she gasps.

'Their mother?' Muriel repeats. Then her square face lights up with comprehension. 'Oh, you sent them home when it turned out the place was rented. Aye, that was wise, of course.' She buckles Agnes in and shuts the door.

As soon as the car door clicks shut, all of Agnes's other thoughts are swept aside by a single one: in a minute they'll be driving away from Port na Bà.

She tries to sit up straight. She can't remember performing the rituals of saying goodbye, the routine final tour of the rooms, checking doors and windows, remembering to take a shell or rock for her fish tank at home in the Netherlands, where for the umpteenth time she'll tell her angelfish and neon tetras about the sunken Spanish galleon outside Tobermory.

How this summer has flown, she thinks, stunned. Every year time seems to pass more quickly. Have I enjoyed it enough, have I paid enough attention and missed nothing? I have to live on the memories the whole of the coming winter.

Muriel slides in behind the wheel. 'I've locked your front door. So, shall we go?' She reaches for the key that's in the ignition, as always. You can do that in Port na Bà. Nothing untoward ever happens there, after all. 'Or do you want me to have a look-round for your eye first? D'you ken where it may be?' She leans across Agnes and touches her cheek, right beneath the empty eye socket.

She can't avoid that hand, and a cold shiver runs up her spine. Suddenly there's the appalling realization that she can't *do* anything any more. She'll never return to Port na Bà on her own. 'No!' she says. 'No!'

Muriel makes a shushing sound. Then she starts the engine.

The tyres have to work hard, spinning on the loose gravel.

They drive off.

Agnes is wrestling with the fog that's filling her head and which is hampering her vision. It won't even allow her one last look at Robert's house, the house in which, all her life long, she expected she would end up living some day with him, needing nothing but each other's company, without children with salt-starched hair sleeping in bunk beds and demanding a glass of water in the middle of the night. Had he lived long enough, it would have happened, too.

She wants to look back. She wants to see the house just one more time.

Look, Robert, our house.

And then she can see it, without turning round. She sees the white walls, the blue window frames, the slate roof. The front door swings open and there are the wellies on the worn linoleum, there's the wall calendar. And there is the living room with the beamed ceiling that makes you feel like a giant, with the creaky wicker chairs, the binoculars hanging from their nail on the window casing, tattered mementos everywhere of generations' worth of Stams. She sees Benjamin's Side Table, groaning with newspapers. She sees the steep stairs, the dusky landing, the dresser with the photographs, the narrow bed in which she used to dream her dreams. She can see it all; for, after all, her glass eye is still there.

Robert gave her a house: a house for an eye. And in that eye, the house will continue to exist, it will continue to behold all the beloved nooks and crannies as they once were – whatever happens to it in the future; through that glass lens, everything that was perfect will be kept forever the way it was.

And some day, a child's hand will find the eye, pick it up and leave it on the windowsill. It will look out at the bay of Port na Bà. It will see the sun go down and the stars flickering in the sky. Seasons will come and go, bees will make honey, birds will lay eggs, the never-ending sea will ripple up and down the beach where Robert's ashes lie scattered, and her eye will be a witness to all of it.

She won't have to miss a bit of it. Ever.

8

The reflected light bounces off the windscreen, and Jaap has flipped down the sun visor. Chris thinks guiltily of his sunglasses, which she threw out of the window a week ago.

He says to her mother, 'The turning for Port na Bà should be coming up any time now. Take a look at the map for me.'

'Mummy,' Tommy cries. 'Muh-hum! I'm so hungry!'

'Dervaig,' says Jaap. 'That's where we turn off. Maybe I can try calling Miller from there again.'

Sonja says, 'As long as there's something to eat for the children.'

Jaap looks at Chris in the rearview mirror. 'All right, Chris?'

In the village they find a pavement café. There's just one table unoccupied under the umbrellas.

'We're all having ice-cream sundaes!' Chris orders. 'It's on me.'

'What a big girl I have,' says her mother. 'Such a big, capable girl.'

Jaap will slip her a ten-pound note to pay with. Or a twenty, in case Sonja wants more than just a sundae.

'You can have a glass of wine too, if you like,' she offers.

'Well, we do have something to celebrate,' says her mother. She's wearing her cheerful, young face, without any hard lines, and she doesn't even mention the fat wasps buzzing round the empty juice bottles on the table. She's pulled Tommy onto her lap and is tickling him in the ribs.

They wolf down ice-cream sundaes as big as rocket ships.

'Could we take one with us for Agnes?' Chris asks hopefully.

Her mother leans over to her, grabs her chin and wipes her mouth with a paper napkin. 'But it would melt in the car, darling.'

'Shall we go?' says Chris, pushing her chair back.

'Oh, come on,' says her mother, 'give me a chance, won't you, to recover from all the emotion! I'd like to smoke a cigarette first. Where's Jaap, anyway? We have to wait for him. He's our driver.' She looks around vaguely.

'Wait till Agnes tells you what I did for her, it'll blow you away,' Chris promises.

'Chris shot a gun,' Tommy says.

'Well now,' says their mother. She laughs. She sucks at her cigarette. 'And what other kind of games did you play?'

Chris, indignant, wants to tell her it was a real gun. But suddenly she remembers what Agnes said: 'People won't believe that sort of thing anyway.' She purses her lips shut.

'Why are you looking so mad all of a sudden, Christine?'

'My name's Chris,' she barks.

Her mother looks at her, startled.

She jumps up, runs out of the café and across the road. There's a large oak across the way. She takes a flying leap, catches hold of the bottom branch, pulls herself up. She's as strong as the Hulk and she chased off the bailiff, whether anyone believes her or not. She is an angel with a double-edged sword. She is the Angel of Justice.

Sonja wonders what she's done wrong this time. Hungrily her eyes follow her daughter scrambling from one gnarled branch to the next.

'Are you guys ready?' asks Jaap, who suddenly appears out of nowhere. 'Where's Chris?'

'Just stretching her legs,' says Sonja. She points. She tries to smile.

'Hey, Tarzan!' cries Jaap. 'Are you coming?'

Tarzan, thinks Sonja, I should remember that one. Christine – Chris will think that's a good one.

Jaap says, 'I tried Miller one more time. I thought it wouldn't be a bad idea for him to be present when we have our little talk with Mrs Agnes.'

'OK, OK,' says Sonja. She squishes a sluggish wasp with her spoon into the remaining whipped cream. 'Well, is he coming?'

Her lover shrugs. 'They couldn't say. The man he's with in the hospital, you know, just died of his injuries, or loss of blood, what do I know, without ever regaining consciousness, so maybe Miller will indeed come and join us when he gets the message.'

'He should be going after the murderer instead!' she cries. 'Come on, Jaap, admit it. We can't possibly expect to take up more of his time, given the circumstances.'

Across the road her daughter has jumped down out

of the tree. She comes running up with pink cheeks. 'Jaap! Jaap! she yells. 'Give me some money to pay the bill, because then we can finally get going.'

'Will you give us a kiss, then?' demands Jaap.

'Blackmail!' cries Chris. She holds out a peremptory hand. He grabs her and flings her effortlessly across his shoulder. She screeches with delight, thrashing her arms and legs.

We always managed perfectly well without him, thinks Sonja, steaming. He mustn't think he – oh, sure! – no way – just wait until Waldo gets back!

As soon as the house comes into view, Chris can tell something isn't right. And she immediately sees what's missing: Agnes's car is gone. 'She isn't here!' she cries.

'Look, Mummy,' Tommy points out, 'that's where we played, on the beach.'

'Isn't our Tommy talking ten to the dozen,' her mother says.

'She isn't here!' Chris repeats. She opens the door and runs towards the house. 'Agnes!' she yells, although she knows it's pointless. She bangs her fists on the door.

'Is there a back door?' asks Jaap.

But that's locked too.

'It's a pretty spot,' says her mother. 'Pity the house hasn't been kept in better shape.'

They all stand a while looking at the splotchy, weathered façade, at the birds' nests in the gutters, the rampant ivy, the slate roof tiles all askew.

Finally Jaap says, 'Well, Chris, it looks as if your friend has flown the coop. You can bet on it she knows perfectly well that you're not supposed to keep someone else's kids hidden in your house. She's taken to her heels.'

'Not true!' yells Chris. 'She said she'd wait for us!'

Her brother complains, 'And she was going to give me a bunny rabbit, too.'

'Oh, come,' Sonja says, 'it wasn't right for her to let you stay here all this time, any way you look at it. No normal person would do that.'

'She's abso-bloody-lutely normal!' Chris yells.

Her mother bends over Tommy. 'My poor darling,' she murmurs, 'she must have made you do all kinds of awful things you didn't want to do.'

'I had to wear a dress,' says Tommy.

'That was for Mrs Jansen, you dummy!'

'Mrs Jansen?' says her mother. 'But that's me! *I'm* Mrs Jansen!'

Chris plops down on the front step. Out of sheer frustration she tries to pry up the tiles. She can't, they're firmly stuck down. Agnes and her brothers did that.

'Come on, Chris,' says Jaap. 'There's nothing we can do now, anyway. But tomorrow we'll come back to see if Agnes is home. I promise.' He holds up his hand.

Sighing, she slaps him a high-five.

When she gets to the car she looks back one more time at the house that Agnes and her brothers built.

It's a bumpy ride over the pasture. Now they're at the farm, where the dirt road begins. Chris presses her nose to the window as if she's seeing everything for the first time. Over there, and here, here she walked with Agnes when they were on their way to the Flynts' for tea. It was raining, but Agnes didn't mind. She told her about Mrs-Jansen-goes-to-market, about the children who used to play the game and about what other fun those lucky kids used to get up to in Port na Bà. Picking blackberries. Hunting for rock specimens. Decorating boxes with seashells. Taking the ferry over to Ulva. Making lemonade.

Morosely she thinks, we didn't even do half of it! And, naturally, next year Agnes will be bringing other kids with her: Agnes has plenty of nieces and nephews, she doesn't need Chris or Tommy at all. She'll simply forget the two of them and then it will be as if they'd never even been in Port na Bà with her. No memory will remain of the summer when she was as strong as the Hulk and as clever as Space Man. It will be as if nothing ever happened.

In the front seat Jaap says to her mother, 'The police will track down this Agnes. If she's still on the island, that is.'

'As long as we're talking to Miller,' says Sonja, 'I'd like to take the opportunity to give him a description of Waldo. I know you think I'm out of my mind, but I do worry about him.'

'Sonja,' says Jaap, 'Miller now has that other little matter to solve as well, remember, the man who just died.'

'Who died?' asks Chris, leaning forward.

'Nobody we know,' says Jaap. Then he turns to her mother again. 'In less than twenty-four hours it'll be swarming with police cars here, you'll see. So you can just forget about someone being available to take a missing person's report on some teenager with fingernails that badly need cutting.'

'His fingernails?' says Sonja. 'Are you off your bloody rocker? It's been almost a week – surely he wouldn't have – he can only – maybe he's injured, lying all alone on a mountain somewhere – I've known it all along. Jaap, we have to take a trip over there ourselves.'

'Aren't you taking this a little too far?' says Jaap.

'Then I'll go by myself, with the little ones,' says Sonja. 'I want to have my family all in one piece again, I've just about had it, in case you're at all interested.'

Chris, in the back seat, sits up in alarm. Whenever her mother puts on that particular voice, the men usually walk out on her.

'Mull's only brought us bad luck,' Sonja goes on. 'And I want to know what's up with Waldo. God only knows what may have happened to him. He's had an accident, I can feel it in my bones.'

'Just this morning there was a gang of murderers after him,' says Jaap. 'Every other hour it seems it's something else again, but it's all equally horrific.' He shrugs his shoulders, as if his muscles ache.

Sonja says, 'You don't have to come. We'll go without you.'

Chris leans forward. She throws her arms round Jaap's neck. 'Come on, let's go to Skye!' she wheedles, into his cheek. Because once they get there, her mother will see with her own two eyes that Waldo is just as indestructible as the bailiff, and at least then she'll be happy again.

'And what about Agnes?' asks Jaap.

Chris slumps back into her seat. Agnes is already on the point of forgetting her, and her mother needs her help. If she really keeps trying her very best for once, maybe her mother will come to see that she does amount to something.

'Chrissie,' Tommy, next to her, whispers wide-eyed, disentangling something from his trouser pocket with his clumsy little fingers, 'I totally forgot to . . .'

298

She looks at the marble in his sticky palm. But it isn't a marble. It's Agnes's eye.

Reverently she picks it up. She closes her fingers over it and then opens them again. Agnes's eye gazes up at her. It will never close on her. It sees her: in Agnes's eye, she goes on existing.

She stumbles over her own words. 'We'll write her a letter, Tommy and me, to thank her for everything. And then we'll invite her to come and visit us in our new house, after the holidays. She's got a car, you know. And then we'll ask Selma to come too, and then everyone can hear it, everyone will hear what Agnes has to say.'

'Well, in that case we can leave for Skye in the morning,' says her mother.

'And what does Tommy think of that idea?' asks Jaap after a pause.

'We don't need his opinion,' says her mother indignantly. 'This isn't a democracy, it's a family.'

'Tommy always does what I want,' says Chris.

'I want a bunny rabbit,' says Tommy.

'You need new shoes, too,' Chris explains to him reasonably. 'There's no way you can have new shoes *and* a bunny rabbit.'

She wraps her fingers securely round the glass eye. She'll keep it safe for Agnes. And at home she'll put it on the windowsill, so it can look out into the wide world, at their street with its fancy pattern of stones and the brand new pavements, and the shopping centre down the way. But first it will get to know Skye, and Waldo, her brother.

It will look at him without passing judgement.

And then they'll go and sit at a pavement café, all of them, and they'll live, yes, they'll all live happily ever after.

* * *

Jaap glances thoughtfully in the rearview mirror at Chris, who's sucking on the ends of her hair in the back seat. Tommy has fallen asleep on her shoulder, his mouth wide open, his cheek resting on a grubby little hand.

Maybe Waldo looked like that as a toddler too, thinks Jaap. He loves Tommy. There's never been any question about his love for Tommy.

He says, 'Misspuckissy?'

His stepdaughter sits up at once. Her gaze meets his in the mirror. Her gleaming eyes, filled with hope. Eyes that harbour no secrets. Just imagine, he thinks, having the whole of your life stretched out before you. He wants to sweep all calamities and troubles out of her way. He says, 'Shall we go to Skye, then?'

Chris gives a squeal of delight. Her hair whips across her face. She jabs two clenched fists into the air. *'Go do it to them before they do it to you!'* she cheers.

THE END